"Your Darkship. It is in Trouble."

Marika leapt up. "Send out . . ."

"Every darkship available is headed that way, mistress. We expect to save them, but it will be close."

Marika settled her nerves carefully, for it would not do to rattle a novice Mistress.

Marika found the darkship, drifting inward, unstable in flight, damaged. Her precious oddball wooden dark-faring ship. It had been crippled. The signs were unmistakable. Someone had attacked it.

She began stalking the passageways of the alien starship, boots hammering angrily. This was it. This was the end of all patience. She would not tolerate any more. Those responsible for this would pay. "I am the successor to Bestrei. Would they have dared this with her? No." She would make them remember. That fact would become painfully apparent to those responsible.

The silth would change if she had to send half the sisterhoods into the dark . . .

Also by Glen Cook

The Starfishers Trilogy
#1: Shadowline
#2: Starfishers
#3: Stars' End

Darkwar Trilogy #1: Doomstalker*
Darkwar Trilogy #2: Warlock*

Passage at Arms*

*Published by
POPULAR LIBRARY

DARKWAR TRILOGY·3
CEREMONY

BY GLEN COOK

POPULAR LIBRARY

An Imprint of Warner Books, Inc.

A Warner Communications Company

POPULAR LIBRARY EDITION

Popular Library® and Questar® are registered trademarks of
Warner Books, Inc.

Cover art by Barclay Shaw

Popular Library books are published by
Warner Books, Inc.
666 Fifth Avenue
New York, N.Y. 10103

A Warner Communications Company

Printed in the United States of America

First Printing: February, 1986

10 9 8 7 6 5 4 3 2 1

BOOK FIVE:
METAL SUNS

Chapter Twenty-Nine

I

Marika's darkship was forty miles from TelleRai's heart when the first sword of fire smote the world.

The flash blinded her briefly. There were more flashes. She did not keep count. The Mistress of the Ship had been blinded, too, and had lost control. The darkship twisted toward the ground.

Marika reached with the touch. *Mistress! Get hold of yourself!*

Her vision cleared. A quarter mile to her left Kiljar's darkship fluttered downward, too, but it stabilized soon after she spied it.

Marika felt Kiljar's touch. The Redoriad second sent, *What has happened?*

I do not know. The strange weapons you mentioned?

Marika looked back to the city so recently and hastily fled. A grisly glow backlighted the snowclouds. The world within, the ghost world of the touch and dark, was filled with terror and pain, unfocused, diffuse, yet centered upon dying TelleRai.

Marika sent, *What should we do, Kiljar?*

Go on. We must go on to Ruhaack. Already the touch tells me there is nothing we can do back there.

How bad is it?

Worse than you can imagine. How did you know?

I just felt something bad coming. Premonition. Silth set great store by intuition. *Not even that much when we started. I just knew we had to get away from the city. Then when* Starstalker *rose above the horizon I knew something terrible would happen. And it is not over yet. I feel a great hot wind coming.*

The Serke will pay for this.

The Serke did not do this, mistress.

They made it possible. It will be impossible to assemble a true convention now, for a while. Perhaps it is best that way. At the moment you could demand and receive anything.

What happened? Marika demanded again.

Kiljar sent a mental picture of what she imagined Telle-Rai must look like now, with the fires raging and the mushroom clouds rising. Marika pushed it away, unwilling to believe the disaster she had predicted.

Her Mistress of the Ship appealed for her attention. *Mistress? Coming up on Ruhaack.*

Go carefully. She shifted touch back to Kiljar. *What do you think? Do you sense any perils ahead? I do not.*

I sense emptiness within the Serke cloister. I sense death. I do not believe what I sense. No Community has committed kalerhag in centuries.

Kalerhag. Ritual suicide. The Ceremony. The ultimate silth ritual. The one that, at one time, had ended most silth lives.

In the packs of the wild, like that of Marika's puphood, the very old were put out of the packstead in hard times, after the less useful males and pups. In the sisterhoods of old the aged had retired themselves through kalerhag. And any sister had done so when she felt honor demanded it.

The two darkships moved in on the Serke cloister, losing

altitude, slowing, watching it belch smoke that rolled up into the clouds, reminding Marika of Maksche aflame after the perfidious brethren attack there.

No sisterhood has committed kalerhag here, Kiljar sent, correcting herself, more distressed. *They took some with them and left the others poisoned.*

Marika instructed her Mistress of the Ship to drop lower still, to approach the Serke Ruhaack cloister below the worst of the heat. Inrushing air tugged at her clothing.

It is safe, Kiljar sent. *Set down.*

Marika had her darkship taken to ground. She stepped off. Her voctor, Grauel, stepped down beside her and stared at the cloister in awe. "What happened, Marika?"

"Kiljar says they poisoned everyone they could not take with them. I suppose the fires were meant to destroy evidence."

"Evidence? Of what?"

The earth beneath their feet was trembling, groaning, carrying news of the destruction of TelleRai.

"Who knows? Let's see what we can find."

As Marika unslung her rifle the hot wind from TelleRai overtook them. Most of its force had been spent, but still it was enough to stagger them. Marika regained her balance. She looked toward TelleRai. "That they could do such a thing," she snarled into the wind. Then, to her Mistress of the Ship, "Stay here. Remain prepared to lift off."

The Ruhaack Serke cloister stood at the heart of the city Ruhaack, surrounded by a broad belt of green. That belt was filling with meth. Marika considered the creatures, Serke bonds all. She felt no danger there. They were nothing more than bonds.

Kiljar left her own darkship and joined Marika. "You intend to go inside?"

"If I can." The cloister gate stood sealed. She ducked through her loophole, caught a small ghost attracted by the disaster, and used it to demolish the gate.

Grauel went in first, behind a short warning burst from her rifle.

There was no one to resist them, silth, voctor, or bond. They found most of the Serke still in their cells, apparently resting peacefully. The stench of death filled the place. Marika could not long stand the sight of dead novices bloating in the heat. She asked Kiljar, "Do you think they did this at all their cloisters? Or just here?"

"Probably just here. This was the beast's head."

"Why, Kiljar?" she asked as they retreated through the gate. "Why would they do such a thing?"

"I suspect to sever all ties that might allow us to trace them."

"But . . ."

"They are running. All the guilty of the Serke and the brethren. Together. I expect to the world where they found their aliens. I doubt that the Serke wanted to do it this way. They are not as wicked as we have painted them. Imagine the pain they will carry with them into exile. It would not surprise me to learn they had turned on the brethren. Bestrei is simple. She has her concepts of honor. She will demand that a price be paid. When we find them . . ."

"Find them?" Marika asked.

"You know we will. Someday. I have not seen TelleRai, but I have sensed it. What was done there cannot be forgiven. Ever. The voidpaths will be filled with silth on the hunt."

"And that explains this, I suppose. The brethren strike on TelleRai compelled the guilty Serke to burn their bridges in kalerhag."

"Exactly. There is nothing we can accomplish here. I suggest we return to TelleRai. We must join the bonds in Mourning. There will be time to worry about settling scores later."

Despite her own cold-blooded excesses against the base and rogue males the rebel brethren had used to attack and destroy her cloister in Maksche, Marika was sickened by what she saw in TelleRai. Broad patches of glassy, glowing desert had replaced miles of once proud and beautiful cloisters—including that of her own Community, the Reugge.

Six of the gruesome weapons, whatever they were, had come down upon the great city. One had fallen upon the convention ground where Marika and Kiljar had thought to disarm the villains forever. It had destroyed the highest sisters of scores of Communities. Others had fallen upon the Reugge cloister and the Redoriad. A fourth had fallen upon the Tovand, the headquarters of the brethren. The remaining two weapons seemed to have fallen where they would.

Touch brought the news that the brethren rebel facility in the Cupple Islands had been vaporized too. Another cutting off of backtrails.

Voidships from several dark-faring Communities had lifted in pursuit of the Serke already, but they would not reach orbital altitude in time. Already the great Serke-brethren voidship *Starstalker* and her convoy of darkships were departing into the great night between the suns.

Kiljar predicted, "We will hear from them again if we do not find and neutralize them first."

Marika did not believe that required any prophetic vision. "I insist on being trained to walk the void. I want to be there when they are found."

"It shall be as you wish."

A cold wind blew out of the north, bringing with it snow that melted as it approached the still hot craters. The winter of the world was a slower enemy, but the fate it bore was as certain. The great glaciers were on the move. Nothing could withstand them.

Nothing? Marika reflected. That was not true. Now she was in a position to do something about the ice age. At last.

II

As years trickled into the well of time it seemed to Marika that her homeworld, and the meth who populated it, drifted backward into their own history, into an era of peace unlike any known since the system had entered the interstellar dust cloud responsible for the cooling cycle. The bonds of brethren who survived the terror after the destruction of TelleRai became extremely conservative and accommodating. They surrendered much of the power they had gained in recent generations and hunted out the heretics among themselves. The vestiges of the Serke Community were absorbed by sisterhoods with claims or were allowed kalerhag. Serke properties became reparations paid to Communities hurt at TelleRai.

The Reugge, with a prior and stronger claim, took the biggest bites. Marika successfully argued her right to claim Serke starworlds for the Reugge, though few of the established dark-faring orders were pleased. Only a tiny fraction of what the Serke had held off-planet, a mere token, those holdings nevertheless legitimized the Reugge as starfarers.

In the early going, while she was trying to take possession of the new holdings, Marika had to borrow voidships and crews from friendly sisterhoods. She had to borrow again in order to properly exploit the new far territories.

"Grauel, alert the darkship crew," Marika said.

The huntress asked, "Where to now, Marika? How much longer must we live paw to mouth, upon the charity of other sisterhoods?"

"Not long. Not long at all. Where is Barlog? Is she recovered enough to make a journey with us?"

"Try to leave her behind. Where are we going, anyway?"

"To visit Bagnel."

"Oh."

"Don't take that tone. I am indifferent to Kublin."

"I do not want to call you a liar, Marika. I do understand. Somewhat. I would have difficulty dealing with a littermate myself. Yet he was at the very root of the crimes, one of the chief criminals."

"He will remain where he is. The rest of his natural life."

Grauel held her tongue, but it was obvious she did not find

the risk of leaving him alive acceptable. Marika let the argument alone. As strength goes. She was most senior of the Reugge. Her word was law. That was enough.

The three bath reported immediately. The Mistress of the Ship delayed a few minutes. Marika was irked by the delay, but said nothing. Mistresses of the Ship were that way, even when they served a most senior. They felt compelled to assert themselves.

She was tempted, briefly, to take the command position herself. She did not get to fly as much as she liked now that she was trying to drag an entire Community out of the despair brought on by the destruction of TelleRai.

The darkship dropped into the landing court of a packfast hidden far to the north, in territories all other meth believed had been abandoned to the ice. Senior Edzeka came out to meet Marika. She did not have much to say. Just another example of the widespread emotional paralysis Marika encountered everywhere.

"How may we serve you?" Senior Edzeka asked, and when Marika told her she wanted to see her friend, the tradermale Bagnel, the senior assigned her a guide and disappeared.

Following Marika's instructions, Bagnel had been treated as an honored guest. "Really more an honored prisoner," he said. "But I should complain? If I hadn't been here I'd probably be among the dead."

"They have kept you posted on the news?" Marika asked.

"Those two arfts still shadow you, I see," Bagnel said, nodding toward Grauel and Barlog. "Yes. It was a form of taunting, I suspect. They were certain whatever favor I enjoyed would be withdrawn." The male looked haggard for a moment, betraying the fact that he feared *that* might be why Marika had come.

"I have come to bring you out of hiding, to send you back to the brethren. Those who destroyed your bond, and Maksche and TelleRai are dead, scattered, or on the run. The brethren need new leaders—rational and reasonable leaders."

"I would be no puppet."

"We have been friends long enough for me to know that, Bagnel. If you pretended to be I would become more suspicious of you than I normally am."

"Of me?"

"Of course. You are brethren. I am silth. There is no way our interests will ever approach identity. But we can live together amicably. We have done before."

Bagnel looked at Grauel and Barlog for a moment. Marika had the distinct feeling that, more than ever, he wished her two old packmates elsewhere.

"So," he said. "Tell me Marika's plans. I hear you are most senior of the Reugge now."

"A temporary inconvenience. I will shed the mantle as soon as I can. I have another destiny. Out there." She pointed skyward. "My dream." She had shared her dream of the stars with no one but Grauel, Barlog, Bagnel, and a few meth whose goodwill would be critical in achieving it. Only the named three knew how much an obsession the stars were.

"I see."

"I have made certain arrangements on your behalf. Wherever you go when you return to the brethren, a small number of aircraft will remain available. The arguments were bitter, and I had to lie to convince some members of the convention, but the fact is, they're there for you. Because I know what my life would be like if I could no longer fly."

Bagnel bowed his head and said nothing for a long time. Then, "I am sure they have said terrible things about you, Marika. After what you did at the base at . . . But they do not know you. Thank you."

"I remember my friends as well as my enemies. The sisters here have instructions to see you prepared for the journey. I have a few things to do here before we depart. I hope you do not mind traveling blindfold."

Bagnel snorted. "I expected nothing else. This place, with

its secret manufactories, would be too precious to you for you to do otherwise."

Marika shrugged. "Darkships are too precious to we silth to allow control of production or distribution to rest in outside paws. Were it not for this place the Reugge would have none left but mine after the battles in the Ponath and the destruction of Maksche and TelleRai.

"I will see you later. We will fly together again, as we did when we were innocent."

Marika was barely out of Bagnel's hearing when Barlog remarked, "You told Grauel you were no longer interested in Kublin's fate."

"I said nothing of the sort. I am no longer interested in making special dispensations for him, but he is still my littermate, even though he turned rogue. He is still the meth who was closest and dearest to me during my puphood years. Those days cannot be regained, but they need not be discarded."

The two huntresses exchanged glances. Marika knew they were thinking they would never understand her. To them she must seem an incongruous and incompatible mixture of sentimentalism and deadly cold ambition, too often subject to masculine weaknesses.

They would never understand. For all they wore the dress of Reugge voctors of the leading rank and were accustomed to the technological and social marvels of the south, at heart they remained neolithic huntresses with a very primitive black-and-white view of the world's workings. Mostly they did not try to reconcile their beliefs with what they saw. They followed orders, often with sullenly silent or formal disapproval, and held themselves aloof from their effete and decadent surroundings and associates.

Their disapproval was graven on their faces, but neither said another word as Marika stalked into the packfast's signal intercept section.

Kublin was imprisoned there, compelled to translate brethren cant and coded messages Reugge technicians stole from the satellite network. "He is as isolated as if he had been sent to rejoin the All," Marika said. "And this way his blood is not on my conscience. Not to mention that we get some use out of him."

Grauel and Barlog did not speak to arguments they considered weak excuses. Blood meant little or nothing to a Ponath female dealing with males.

Kublin was at work when Marika arrived. She stood out of the way of the small team on duty, and signaled the supervisor to continue as though she were not there. She watched Kublin.

He did what he was supposed to do, no faster than he had to. He looked much older than he had when she had captured him. When she mentioned that to Grauel the huntress remarked, "You look much older too. And you two look very much alike. Persons who did not know you nevertheless would suspect you were littermates."

The discussion, though whispered, caught Kublin's attention and he noticed Marika for the first time. Their gazes met. He betrayed no expression whatsoever.

Marika did not try to speak to him. There was nothing to say anymore. After a few minutes she left and collected Bagnel, and returned to warmer southern climes and the business of righting a Community decimated by the attack upon TelleRai.

III

The initial fury of the hunt for the fugitive Serke and brethren faded, but the search never ceased entirely. Nor did it enjoy any success. The villains had vanished as though they had never been, and surviving members of the Serke Community could provide no hints as to where they had gone.

Contrary to her announced intentions, Marika did not immediately step down as most senior of the Reugge Community. She claimed that was because there was no one qualified to replace her. All the Reugge ruling council excepting herself had been in TelleRai when death fell from the sky. So she remained on till she was confident that the order was no longer is disarray, by which she meant till it was made over to her own specifications. She sorted through the ruling councils of the surviving cloisters, identifying and elevating sisters whose philosophies mirrored her own.

In time she did yield first chair, to a silth named Bel-Keneke. Bel-Keneke hailed from a frontier province as remote as the Ponath. Her attitudes were very much like Marika's, though she was nowhere near as strong in the talents.

Marika collected Grauel and Barlog and retreated to the secret darkship factory in the snow wastes, there to continue interrupted studies and to pursue her slightly paranoid watch on signals traffic.

At first Marika came out of hiding regularly, to study with Kiljar, to fly with Bagnel, as had been their custom for years, except when broader events interrupted them. She learned to handle a voidship with the best of the starfaring Mistresses of the Ship, though she never actually pursued her dream and traveled to any of the starworlds. She did not, in fact, go much beyond the orbits of the two larger moons, Biter and Chaser.

Once she had become proficient with the voidships her ventures out of isolation became even more infrequent, then not at all.

She fell out of the public eye for nearly three years.

The permanent snowline crept southward steadily till it reached the remains of TelleRai. The land of Marika's birth lay buried beneath a hundred feet of ice and snow. The ruins of Maksche were little more than lines beneath a cloak of white.

Hunger stalked the world for all the effort of the silth to care for their bonds, for all the abnormal cooperation that developed between disaster-besieged sisterhoods. Too many meth were being compressed into too little territory.

The population of the meth homeworld had never been large, but neither was much of its surface developed agriculturally. Development efforts started after the destruction of TelleRai were too little, too late. Land could not be brought into production quickly enough to support the shifting populace.

Marika watched from isolation. In time she lost patience with the efforts of others.

"Grauel, send word up to have my darkship prepared. Find Barlog. Arm yourselves."

Surprised, Grauel asked, "What are we doing, Marika?"

"We're going out. It is time I stopped waiting for others to do something. No one seems inclined to act."

"Really?" It had been three years since Grauel had been out of the fortress, which Marika had renamed Skiljansrode in honor of her dam, and which she had made over into an independent packfast populated by refugees, fugitives, and malcontents from a dozen sisterhoods. Viewed from a traditional silth perspective, Skiljansrode could be considered the germ of a new Community.

Marika never thought of breaking away from the Reugge.

Other silth contemptuously called those of Skiljansrode the brother-sisters because they worked with their paws. The principal product of the fortress remained darkships, but other, more technical items went out as well, increasingly in competition with the brethren. Most of the meth at Skiljansrode were curiosities like Marika herself, little interested in the fashions and forms of silthdom.

"Really, Grauel. Really. Have Kloreb message the cloister at Ruhaack that we'll be coming. I will want our quarters warmed. I will want a précis of the current political climate prepared. And I will want Kiljar of the Redoriad told that I will be in Ruhaack and that I would like an audience."

"Is something afoot, Marika?"

"In a sense. It's time we tried to do something about reversing the winter of the world."

Grauel looked at her long and hard. Finally she said, "Not even you have the witchcraft to make the sun burn hotter."

"No, but there are ways. What do you think I have been working on all this time? It can be done. I think the brethren knew that in the old days. Had they won, they might have taken steps. I suspect many of them know what to do even now, but they allow the long winter to go on because it weakens us."

"I believe you when you say . . . It's just . . ."

"Just?"

"I haven't been out of here for so long. I find I am very uncomfortable when you talk about going."

"I'm uncomfortable too, Grauel. And that is a sign that we have sat still too long. We have allowed ourselves to become sedentary. We have become like our dams. We have reverted to being the pack meth we once were. I think we're overdue to reenter the active world."

"Shall I have Bagnel messaged as well?"

"That can wait till after we reach Ruhaack."

In the past three years Bagnel had risen high among the brethren. Marika found she was excited about seeing him again. More excited than she was by any other prospect, including the possibility that she would mount a voidship again, and this time maybe actually fly off in pursuit of her dreams. After, of course, she had won the struggle to get a program started to reverse the long winter.

How many more years might that take?

She knew the exact cause of her excitement. She examined it with sardonic self-mockery.

Toghar ceremonies or not, she was female. And she was into a female's prime pupbearing years. Some hormones were produced despite Toghar.

"Not a distraction I need," she murmured to herself. There were silth who assuaged that natural need, who enjoyed a sort of false esterus, using male bonds. Marika refused. She considered that degraded, despicable, even perverted. She forced the need out of mind.

"Go on, Grauel."

She paced after the huntress departed, concerned that she had been gone from the world too long, that it might have passed her by during her three-year sabbatical.

Chapter Thirty

I

Ruhaack had become the site of the new dam cloisters of several Communities bombed out of TelleRai. The city was a welter of construction. TelleRai itself had been abandoned. It was no longer healthy.

The Reugge had been awarded possession of the former Serke cloister. The reconstruction and refurbishing begun during Marika's administration were finished. The Reugge Community was back to business as usual—as much as it could be.

The Redoriad were building their new main cloister in one of Ruhaack's satellites. Construction was far advanced from what it had been at the time of Marika's last visit.

Though Marika had departed the immediate equation, the two orders remained closely allied. For a time, soon after the bombs, there had been talk of a merger. The main talkers had been Marika's enemies, who wished to keep her from taking control. Nothing had come of it. Marika's supporters and other conservatives within both Communities had scuttled the proposal.

15

The same conservatives supported the alliance, though. It had proved of great benefit to both orders. The Reugge, particularly, were now considered a force to be reckoned with in everything.

Marika nervously stalked around a hastily prepared apartment. Kiljar, now most senior of the Redoriad, was coming to see her. She felt like a pup again, as unsure of herself as she had been when first she had arrived at Akard.

"I shouldn't have locked myself up in Skiljansrode," she told Barlog. "Not so thoroughly. I've lost something."

Grauel entered. She looked sour. "Bagnel the tradermale is here, Marika." Which explained that. Grauel never had approved of Bagnel. "And the Redoriad say that mistress Kiljar has departed the Redoriad cloister."

"Good. Good. What of Bel-Keneke?"

"She will be here soon, I think more out of curiosity than because you implied that you were about to call in her debt to you."

"Fine."

Both huntresses considered her. She continued to pace.

"I spent too long in the safety and nonpressure of Skiljansrode," she explained again. "I have lost my edge. I am not comfortable being Marika. The weapons . . . I feel almost silly carrying them. But they were our sigil. Going around armed, making dramatic gestures. We are too old. I'm almost ready to become one of the Wise."

Grauel snorted. "Maybe in another twenty years. You're still hardly more than a pup." She spoke thus in defense of herself. She was much older than Marika, but she was not ready to lay down her huntress's role.

Barlog said, "I think I understand, Marika. When I am out in the cloister I too get the feeling that the world has left me behind."

Grauel agreed. "I encountered young voctors who didn't know who we are. Or were, perhaps I should say. Not that we were ever that famous. But there was a time when our being Marika's bodyguards meant a lot more than it does now."

"It slips away," Marika said.

"It hasn't been that long, Marika."

Bagnel arrived first. A group of baffled novices delivered him to Marika's door. A male in the cloister? Impossible. They were scandalized. They had heard stories about the bizarre doings of this silth called Marika, but had not believed them before this.

Marika was amused.

"Well," Bagnel said as the door closed behind him. "The living legend herself. Where have you been, Marika? We agreed to fly together at least once a month. One day there wasn't any more Marika. No message. No excuse. No apology. Nothing for years. Then out of nowhere a typically peremptory summons. And here I am, though I should have requited indifference with indifference."

It took Marika a moment to realize he was teasing, that he was glad to see her. "You're looking a little gray around the fringes, Bagnel."

"I have not had the privilege of taking an extended sabbatical. My brethren would gray the fur of a statue." He looked troubled.

"What is it?"

He glanced at Grauel and Barlog, as always disturbed by their presence. "Are they immortal?"

"They are as safe as ever, my friend. The Redoriad will join us presently, though I do not expect her immediately. Most Senior Bel-Keneke will wait till Kiljar has arrived before she makes her own entrance." She did not add that the room itself was safe, for she, Grauel, and Barlog had made independent sweeps in search of the sort of listening devices Marika herself had once used habitually.

"Nothing really remarkable. Just the persistent element that wishes the sisterhoods ill. It has been growing stronger recently. Nothing to be concerned about, mind you. Just aggravation enough to keep me on edge."

Marika considered him closely. "There's more than that, isn't there?"

"You read me better than ever. Yes. I have found evidence that those who fled have not broken entirely their ties to their homeworld. Evidence that they are in contact with those who are driving me gray."

"What?" A tendril of fright touched Marika. "How can that be?"

"It is easy enough. It is not difficult at all to slip a darkship through to the surface, to some remote rendezvous. Especially when I have no advance warning."

"Then it isn't over."

"It never was. You knew that. The Serke just fled to a safe place. I suspect their overall goals had to change somewhat once they were driven off the homeworld, simply by force of circumstance, but there was no reason for them to give up trying to seize control of everything."

Marika paced, mused, wondered that the Serke had gotten so entangled in a brethren scheme that they had allowed themselves to become the tools of their own destruction.

Bagnel added, "Unfortunately, nobody takes the threat seriously anymore. They have been quiet, so are forgotten. Nobody even hunts them now, except as a convenient side flight on a trip to the starworlds. But if they were hiding anywhere convenient they would have been found already."

"They aren't strong enough to try a comeback," Marika said. "Even with help from their supposed aliens."

"You think not?"

"If they were, they would have tried. Right? They have not. Therefore they are not."

"Irrefutable logic."

"Smart, Bagnel. I suspect they have no support from any alien—if one even exists. If one does, that relationship must be less intimate than we once thought. In my reflections I have begun to suspect that they may have no direct contact at all."

Bagnel looked startled.

"Yes?" Marika asked.

"You continue to amaze me."

"How have I managed that now?"

"You just struck close to the picture we have developed by questioning prisoners and others who may be in the know one way or another. What seems to have happened is that they did make a contact, but they could not deal with the alien because the alien *was* alien—though from other things we have learned they don't *seem* that alien. If you are following this."

"I'm trying."

"Apparently being unable to deal with the alien, they stole, possibly by killing the alien and appropriating everything that belonged to them. So it's possible they're hiding from the alien race too."

"If you are going to go rogue, why do it halfway?" Grauel asked. "Marika, mistress Kiljar is about to arrive. I hear the novices shuffling in the hallway."

"We'll talk more later, Bagnel. I'm happy to see you have become so important among the brethren. I cannot think of anyone more deserving."

Bagnel snorted derisively.

II

Kiljar, too, had aged, but she had been old when Marika had seen her last. She was shocked by what time had done to the Redoriad. Kiljar had lost large patches of fur, and what remained was mostly gray or white. She had lost a lot of weight, too, and begun to stoop, but her eyes remained brightly intelligent.

More than age, long-term ill health had diminished the Redoriad most senior. She had to walk with the aid of a cane. One side of her body was partially paralyzed. She responded to Marika's horrified glance with a lopsided expression of amusement. "A stroke," she explained, slurring her words. "Weakened the flesh but did nothing to the mind. I am recovering slowly."

"Could the healer sisters not . . . ?"

"They assure me there is nothing more they can do without killing me. That seems too heroic a measure to effect a cure."

"At least you have been able to take it in good part."

"The hell I have. I resent it. It angers me so much I go into howling rages against the All. They think me quite mad at the Redoriad cloister. But none have yet found the courage to try ousting me from first chair. They think I am dying anyway. They spend their time trying to outmaneuver one another so as to stand at the head of the pack when I go. But I am going to disappoint them. I am going to outlive them all. You look good, Marika. I suspect that a few years beyond the edge of the world were just what you needed. You seem less driven, less saddled by doom."

Marika looked at her sharply, surprised that Kiljar read her so easily.

She suspected one unconscious reason she had isolated herself was because of self-doubt, an inclination, following the destruction of TelleRai, to credit those sisters who called her Jiana and doomstalker. Four sequential destructions of the place she called home, with those who dwelt there, was enough to make anyone ask questions.

"The most senior is approaching, Marika," Barlog said from the doorway.

"Leave it open. Sit somewhere." Barlog still had difficulty getting around, all these years after recovering from the wounds she had suffered at Maksche.

We have all been injured and left crippled, Marika thought. In the heart if not in the flesh.

Bel-Keneke arrived. Marika reached back in time to find greetings appropriate to a most senior of the Reugge. There had been no formalities, no ceremonials, no obsequies, observed at Skiljansrode. Marika held them in contempt because she considered most of them unearned.

Bel-Keneke, too, had changed, though now she seemed

more secure in her role than when last Marika had seen her. "You can dispense with the ceremonials, Marika. I know they do not come from the heart. You are looking well." She ignored Bagnel and merely nodded to Kiljar. "You should be seen here more, Marika. There are times when we could use your slant on the world."

"I will be seen more," Marika said. "That is why I have come back."

"Direct as always. So. We are all here. Let us get to it. Tell us about the grand project you want to attempt."

Marika prowled while Bel-Keneke seated herself. Barlog, in the background, in her customary array of weapons, looked increasingly uncomfortable. Marika gestured for her to sit, as she had directed earlier.

She did not sit herself. She could not. She was about to broach the result of many years of thought and felt shy about doing so. It was not the usual sort of Marika idea, full of fire and blood and doom for enemies of the Reugge. She was afraid for its reception.

She moved to the center of the room and stood there with her guests watching from three directions. She ordered her thoughts, ran through calming mental exercises. Finally she attacked it. "I have an idea for stemming the snow and cold."

"What?" That was Bel-Keneke, who was least accustomed to Marika's ways. But the others looked at her askance.

"A major engineering project that might allow us to turn back the ice."

"Major?" Bagnel murmured. "You have a gift for understatement, Marika."

Kiljar said, "If you managed that you would be immortalized with . . ."

"It is not possible," Bel-Keneke said. "You are talking about halting a process of such a magnitude that . . ."

Bagnel added, "Perhaps we ought to hear her idea before we tell her it is impossible."

Marika gave him a nod of gratitude. "Excuse me, mistresses. I know it would be a large project and extremely difficult, but it is not impossible—except perhaps in that it presumes the cooperation of all the Communities and all the brethren bonds, working toward one end. Achieving that will be more difficult than the actual engineering and construction."

"Go on," Kiljar said before Bel-Keneke could interject negative comments.

"Review: The problem is that insufficient solar energy penetrates the dust and falls upon the planet. The solution—my solution—is to increase incident radiation."

"Do you plan to sweep the dust up?" Bel-Keneke asked. "Or to stoke the fires of the sun?"

"Not at all."

"Why so negative, sister?" Kiljar asked. "Do you feel threatened because your predecessor has come out of hiding?"

Marika ignored the sparks. Those two old arfts never had had much use for one another. She said, "We collect solar energies that are flinging off into the void and redirect them toward the planet. We do that by constructing large mirrors."

"Large mirrors," Bagnel said.

"*Very* large. Wait. I admit there will be difficulties. The orbital mechanics of our situation, because of the presence of so many moons, will make maintaining stable orbits for the mirrors difficult. But I have been studying this matter for some time. It is not impractical. If we can install the largest mirrors in the planet's leading and trailing solar trojan points and keep them stable . . ."

"Pardon me," Bagnel interrupted. "The idea is not original, Marika."

"I did not think it was. I assumed the brethren had thought of it long ago and had not brought it up because it was in their interest to have the weather help destabilize the social structure. It was no coincidence that the inclination to rebellion grew stronger as the cold crept down. I believe the factors behind the planning failed only because they got overeager."

"You are, perhaps, half right. In such an engineering program the brethren would have required the same level of cooperation you already mentioned. We would not have gotten it. There is, too, the sheer magnitude of the thing. I have heard that the necessary mirrors would have to be thousands of miles across. If you mean installing them in the trojan points where the sun's gravity and the world's balance, rather than in the lunar trojans, they would have to be almost unimaginably huge to reflect enough energy to make a difference."

"Those are the points I mean, as I said. The main mirrors would require less stabilization there. But, as you say, they would have to be more huge than anything any meth has imagined. I picture them on the order of five thousand miles in diameter."

"I fear you underestimate considerably."

"Utterly impossible," Bel-Keneke said.

"Let her talk, sister," Kiljar countered. "Marika is no fool. She would not have brought this up had she not worked most of it out already. If she says it can be done, then she has done enough calculation to convince herself."

"Thank you, Kiljar. Yes. The idea first occurred to me while I was still a novice, many years ago. There were too many other demands on my attention then, so I did not pursue it. Later, when I retreated to Skiljansrode, I did have the time. It is the major reason I have remained out of touch so long. I will admit that I have not done all the calculations necessary. The orbitals require calculations all but impossible with pencil and paper. But the brethren once developed a system for rapid calculation, else they could not have orbited their satellites. I am hoping that the system, or at least the knowledge to replace it, survived the bombing of the Cupple Islands. That system, skilled labor, the metals, technology, and such would be required of the brethren. The Communities will have to lift the materials into the void—

and contribute the talent where necessary. Skiljansrode will provide the reflecting material."

"A grand stumbling block in the scheme as the brethren worked it out," Bagnel said.

"As I see it, we would need a web of titanium metal-work—or possibly one of golden fleet wood if that proves either impractical or the titanium cannot be produced in sufficient quantities—supporting an aluminized plastic surface no thicker than a hair."

"It's a possibility," Bagnel said. "I am amused by the notion of wooden satellites. But that is neither here nor there. Discounting for the moment all the other problems, where do we get this plastic? The same notion occurred to those who toyed with this among the brethren. They were unable to produce such a plastic and were reduced to thinking in terms of a heavy aluminum foil that proved too brittle in actual trials. The breakage ran better than fifty percent."

"We have developed the plastic already. You will be amused to learn that it is a petroleum derivative. I felt I had to have that before I broached the larger idea."

Bagnel began to look truly interested, not just speculative.

"Two main reflectors, as I said, to provide a steady, gross energy incidence. Then smaller ones, in geocentric orbit—and lunar trojan orbit—with which we can fine-tune the amount of energy delivered. With which we can deliver extra energy to specific localities. For instance, to keep threatened crop lands in production. We will want more energy in the beginning, anyway, to initiate the thaw cycle."

"It is crazy," Bel-Keneke said. "You have gone mad in isolation."

"It's not impossible at all," Bagnel countered, now so intrigued he forgot to use the formal mode. He got up and started pacing and muttering to himself.

"Do you really believe in this, Marika?" Kiljar asked. "Have you convinced yourself that, despite the obvious problems, it can actually be done?"

"My conviction is absolute, mistress. I have yet to find an insuperable barrier, though there were more problems than

I at first expected. Yes, it can be done—if the Communities and the brethren are willing to invest the resources and the energies."

Bagnel's pacing took him to a window. He stared out at the frigid world. The most seniors watched him uneasily. "You have done it again, haven't you, Marika?"

"Done what, Bagnel?"

"You have overturned everything. And bigger than ever before. No wonder you had to take a few years off. You needed that long to wake the earthquake."

"What are you talking about?"

"Three meth are going to leave this room with your notion fixed in their minds. All three are going to find some reason to consult others about it. Those others will tell others. The news will spread. In time it will have reached those for whom it will represent an almost religious opportunity for salvation. It will become impossible for us, brethren and Communities alike, to do anything but attempt it, even if it proves impossible. For the alternative will be destruction at the paws of outraged bonds who will believe themselves betrayed."

"What are you talking about?"

"I am saying you have let a devil loose. That you proposed this with no thought for the social implications. I am saying that you have made undertaking the project mandatory simply by stating that you believe it is feasible. I am saying that such a project will reshape society as well as weather. I ask you to think about what you are asking."

Taken aback by his vehemence, Marika said, "Tell me."

"You are asking that the brethren be restored to grace. You are asking two dozen dark-faring Communities to join forces in one grand project instead of flying off in all directions, spending half their energies sabotaging and one-upping each other. You are proposing a project of such vast magnitude that bond meth will have to be given technical training because the brethren available to do the work are not numerous enough. You are letting devils out. Those are things I foresee just off the top of my head. More thought would produce more, surely. And the project is bound to have repercussions that cannot be foreseen at all—some just because of its scale. Did none of this occur to you?"

"No. I was not concerned with anything but the practical considerations." Marika took a turn at the window and thought of Jiana the doomstalker, reflecting on the fact that destruction need not be physical, as it had been with the Degnan packstead, Akard, Maksche, and TelleRai. She turned. "You really think so?"

"Yes."

"Given that, do you think it would be worth the effort?"

"Actually, I do. Because the alternative is a longer, slower, more certain doom. This cooling cycle is going to continue till the whole planet becomes too cold to support life. The permafrost line is within three thousand miles of the equator today. It shows no inclination to slow its advance, though I am sure it will in time—after it is too late for us. I suspect that we dare not waste many more years or for the meth it will be too late for anything but awaiting the end. Which will not come in our time, of course. But it will come."

Marika looked at Bel-Keneke and Kiljar. "Mistresses?"

Kiljar said, "I approve pushing ahead. Tentatively. Trusting your judgment, Marika, and that of your friend. I will want to see more solid data before I approach my Community with the proclamation that this project is the only way we can save our world."

"I understand. Bel-Keneke?"

"You are outside my expertise. You know that. All I know about the void is that it is cold and dark out there. I do very much share the male's social fears. I foresee great troubles and terrible changes. But I am in your debt, and I respect the opinion of mistress Kiljar. If you can convince her, I will follow her lead and back you."

Marika walked back to the window and stared out at the chill landscape. Once Ruhaack had been warm and lush. Now it was barren, except where meth had planted vegetation adapted to a near arctic climate. After a moment she turned.

"Bagnel may be right, about the social upheaval. I plead guilty to failing to consider that aspect. But we are in a corner from which there is no escape. There is no future without trying. If the race is to survive, we must pay the price."

She was amazed that the most seniors were so agreeable. Perhaps the world had grown more desperate than she knew.

"Bagnel, can the brethren provide the necessary calculators?"

"We call them computers. Yes, we have them. We may have to develop a breed designed specifically for the project, but that would not be an insurmountable problem. A matter of increasing capacity, I expect." ·

"What about the engineering? Do you have anyone capable of designing the mirrors?"

"That I cannot say, but I can find out. Given adequate time, I am sure, someone—more likely many someones—could be trained. I will find out and let you know."

"So that is that. We are agreed. We go ahead a step."

III

Marika gaped at Bagnel. "Eight years? Just to get the materials together?"

"It's a big project, Marika. I think that's too optimistic a figure, myself. It assumes total cooperation by all the Communities in providing the labor we'll need for getting the titanium out, building new plants to process the ore and metal, building new power plants to provide energy for those plants, and so on and so on and so on. I told you it would reshape society. And it *will*. My guess is that we'll be extremely fortunate to get even one mirror functional within ten years. There will be hitches, hang-ups, problems, delays, personality conflicts, bottlenecks, shortages. . . . "

"I get the picture."

"The word is spreading already, just as I forecast. I keep running into brethren who know before I consult them, though I swear everyone to silence when I do consult them."

"We expected that. We chose to live with it."

"I have another scenario for you. In this one your old enemies get wind of the project. As inevitably they must."

"You think they would try to sabotage it?"

"I am certain they'll try. Wouldn't you? The cold is on their side."

"Then we must neutralize them."

"How, when no one has been able to find them?"

"No one has tried hard enough. A truly major effort . . ."

"There. You're talking about diverting energies from your project. Which means having to stretch it out a little."

Marika sighed. "Yes, I guess I am."

"You see? One thing affects another."

"We'll do what we have to. Are you ready to face Kiljar and Bel-Keneke? And beyond them, a convention of all the Communities?"

"I believe so."

"Good. Because Kiljar is failing and I believe that to have a chance the thing has to get rolling before she dies."

"Arrange for me to see her. I'll sell her."

"Just give her the truth. Let it argue for itself. You cannot mislead her. And she'll have to sell it to others on its provable merit."

"Of course. That's understood. Did you happen to notice that I flew down here in a Sting? We haven't flown together for a long time."

"I did notice that. And I was thinking of stealing you and it if you didn't come up with the suggestion yourself."

"This afternoon, then? After I have seen the most seniors?"

"Yes. Don't let them intimidate you. They may try, just to see what you're made of."

"Those old artfs? Not likely. Not when I have to deal with my factors and bond masters every day."

Bel-Keneke and Kiljar needed very little convincing. They had done their own investigating. "I am amazed," Kiljar admitted. "The response among the Communities has been almost messianic in intensity. They believe you are going to show them the pathway into a new age, Marika."

"It must be timing," Bagnel remarked. "Purely a matter of timing. Everyone is just frightened enough, just certain enough. Ten years ago no one would have taken the project seriously. Conservative elements would have killed it. But now the world is in desperate need of a hope, and this one fills the need. I find extremes of enthusiasm everywhere within the brethren. All the factors and masters, once they examined the data, showed uncharacteristic excitement. Even some who were very suspicious before. It has softened the appeal of the rogues tremendously. There have been almost no incidents at all this past month."

Bel-Keneke added, "I have consulted a number of senior sisters from a number of orders. My experience has been the same everywhere. Tremendous enthusiasm, discovering a hope where none was thought to exist, except in that the dark-faring sisterhoods might have established a few feeble colonies upon the starworlds. How long the enthusiasm will persist I cannot tell. Seldom has any meth devoted herself to a project for as long as this will require."

"There will be problems," Marika agreed. "The project will hurt some orders more than others. It will draw attention and energy away from the starworlds. None of those sisterhoods will be pleased by that. I do have a suggestion, though it may not prove popular."

"Yes?" Kiljar inquired.

"We could survey all the sisterhoods, including those without rights in the void. Then conscript every sister capable of serving aboard a darkship out there. We could even retrain some of the strongest bath as Mistresses for workships. We would then have to depend less heavily on those sisters normally preoccupied with the starworlds. Too, we will have to lift the ban on the brethren so they can participate as fully as possible. That is an absolute necessity. We will get nowhere without them because of the traditional silth resistance to becoming involved in physical labor. Also, ships of the sort that were associated with *Starstalker* before she vanished would be valuable if we could build them. That would ease our dependence upon a very small supply of void-capable Mistresses of the Ship."

Bagnel said, "We should be able to develop construction ships. I have suggested that it be given some thought. I doubt that anything we came up with would be as good as those rogue vessels, but because some saw them we know what has to be done. There are problems, though, Marika. Fuels. Energy. We're right down to it now, and you may not want to hear this. The fact is, one way or another, we have to tap the resources of the Ponath. It is going to take a tremendous amount of energy to produce the necessary titanium."

"You were going to look into the possibility of producing it in orbit, in solar-powered factories."

"I was and I did. There are no adequate titanium ores available anywhere in the system other than right here on the planet. I'm sorry. The girderwork will have to be produced down here and lifted into orbit."

Kiljar asked, "Who will manage all of this? Consider the politics. It will be an alliance of all the Communities and the brethren, and will represent and include most meth bonds. With that many interests, there is no hope of working in harmony for the time required. Many sisters will not tolerate taking orders from old enemies or from competitors in other orders. None will take directions from brethren, even where brethren are the competent experts. None will work with bonds as though they are equals."

"Setting this in motion will require a formal convention, as Senior Kiljar has said," Marika said. "Most of that will have to be fought out there. One possibility would be for the Communities to elect a most senior of most seniors for a fixed term and give her absolute powers and a group of judges to enforce them."

"The smaller sisterhoods would object strenuously," Kiljar said.

"Then, perhaps, a continuous convention in which grievances can be aired as they arise, given the understanding that work must go on uninterrupted."

Bagnel snorted derisively. "No, Marika. I see time stretching and stretching already. Nothing ever gets done while silth argue. The arguing has to be done before. During, there can be nothing but the project."

"Just how critical is the time frame?" Bel-Keneke asked. "Is there a time of no return? Of too late? We will be inside this dust cloud for millennia."

"I do not know exactly, mistress," Bagnel said. "One thing we will have to do is chart the density of the dust, just so we can estimate such things. I do know that we do not have millennia. Even now, tapping the petroleum in the Ponath will demand the creation of new engineering techniques. The longer we wait, the deeper the ice. And the greater the difficulties. Everywhere."

"No matter what we do there will be problems," Bel-Keneke mused. "No matter what else, then, we have to keep muddling ahead. An inch gained now may mean a foot saved later. Any progress will be better than none."

Kiljar said, "Our first trial will be assembling a convention capable of acting. That chore I will assume myself, being, you will admit, somewhat more tactful than any of my fellow conspirators."

Marika was startled. Humor? From Kiljar? You never learned everything about anyone.

Bel-Keneke remarked, "If the project takes twenty years instead of eight, so be it. The Reugge are committed."

Marika turned from one more look at the icy world. "Bagnel, I believe you promised to take me flying. Let's do it."

Chapter Thirty-One

I

Marika's voidship drifted slowly through the clutter and confusion of the leading trojan point. She could make better speed down on the surface of the planet. Here she dared not fly herself, trusting only herself, for there were so many obstacles to navigation. Passage through the site required the combined efforts of a Mistress of the Ship and a Mistress-qualified pilot-passenger working from the axis. Marika could not imagine how the brethren kept track.

Three years had passed. Initial construction was just beginning. The support industry down on the planet's surface was not yet more than thirty percent of what it would have to be. Ninety percent of the off-planet effort, so far, had been devoted to the leading mirror.

It would be a demonstrator, in a sense. If it went active and did no apparent good, the rest of the project would collapse.

Marika reached with her touch and scanned the confusion. She remained awed by the magnitude of what she had set in motion. Designing it, planning it, talking about it was not the same as seeing it.

Flares of light speckled the night as crude brethren ships moved materials. Already Bagnel was complaining that they had chosen the most difficult way possible of building the mirror. He was agitating for a giant pack of balloons in the trailing trojan. His brethren had orbited a two-hundred-mile gas-filled reflector the week before. Its energy yield was directed at the developing oil field in the Ponath. Its value might have been more psychological than actual. The workers there claimed they sensed a change in the bitter cold already. Marika had visited and had been able to find no evidence of any local temperature increase. She suspected most of the energy was being absorbed before it reached the surface.

A remarkable vigor and an even more remarkable spirit of cooperation still animated the venture. There had been far fewer conflicts than anticipated. Yet even now Bagnel's best estimate had the leading mirror eight years from completion.

That protracted unity, in part, sprang from the project's single biggest problem, which existed down below—a sabotage campaign by those residual brethren still committed to the cause of the departed villains.

These criminals were more subtle than their predecessors. Marika's old tricks for digging them out did not work nearly as well. But still, enough were taken to keep the mines working at capacity.

Few of the taken had any direct connection with the brethren. More and more disturbing to Marika was the fact that the criminals were able to continue recruiting. And that they now were taking a few females into their ranks. The great hope of the mirror project had not adequately fired the hearts of the mass of bond meth. Marika was distressed, but did not know how to convince ordinary meth that they had as great a stake as the powerful who ruled their lives.

The mines were a problem not yet unraveled. In the past there had been no need for mechanization there. The structure of society had been such that no demand for ores had been so great that plain physical labor could not meet it. Meth did not mechanize simply for the sake of efficiency. They did so only where a task could not be performed by meth alone. But now . . .

Bagnel had been correct. The project was restructuring society. Traditionally labor intensive areas like mining and agriculture had to be mechanized either to up volume or release labor for the project. Marika was, she feared, creating the possibility of compelling some of the changes the rogue brethren had aimed toward. Some could not be avoided. There were times when she agonized. She was in the incongruous position of being the principal defender of the silth ideal while not believing in it herself.

Marika's Mistress of the Ship reached the sunward position she desired, just miles from the heart of the expanding framework. The titanium beamwork sparkled, arms radiating from the anchor point. Marika recalled some old steel bridges, brethren-built, that spanned the river at TelleRai. Bridges constructed with incredibly complex girderwork intended to distribute load stresses. Bridges built in later times were much simpler in design. Was there a similar design problem here? Was the framework needlessly complex? Or, like those old bridges, was the design state of the art for the knowledge available, for the metallurgy of the moment?

Rotate your tip so the framework is overhead, Marika sent. *Your glow is obscuring my view.*

The framework rose, filling the sky,.

A tinny voice spoke in Marika's ear, from the tiny radio earplug there. "Hello, the darkship. We will need you to pull back a few miles. We are coming through your space with girderwork."

There was a time when no male would have dared think of speaking so to silth. But in space the laws of physics often overruled tradition. Maybe these brethren would have to be destroyed in the end, lest their easygoing, not so subtly insubordinate ways infect the rest of the meth race.

Marika scanned the night for a brethren workship towing a string of bundles and spotted its flare. She touched her Mistress, relayed instructions. The darkship began to drift backward.

She was pleased with what she saw at that trojan.

She would be remembered. The meth race would recall that Marika the Reugge, wild silth of the Degnan pack of the upper Ponath, had lived. Even if the project failed, if it died in squabbling between the sisterhoods, it was something that would not be forgotten. She, its instigator, would be remembered with it.

Already the mass of materials reflected enough light to be visible from the planet's surface. In a few years it would be the brightest object in the heavens, bar the moons. When it was complete only the sun itself would outshine it.

There was nothing she could contribute here, other than encouragement. She touched several senior sisters who were working the site and sent her wholehearted approval, then touched her Mistress. *Proceed to the other site now, please.*

The darkship began easing out of the clutter.

It took an hour to reach space where the Mistress dared move swiftly. During the wait Marika ducked through her loophole into the realm of ghosts, through which she worked her silth magic, and continued a long-term effort to further familiarize herself with the odd those-who-dwell of the void.

She was accustomed to them now, and used them as she did the ghosts down below on her homeworld. Their immensity and power no longer disturbed and intimidated her, perhaps because by dealing with them she developed her own strength and power. There were none of them so mighty she could not take them into control and use them to pull her voidship or perform some task ordinary meth would perceive as witchery.

She knew them, and the void, but still she had not realized her dream. Still she had not traveled to an alien star, even as a passenger upon another Mistress's darkship. Still she had not dared breach the Up-and-Over, where light became a lagging pedestrian. For reasons deep within her, reasons she could not fathom herself, she was frightened of what she might encounter there.

Darkfarers told her hers was a problem all voidfaring Mistresses and bath faced before faring the Up-and-Over. They called the fear the Final Test. Those who conquered it joined the most elite sisterhood of all, the few score who flew the darkships to the starworlds. Those who did not conquer it seldom fared past the orbits of the meth homeworld's major moons.

Marika extended her touch, her sensing, farther and farther outward. . . . There it was, that dark something—remote, lying outside the system itself, vast, colder than the indifferent void. A sense of darkness radiated from it. And it terrified her.

She sensed it every time she passed outside Biter's orbit. Kiljar had told her it was the ultimate in those-who-dwell, more vast and powerful and deadly than anything she had yet experienced. It lurked in the gulf between the stars, and had to be appeased by any voidship that passed out of the system. It had appeared there soon after the first silth had penetrated the deep.

It was the thing that made Bestrei, the Serke champion, the most terrible of living silth. Three living silth could manipulate that great darkness. Bestrei could control it better than any other. She could call it and hurl it against any challenger. None had the strength to steal her control and drive it away.

Kiljar said Bestrei meshed with it so well because inside she was just as cold, deadly, and vacant.

Marika feared it because she sensed it in her future. The script was written. The very nature of meth, silth, and the silth ideal made certain eventualities inevitable.

Someday . . .

Unspoken by anyone, tacitly assumed and accepted by every silth, was the fact that one day Marika would have to meet Bestrei in darkwar. The confrontation was fated by the All. There was no escaping it.

When Marika reflected upon that chance she was afraid,

for she was unsure of herself with the great black, with
Bestrei. Most of her life she had been hearing about Bestrei
and how terrible the Serke was. The one time their paths
had crossed she had been awed by the raw power in the silth.

The Serke and their rogue brethren allies had mounted
several incursions into the home system the past few
months, attacking the mirror project. Bestrei had not participated. Bestrei would not pariticipate in such trivialities, in
the estimation of silth who knew her. She would be con-
temptuous of such nuisance tactics. She would not be seen
till she was offered a traditional challenge with dramatically
high stakes.

As seemed inevitable, fate stalked Marika's trail. As her
Mistress of the Ship began to put on speed toward the
trailing trojan point, Marika received a generalized touch
from a fartoucher sister riding a picket darkship far out in
the direction from which *Starstalker* and the raiders always
appeared. It was brief, cut short.

Turn about, Marika sent to her Mistress. *Starwalker is
coming.*

The plane of the touched reeked with the fear of the
Mistress and bath. The Mistress returned, *This is not our
proper task, mistress.*

Turn about. Set course upon the Manestar.

The darkship wheeled.

The speaker in Marika's ear began to babble as slower
electromagnetic waves brought the warning.

II

They are very daring this time, Marika sent. Many minutes
had passed. *Starstalker* and the raiders were closing with
the leading trojan. Never before had *Starstalker* come in so
close. The Serke had been afraid to risk her. Losing her
would mean losing the brethren she had brought aboard her.

Marika's Mistress of the Ship returned, *They must be armed with more powerful weapons.*

The possibility had occurred to Marika. A few bombs of the kind that had destroyed TelleRai could kill the project. Having them delivered might seem worth risking *Starstalker.*

She opened to the universe, sensed the movement of everything nearby. A dozen brethren ships and five darkships accompanied *Starstalker.* For the moment Marika was alone, the only defender capable of intercepting the raiders. The sisters down below remained confused, as always. Those within the work site could not get out into free space in time to save themselves, let alone do any defending.

Did the Serke know she was here? Had they recognized her? There was no indication in their behavior. The rogue ships were headed toward the mirror. The silth were forming a screen meant to intercept help coming up from the planet. Marika was tempted to strike at *Starstalker* itself, to destroy any chance for the criminals to escape, but she feared that might allow the rogues a chance to kill her project.

The rogues had to be halted first.

She went out the long arm of the darkship, her specially built wooden darkship, her darkship that so amused the sisters of the great titanium crosses. The struts bore shields showing her own personal and Degnan witch signs instead of those of a particular cloister, as was the case with all other darkships. She reached the Mistress of the Ship and sent, *I will take it now. I am fresher. You guard while I attack. Do you understand?*

Yes, mistress. The silth responded with an absolute lack of enthusiasm, despite understanding the necessity presented by the situation.

Marika assumed control, urging the darkship onto a course that would cut that of the rogue vessels from behind.

She put on velocity till she felt her bath begin quivering with the strain of her demands, felt the displaced Mistress shuddering, wanting to tell her to ease back, that they were too near space cluttered with materials for the mirror.

Marika swooped into the wake of the rogues and tasted the bitter flavor of ions from their exhausts. She gained rapidly, reaching ahead to see what she faced.

Two ships carried no crew at all. She allowed the darkship to drift while she captured a stronger ghost and took it forward for a closer look.

The uncrewed two were loaded with what must be bombs, great cumbersome devices with a jury-rigged feel. She explored one rapidly, but could find no way to disarm it or to detonate it prematurely.

She took the ghost into the fuel stores of those two ships, compressed it to marble size, put spin on it, and used it to perforate the tanks. She returned to flesh in time to watch the second flower of fire blossom against the night.

She felt the rage explode among the thwarted rogues, felt them begin sweeping the surrounding night. She returned to the otherworld and began stalking them.

They could not see her! Their radars could not pick up her wooden darkship. She was running right up to them, and they could not see her!

She hit one ship after another, just as she had taken the bomb drones. They scattered so she could not massacre them all.

Mistress. Come out. The Serke have turned our way.

She had known that would come and had ignored it.

Five of them to her one plus a spare Mistress. The odds were too long, strong as she was. Yet there was no way to hide from them. To do that she would have to abandon the talent entirely. To do that in the void meant instant death.

She curved after a rogue ship belching flame in an effort to escape, closed up, killed it, began looking for another.

Mistress . . .

There is time. Do not distract me again. Six brethren ships had been negated. They would remember this raid as a disaster. *Just guard me.*

Let the Serke come. She was strong and treacherous. If nothing else, she could outrun them.

She was closing on another rogue when the Mistress touched her again. She suppressed her anger at being interrupted.

She did not need the warning.

Astounded, she forgot the rogue as she stared at a glowing darkship that had materialized only a few hundred yards away. She recovered barely in time to help the Mistress turn the attack.

This Serke Mistress was weaker than she. Grimly, Marika ducked through her loophole and seized a ghost, hurled it back.

The darkship vanished.

Another appeared an instant later, in another quarter, and vanished again before she could do it harm.

She finally understood. They were trying to attack her through the Up-and-Over.

How could she get out of this?

She could see no escape.

Decision came instantly. She swung the tip of the wooden dagger toward *Starstalker* and accelerated.

The Serke recognized her intent. They flung themselves into her path. She and the Mistress brushed their attacks aside and continued the drive toward the great voidship. Soon the sisters there would have to move or be rammed.

The Serke tried placing a preponderance of strength in Marika's path. But once they did that she knew where to expect their appearances. She recovered her advantage of her superior grasp of the dark side.

Short, sharp touch-shrieks filled the void as a Serke Mistress's heart exploded and her bath realized they had no hope.

Marika continued gaining velocity.

Starstalker vanished.

Marika searched the void, wondering where it would return from the Up-and-Over. If she chased it hard enough it might not be able to recover the rogues before darkships rose up from the planet's surface or came from other work sites. The rogues might have to be abandoned.

A lance of fire cut past her. She had not kept close enough track of the rogues. She had allowed one to sight her visually. Hurriedly, she threw a ghost its way, destroyed it, and returned to flesh to find her Mistress almost overwhelmed by the Serke. A pair of darkships drifted nearby, radiating elation, thinking they had her.

Marika hammered at one. Again the dark filled the despair.

The second darkship vanished.

Marika spotted *Starstalker* again, far away, and darted toward it.

It was going better than she had expected. She was as strong as ever she had been, as quick, as deadly, as finely tuned in her instincts. She had won the victory already, even if she were destroyed. The raiders could no longer damage the project.

The surviving Serke were gathering at extreme range. She suspected they would jump at her together. She could not see herself and one sadly weakened Mistress fending off all three.

She had to shatter the fear barriers and hazard the Up-and-Over herself. There was no other exit. They would make no more mistakes.

How long before help arrived? Surely there had been time for darkships to complete the long, slow climb from the planet's surface. Surely someone could have arrived from the moons or have wended her way out of the jungle of metal at the trojan point.

But a quick fling of the fartouch brought no response.

It was the Up-and-Over or death.

She knew what she was supposed to do. Technically. She had reached out and collected the appropriate ghosts occasionally, but had come up short on nerve. And never had she allowed herself to be taken through by someone else, though that was the customary way of learning.

There was no option. The Serke were poised.

She gathered ghosts.

The Serke darkships vanished.

Marika sealed her eyes and opened to the All, twisted her ghosts, and bid fear be gone. She reached for the Up-and-Over, twisted again.

The stars vanished. Everything vanished. For several seconds nothing surrounded her but a chaotic sense of ghosts and screaming. She had penetrated a vacancy that made the void seem warm and homey.

Stars reappeared, spinning. The darkship was tumbling. Marika looked for landmarks, and nearly panicked when she could spy nothing familiar. The world! Where was it? Where were the Serke darkships, the brethren ships, the mirror, *Starstalker,* the moons? She saw nothing at all. Only stars, distant stars. Had she hurled herself into the gulf between?

Something huge and dark stirred nearby, aware of her presence, so powerful she could feel it without reaching into the plane of ghosts. It was the great grim dark thing she had so often sensed waiting at the lip of the system. Her skip through the Up-and-Over had thrown her almost into its grasp!

Still battling panic, she steadied the darkship, polled her companions, found them frightened but safe. Her Mistress had no experience of the Up-and-Over either. *What do we do now?* she sent.

Find the direction home.

Marika scanned the void opposite the crawling darkness, and found a star that seemed brighter than any other. *That one?*

The Mistress knew where they were too. *Must be. Only the sun would be so bright from here. Hurry. It knows we are here and it is coming to see . . .*

The darkness had begun to move.

Marika turned the darkship toward the sun and began moving inward, accelerating. *Can we make it?* She did not have the courage to hazard the Up-and-Over again.

We must try. We cannot go through again. Another time,

now knowing what we are doing, and we could be too far away to find our way. In the face of a problem less savage than the Serke the Mistress was perfectly calm. More rational than she, Marika thought.

The homeward passage took three days, despite the incredible velocities Marika attained. She reached lunar orbit at the edge of exhaustion, with her bath and Mistress all but burned out, and had to be rescued by brethren ships working the mirror, for she and her meth did not have enough left to take the darkship down.

III

Bagnel came to Marika where she lay in a bed aboard the workstation the brethren called the Hammer because of its shape, two pods upon the end of a long arm rotating to create an illusion of gravity. He said, "I heard you cut it pretty close this time."

She had not been awake long and he was her first visitor. "Very close. I wasn't sure I would make it this time."

He eyed her intently while shaking his head.

"I tried something I didn't know how to do and almost did myself in. Is that what you want me to say? I've said it. But I'll also say I didn't have any choice. It was the Up-and-Over or die. The Serke were closing in."

"I understand."

"How bad is it? How much damage did they do?"

"The raiders? None at all. Unless you count a little caused by one of the wrecks. It ploughed through an area where we had some materials tethered. We'll have to replace a few hundred sections of beam that got warped."

"That's all?"

"Evidently you took them completely by surprise. I hear there's a great deal of despair among the recidivists down on the planet. This was supposed to be a killer blow."

"Then the other darkships did get there in time to keep them from wrecking everything."

"Not exactly."

"What?"

"They ran away. The Serke. Before the darkships ever arrived. We heard the warning, but for a long time we did not know what had happened. Actually found out from a captured rogue.

"But . . ."

"Marika, nobody knew you were out there. I mean, some of the workers remembered a darkship nosing around, but they didn't know whose it was. You didn't tell anybody where you were going or what you were up to. Meth only started wondering about where you were after we captured the rogue and could not find any silth missing who were supposed to be out there at the time. Meth were talking about a ghost darkship for a while. Then when nobody could find you anywhere down below . . . Marika, you have to stop doing that kind of thing. You could have died trying to get back. If you had told somebody what you were up to, anybody, silth could have gone looking for you. It's hard to save somebody when you don't know they're in trouble."

"All right, Bagnel. Don't get excited. I get the message. It doesn't matter now, anyway. Everything turned out for the best. I'm safe."

He scowled. There was much more he wanted to say, but he held his tongue.

Marika said, "The problem has become how to protect the mirrors. They would have destroyed the project but for the accident of my having been out there. Two of those ships were carrying bombs like the ones they used on TelleRai."

"Accident? What accident?" There was an odd glint in Bagnel's eyes.

"What is it? I don't like the way you're looking at me."

"You always discount the notion that you are fated. I don't like superstition any more than you do, Marika, but this time I really have to wonder."

"Don't you start. I get enough of that nonsense from silth.

Anyway, if you assume I am a fated thing then the mirror would have been destroyed. Isn't the pattern one of destruction? That's what they keep telling me."

"Maybe that was to prepare you for the turnaround."

"Enough of this, Bagnel. I won't have it from you. It's pure silliness."

"As you wish. I came to see how you are. I have my answer. You're as nasty as ever. And those who had hopes of your early demise will be disappointed again."

"Right. I intend to keep disappointing them, too, because I intend to outlive them all. I have too much to get done to waste time dying."

He looked at her hard, surprised by her intensity. "Things such as?"

"The project has reached takeoff. It is running itself. Not so?"

"Pretty much."

"This misadventure got me to thinking. There is very little I can contribute now, unless it's protection. Or if I just help lift materials from the surface. The rest of the engine is running on its own impetus."

"So?" He sounded suspicious.

"So I think it's time I went looking for trouble instead of waiting for it to come to me. No smart remarks! Remember when I was young? Remember how the novice Marika always jumped to the attack? She hasn't been doing that since she got older. That antique factor in your quarters that time was right."

"You're so old now? About to turn into one of your Ponath Wise meth? Eh? Eh? I know. You attacked even when you didn't know what you were attacking. Yes, I remember that Marika very well. She was a fool, sometimes. I think I like today's Marika a little better."

"Fool. *That* Marika made things happen. This Marika just sits around reacting. Mainly because she has been too cowardly to take what she knows to be necessary next steps. Before Kiljar finally gives up dying and actually yields up her spirit to the All—which may not happen for another century, the rate she's going, always going to die tomorrow and going on for another year—and maybe leaves the Redoriad Community in the paws of somebody less sympathetic, I'm going to learn the ways of the gulf and the Up-and-Over. I am determined. I will defeat fear, learn, then go hunt those who would destroy us."

"Marika, please understand when I say I don't approve. I don't think . . ."

"I know, Bagnel. And I appreciate your concern." Marika close her eyes. For several minutes she did nothing but relax, comforted by his presence. Much of their friendship remained tacit, undefined by confining words.

"Bagnel?"

"Yes?"

"You have been a good friend. The thing we mean and wish when we use the word friend. The best . . . Oh, damn!"

Bagnel was startled. Marika so seldom used words like damn. "What is the matter?"

"There are things I want to say. That should be said, for the record. But I can't pry out the right words. Maybe they don't even exist in the common speech."

"Then don't try to say them. Don't look for them. I know. Just relax. You need rest more than talk."

"No. This is important. Even when we know things, sometimes it takes words to make them concrete. Like in some of our silth magics, where the name must be named before the witchery can be." She paused a time again. "If we had been anyone but the meth we are, Bagnel. Anyone but silth and brethren, southerner and packsteader . . ."

He touched her paw lightly, diffidently, actually squeezed it gently for a second, then hastened out of the cubicle.

Marika stared at the cold white door. Softly, she said, "They might have made legends." She could recall him having touched her only once before, for all they had been in close contact for so many years. "We will have to make them for them, for they will never be."

He had dared, at last. And fled.

One did not touch silth.

She had touched him once, before she had known him, atop a snowy ridge as they stared down upon the nomad-gutted remains of the place he had called home. It had been his responsibility to defend that place, and he had failed.

Silth did not show fear. Ponath huntresses did not show fear. Neither did either weep.

Marika wept.

Chapter Thirty-Two

I

For the first time in nearly six years Marika put the mirror project out of mind—though she debated with herself many days before admitting that it could get on without her there trying to run everything herself.

Kiljar allowed her to draft whomever she wanted from among the Redoriad dark-faring Mistresses of the Ship. She took the best as her instructresses.

She went up into the dark, out into the deep, and drove herself to exhaustion again and again, learning the Up-and-Over. She pushed herself as relentlessly as she had when she was younger, and she regained some of the enthusiasm that she had had then. She forced herself to learn the guile and craft that were needed to placate or elude the great darkness lurking at the edge of the system, waiting for no one knew what, filled with a hunger so alien it was impossible to comprehend.

"While we perceive them in countless ways they are all much the same, what you call ghosts," Kiljar said. Not once in all her years had Marika encountered another silth who

called them that. Most called them those-who-dwell. A very
few did not believe in them at all. "The farther from the
world's surface you get, the larger they are, and fewer, till
out in the gulf you find the rare black giants.

"Most of us do not worry about what they are or why. We
just use them. But there are those sisters, seekers after
knowledge, who have been debating about them for centuries. One popular hypothesis about their distribution says
that they feed upon one another, like the creatures of the
sea, larger upon smaller, and the largest are least able to
withstand the distortion of space that occurs near large
masses. The perceived size gradient does run right down to
the surface here, each ghost seemingly pushing as close as it
can. The feeding theory would say for safety from larger
ghosts and because if they get closer they might catch
something smaller.

"I do not accept an ecological-feeding hypothesis myself.
I have been silth more years than you care to imagine and
never have I witnessed one ghost preying upon another. And
I know for a fact that the gradient, while generally true, will
not hold up to close examination. Among the several thousand forms ghosts take there are those who refuse to follow
theory. Even out near the big black there are several different small forms. I have seen them. Ones no bigger than my
paw flashed about in swarms of millions.

"The hypothesis of our age, perhaps growing out of brethren disbelief in anything not subject to measurement and
physical analysis, not yet widely accepted but becoming
more so, is that they do not exist at all. This hypothesis says
they exist only mentally, as reflections of silth minds trying
to impose patterns upon the universe. The hypothesis makes
of them nothing more than symbols by which powers
entirely of the mind are able to manipulate the universe.
This hypothesis would have it that silth trained that way
could do everything the rest of us can without ever summon-
ing those-who-dwell."

"No one actually has done that, though. Right?" Marika
asked. She like to believe she had an open mind, but she

could not see this. She had seen ghosts before she had heard of silth or silth powers. Her very conception of them, as supernatural entities, came from that time, when nothing else in her experience could explain what she had sensed and experienced.

"Silth tend to be conservative, as well you know. They remain devoted to methods that work. From a purely pragmatic point of view it does not matter if those-who-dwell are real or symbolic. What counts is the result of the manipulation."

Marika reminded Kiljar, "I saw ghosts before I ever heard of silth. I still recall the first instance vividly. It was right after we found out that the nomads were watching our packstead. I had developed a feeble grasp on the touch and was trying to track my dam while she was out hunting them."

"That has been explained away as genetic imprinting, the argument being that the touch itself is proof enough that we rely on the powers of the mind. It has been pointed out that we never summon those-who-dwell to make a touch, only to physically affect our surroundings. And the summons itself is with the touch."

"Mistress, we are entering an age when meth, even silth, prefer explanations that are not mystical or magical. They will search for new reasons. I am content to accept what is, without explanation. If it works, I am satisfied. I do not need to know *how* it works. But, to change the subject, I believe I am ready for my solo star flight. What do the Mistresses who have been instructing me say?"

"They agree with you. Almost. But you have yet to make a supervised crossing to another star. It is a rule: The first time you go you must take someone with you who has experience. Just in case."

Marika was mildly irked, yet could not understand why she should be. Kiljar made perfect sense. She supposed it was the rebellious pup within her still, the pup with the overweening self-confidence. "Very well. I will go do that. If I can find a Mistress willing to go with me."

"Be careful, Marika."

"I shall. I have goals I have not yet achieved."

Kiljar's ragged face tightened momentarily. She was not pleased by the way Marika had fixed herself on stalking the Serke and rogue brethren. "Be very careful, pup."

"Pup, mistress?"

"Sometimes you are. Still. You came to your powers too early."

Grauel and Barlog looked grim as they took their places. They controlled the appearance of fear, but they were afraid. Grauel had been into the void only once, and that time she had not passed beyond the orbit of Biter. Once returned to the surface, she had stated a strong preference for remaining there the rest of her life. Barlog never had been up.

Now Marika wanted to drag them with her to one of the fabled starworlds. Worlds in which they still did not wholly believe.

"Relax," Marika told them. "It will seem strange, but it will be no more difficult or dangerous than a surface flight from Ruhaack to Skiljansrode."

"It isn't the same," Barlog insisted. "Not the same at all. Inside."

"We're still Ponath huntresses, Marika," Grauel said. "Very old ones, too. Very near the end of our value as huntresses. If we were in the Ponath still we would be on the edge of becoming Wise. A year or two more at the most. And you know the Wise. They are not inclined toward risk."

"I'll do my best to keep it from becoming too harrowing. After all, the purpose is to instruct me, not to take off on an adventure. That time lies a way down the river yet." She beckoned the senior bath, who brought a bowl of the golden drink. "Each of you drink about a cup of this elixir."

The Mistress who was to share and chaperone the journey tossed off a drink after Grauel and Barlog finished, then settled her tail upon the axis platform. She had been to the starworlds countless times. For her this journey would be routine.

The bath drank, then their senior brought the bowl to Marika. She finished it, feeling the drug taking effect immediately. "Have you finished your rites?"

The senior bath said she had.

"Good. Is everyone strapped?" She noted the tight grips Grauel and Barlog had upon their weapons. This was one time she had not needed to remind Barlog. The huntress had brought her arms as talismans against the unknown.

Marika touched her own weapons. Rifle across her back. Revolver inside the tattered otec coat that had been with her almost forever. She carried a knife in her boot, another on her belt, and a third concealed under her arm. She had ammunition enough for a small battle and dried meat enough for a week.

She felt foolish when she gave it a thought. She, too, was carrying amulets into the unknown.

"Take it up," the practiced Mistress said. "Time is wasting."

Marika closed her eyes, gathered the strongest of those-who-dwell, and began the long ascent into the void.

The dream of a lifetime was coming true. Her feet were upon the path to the stars.

She was terrified.

Though during the long climb she attained velocities not to be imagined onplanet, she became impatient. She wanted to get into it in a hurry, get through it, get it over, get the fright thoroughly tamed.

The void demanded new realms of thought of those who would navigate it. Mental habits from the surface could not be transferred. Often dared not be, lest they be fatal.

It was traditional not to enter the Up-and-Over before passing the orbit of Biter, the outer of the major moons. Seldom were the appropriate ghosts numerous enough closer to the planet. Impatient as she was, Marika began seeking those-who-dwell long before the proper time. Her guide refused to allow her to gather them. She pushed the

darkship hard till she reached a point where her tutor found
the ghost population acceptably dense.

Marika felt she could have called them to her much
earlier, but she did not argue. She had not come to argue.
She had come to get a final test over so she could walk the
stars alone.

Sight on the star, the Mistress sent, and Marika fixed her
gaze upon the Redoriad star she had chosen as her destination. *Gather those-who-dwell. Keep that star firmly fixed in
your mind. Do you have them? Star and those-who-dwell?*

I do.

*Make the star grow slowly larger in your mind's eye.
Squeeze those-who-dwell with all the will you have. Let
them know that you will not release them till that star has
become a sun.*

The horde of ghosts Marika gathered was larger than any
she had seen any void-faring Mistress gather before. She did
as she was instructed, squeezing down with a mind strong on
the dark side.

The stars around her went out like electric lights suddenly
extinguished. For an instant she almost lost the spark that
was her destination. She resurrected it in imagination,
pounded it into those-who-dwell, who boiled around the
darkship, frenzied by the effort she exerted, furious in their
effort to escape.

The spark swelled swiftly in sudden jerks, as though she
and the darkship were skipping vast tracts of intermediate
void. That star became the size of a new coin.

Let go! the Mistress sent. *Let go now!* Marika had
become so fixed upon driving toward her destination that
she had not thought to release her bearers.

What did I do wrong?

You almost hurled us into that star. The Mistress was in
a state approaching shock.

*I apologize, Mistress. I was concentrating upon control-
ling those-who-dwell.*

*You did so. You definitely did. Never have I seen a
passage made so swiftly, so suddenly. We will see how you*

manage the return journey. If you are more aware of your destination. If so, I will tell the most senior you are ready to fare on your own.

You seem distressed, Mistress.

I have experienced nothing like this. I have encountered no such overwhelming demonstration of power. You hardly needed the bath. She then let it drop, and refused to be drawn forth on the matter again. *Feel for the world. You are on the sunward side of its orbit.*

Marika found it, to the left of and slightly beyond the sun. *Up-and-Over?*

Carefully. You do not need to set records getting there.

Marika repeated her performance, though with a gentler touch. *How was that, Mistress?*

Less unsettling. But you need to develop a subtler touch. Take the darkship down. The Mistress presented a mind picture of their destination.

From orbit the planet looked little different from Marika's homeworld. Less icy, perhaps, but even here, according to her tutor, the interstellar cloud had begun to have its effect. In a few hundred years this world, too, would be gripped by an age of ice.

As steller distances go, Marika, we are still very close to home. We see very few stars in our home sky. If we go out in the right direction, so that we pass beyond the cloud, we can see stars by the tens of thousands.

As Marika watched the world expand and become down, she realized, with a chilly feeling of déjà vu, that she had fulfilled her dream. She had walked among the stars. As a dream it had lost meaning and impact in the pressure of more immediate concerns.

"Stars beneath my feet," she whispered.

The darkship dropped through feeble clouds and turned out over a desert, an environment familiar to Marika only from photographs and tapes. There were no deserts in those parts of her own world that she knew. She realized that she had no broad, eyewitness familiarity with her native planet. She knew only a long, narrow band running from the Rift through the Ponath, Maksche, TelleRai, and on south to Ruhaack. She had seen perhaps a thousandth of her world. And now she was stalking the universe!

Toward the sun, Marika. Two points to your right. Can you feel it?

Yes.

This world felt nothing like her own. It felt incredibly empty, lonely. Her touch rang hollow here, except in one very well-defined direction, sharp as a knife stroke. She pushed the darkship forward, through a wind she found unnaturally warm even at that high altitude.

Barren mountains rose above the horizon. They were bizarre mountains, naked of vegetation, worn by the wind, each standing free in a forest of stone pillars. Some reached five hundred feet into the air, striated in shades of red and ocher, and each wore a skirt of detritus that climbed half-way up its thighs.

She found the cloister without further aid from her tutor. It lay atop one of the pillars. It was a rusty brown color, built of blocks of dried mud made on the banks of a trickle of a river running far below.

Sisters came into the central courtyard as the darkship slowed, hovered. They peered upward. Marika let the darkship settle.

"Welcome to Kim," her tutor said once the darkship had grounded. "We will rest for a day before we start back."

Marika stepped down onto alien rock, hot rock, under a sun too large and bright, and shuddered. She was here. There. Upon a starworld. The pup who had shivered in the chill wind licking the watchtower at the Degnan packstead and had stared at the nighttime sky, had achieved the impossible dream she had dreamed then.

She watched Grauel and Barlog dismount, their fur on end, their weapons gripped tightly, their eyes in unceasing flickering motion. They felt the strangeness too. They felt the absence of the background of unconscious touch that existed everywhere at home.

Marika met Redoriad silth whom she did not remember

five minutes later. They asked questions about the homeworld, for their cloister was off the main starpaths and they had little news. She and the Mistress answered, but she paid little heed to them or what she said. She was unable to get over the fact that she had done what she had done.

Marika did not sleep much during the time set aside for resting. Her curiosity was too strong once the impact of achievement began to lessen. She spent hours learning everything she could about the world.

That was not much. The silth had little commerce with the natives, who were very primitive and had nothing to offer in trade. The Redoriad maintained the cloister on Kim only as a means of enforcing their claim upon the planet and as an intermediate base from which further starworlds could be explored and exploited.

II

The homeworld flashed into being. *Very good,* Marika's tutor sent. *Almost perfect this time. You will do, Marika. You will do. You need to study your stars now, so that you can recognize them from any distance and angle. Then you will be ready to roam on your own.*

Do darkships get lost?

Sometimes. Not so much anymore. The sisterhoods do not do much exploring these days.

Why not?

In the early days the voidfarers visited more than ten thousand stars and found little worth finding. There is little out there. Certainly little that can be profitably exploited. Nevertheless, in ten thousand stars there has been enough found that the few silth with the star-faring skill are kept quite busy. It has been a generation since anyone has had time for exploration.

Except for the Serke.

Perhaps. They found something, certainly.

Did they not, though.

Marika had her next step already planned. A thorough search of everything salvaged from the Serke before their disbandment. Somewhere in the records there might be a clue—though no one had yet found it.

The homeworld swelled, and with it a feeling of welcome, of returning to where she properly belonged, as the unconscious touch-world of all meth gradually enfolded her. She looked back at Grauel and Barlog, but could not see their faces. She sent a tendril of touch drifting over them, found them relaxed, pleased, almost comfortable. Out on the world called Kim they had been nervous and irritable all the time.

The darkship settled into the court of the new Redoriad cloister. There Marika's tutor immediately took her leave, heading for Mistress's quarters without a backward glance. As she rose to go on to her own cloister Marika wondered what new rumors would be spread about her now.

Hardly had she settled into the Reugge landing court, dismounted, formally thanked her bath, and begun soothing Grauel and Barlong, when Edzeka of Skiljansrode appeared. She hastened toward Marika with a portentious step.

"Something is wrong," Grauel said. "Bad wrong. Else she would not have come out of her den."

The joy had gone out of Barlog too. "I have an awful feeling, Marika. I do not think I want to hear this. Whatever it may be."

"Then go. It is time you took a ceremonial meal with the voctors anyway. Isn't it?"

Both huntresses gave her looks that suggested she was mad for saying they should leave her.

"Edzeka. What are you doing here? You look grim."

"A nasty problem, mistress. Very nasty."

Marika dismissed everyone else who had gathered around, who took it as a slight. She did not care. Never would she let herself fall into the manners and stylized forms of silth relationships. "Trouble at Skiljansrode?"

"Major, perhaps, mistress. The prisoner Kublin has escaped."

Marika did not permit her feelings to show. "How did this happen? And how long ago?"

"Shortly after you departed for the stars. Or maybe just before. It is not absolutely certain yet. There is some evidence he chose that moment to move specifically because you would be out of touch. There were copies of intercepts at his workstation mentioning you going out. We have not pinned down his time of escape because it came during his off-hours. When not at his workstation he remained in his cell, even if offered an opportunity to move around."

"I see. How did he manage it? Who was lax?"

"No one was lax, insofar as I could determine. He did it with the talent. There is no other explanation that will accommodate the facts, though not all of them are clear yet. Several voctors were injured or slain, and their injuries are all of the sort caused by one who wields the talent. It was the failure of those voctors to report that alerted us to the fact that something unusual was happening. We first thought someone had gotten in from outside, it making no sense for a prisoner to attempt escape. It was a while before someone noticed he was absent—by which time we did at least know that no one had come in from outside."

"A search is being made, of course?"

"Every darkship we could lift. I myself came here aboard a saddleship so no bath would be wasted on the carrying of a message. I thought you would want this reported directly, without it passing through the paws of anyone else."

"Thank you. That was thoughtful. How is the search progressing?"

"I do not know. I have been here awaiting you. Not well, though, I fear, else someone would have followed to tell me he has been recaptured.

"He will be difficult to take if he has been honing wehrlen's skills all this time." Already Marika had begun consulting a mental map. These days Skiljansrode lay far up in frozen country. It would be a long walk for anyone, getting from that packfast to country where one could live off the land. Almost impossible even for a skilled nomad huntress accustomed to the ways of the frozen wastes. Due south would be both the shortest and easiest route.

Edzeka would know that. No point telling her what she knew, or upbraiding her for what could not have been her fault. "How much food did he take out with him? What sort of clothing and equipment? Has that been determined yet?"

"It had not at the time I left, mistress."

"I know him. He would have prepared extensively. He would have made sure he knew all the risks and all the needs he would face. He would have prepared to the limit allowed by his situation. And he would not have moved unless he was convinced his chances were excellent, even with silth hunting him. He is a coward. But he doesn't make desperate moves. Knowing the fickleness of the All, we would be utter fools to hope the winter would take him for us. What is your method of search?"

"I positioned three of my darkships twenty miles farther south than I believed he could possibly have traveled, even with the best of luck. The middle darkship I stationed right on top of the base course he is going to have to make. The other two I placed to either paw, at the limits of sight, within strong touch. All three darkships are at one thousand feet. That places a barrier forty miles wide directly across his path. He cannot avoid being seen or sensed without going at least twenty miles out of his way. In that country, in that ice and snow, that would mean at least three days of extra work. That should give winter's paw a little extra edge."

"I like that. Go on."

"The other darkships are searching for him or physical evidence of his passage. The wind is blowing hard and there is fresh powder snow, but even so he cannot help leaving a trail."

"Very good. Very good indeed. Logically, that should do for him, one way or another. Keep pressing so that he has to keep going out of his way. He will not dare light a fire. His food supply will dwindle. When he becomes weakened and tired he will have more difficulty hiding from the touch."

Marika was not confident of that. She ought to claim a favor from Bagnel. His tradermales had tools more useful than silth talents. A few dirigibles prowling the wastes searching with heat detectors might locate Kublin more quickly than any hundred silth.

"Edzeka. The hard question. What chance that he had help? From inside or out?"

"From inside, none whatsoever. Any helper would have fled with him, knowing we would truthsay every prisoner left behind. Which we did, without result. And there never have been any friends of the brethren or Serke among the sisters. Help from outside? Maybe. If someone knew he was there and had a means of getting messages to and from him."

"A thought only." Another thought: the means of communication might have existed right inside Kublin's head. In all the years of isolation he would have had ample time to practice his fartouching. "Nothing came of the truthsaying?"

"Nothing had as of my departure. Final results will be available upon my return. Had they amounted to anything I am sure I would have heard."

"Yes, Well. You may break radio silence if anything critical develops. If you do not have the necessary equipment, requisition it before you leave."

"Thank you, mistress."

"Have you enjoyed Ruhaack? You ought to get out more."

"I have my work, mistress."

"Yes, as we all do. Thank you for the report. This bears thought." Marika extricated herself and hurried toward her apartment, lost in contemplation of what Kublin's escape might portend.

If he did make it out, he could become especially troublesome if he did know what had happened to Gradwohl. She could not be certain he had been unconscious throughout their confrontation.

She had to consult Bagnel. Bagnel knew a little about Kublin. He could judge what Kublin's escape could mean within the brethren.

Silth and huntresses who had survived the destruction of Maksche controlled that wing of the Ruhaack cloister where Marika dwelt. They were few, but intensely loyal to Marika, for they knew that she had tried to avenge their injury and knew she had not given up hope of further vengeance. They guarded her interests well. It was something of an amusing paradox. Marika had not been popular at all before the attack on Maksche.

A sister named Jancatch, who had been but a novice at the time of the Maksche disaster, awaited Marika at the entrance to her cloister within the cloister. Her face was taut. Her ears were down.

"Trouble?" Marika asked, thinking, what else?

"Perhaps, mistress. There was an urgent appeal for your presence from Most Senior Kiljar of the Redoriad some hours ago. An almost desperate call. We replied that you could not come because you had not returned from your travels. We were asked to inform you immediately you did arrive, and to ask you to waste no time. No reason was stated, but there are rumors that she is dying."

"Kiljar has been dying for most of the time that I have known her. With one breath she predicts that she will not live to see the sun rise again, and with the next vows to outlive all the carrion eaters waiting to grab the Redoriad first chair."

"This time I believe that the crisis is genuine, mistress. The Redoriad have called in all their cloister councils and all their high ones who are inside the system. They have closed their gates to ordinary traffic."

"Call them back. Speak to Kiljar herself if that is possible. Tell her or them that I have returned. That I am available immediately if necessary. Grauel, Barlog, assem-

ble my saddleship. I will go over right now if that is what she
desires."

It was. Marika departed within minutes.

She was not welcomed at the Redoriad cloister. The halls
were thick with important silth. One and all, they eyed her
with hostility. She ignored them and the growls that came
when she was granted immediate entry to Kiljar's apartment. Even the most powerful of them had not been permitted that.

III

Kiljar appeared very near the edge. Her voice was little
more than a whisper. She could not lift her head, nor more
than slightly stretch her lips in greeting. But she did manage
to issue strong orders to her attendants to leave them alone.

Marika felt a sadness rise within her, a rare sadness, a
rare sorrow. Few meth meant much to her, but Kiljar had
become one of those few. She took the old silth's paw.
"Mistress?"

Kiljar called upon her final reserves. "The All calls me,
pup. This time there will be no deafening my ears to the
summons."

"Yes." One did not hide such a truth from a Kiljar. "My
heart is torn." One should not hide that truth either.

"It has been good to me, Marika. It gave me more years
that I expected or had the right to hope. I hope I have used
them as well as I believe I have."

"I think you have, mistress. I think you may have accomplished more than you suspect. I think you will be recalled
as one of the great Redoriad."

"I am not sure I wish to be recalled that way, pup. I think
I want to be one of the remembered names in your legend. I
think I want to be remembered as your teacher, as the one
who brought you to see your responsibilities, your importance, as she who taught you to harness your inclination to

excess. . . ." Kiljar succumbed to a racking cough. Unable to help, Marika clung to her paw and fought back the sorrow bringing the water to her eyes.

Kiljar's paw tightened upon hers. "I do not want to go into the darkness riding the fear that I have failed, Marika. You are not of my sisterhood. You are not of my blood. Yet I have made of you the favored pup of my pack. I have done much for you that you know, and much more that you do not. I have watched you grow, and have clung to life desperately in hopes that your growth would become complete and you would mature into a silth fit to stand beside Dra-Legit, Chahein, and Singer Harden. You are in the position, and these are the times. You have the power and the talent to shape the entire world. You are doing so, with your great metal suns. They are the one regret I know I will be carrying into the darkness. I would have lived to have seen them shedding their warmth."

Marika's throat had tightened till she could scarcely speak. She had to struggle to croak, "Mistress, you have been a true friend. I have found few of those. It is not a world for making friends."

"The great never have many friends, pup. Perhaps I have been less a friend than you think, for I have had the temerity to try to shape your destiny. One friend does not try to force a role upon another."

"You are a friend."

"As you will. You know what I want, do you not?"

"I think I do."

"You would, yes. You always know. But I will say it anyway. I do not want you to return to old hatreds once I can no longer be here to peer over your shoulder and be the whisper of your conscience. We have made a sound peace with the brethren. A peace that can last if it is given a chance. An accommodation with which the majority of silth and brethren both are content. To take up old grievances now would . . ."

"I will not, mistress. Though my stomach sours and my heart still fears their power, I will do nothing to alter the balance. I have reoriented my future toward the stars, as I had aimed during my novitiate. I have done what I can here. I will take my anger into the void in my search for the rogue Serke and their brethren masters. I will do nothing here unless others force me."

"Yes. That is well. Go stalk the stars. Find the criminals. That is where the true danger lies—though it must be growing weaker. They have not been back, except to sneak messengers in, since you drove *Starstalker* into the void. But do not allow that hunt to rule you entirely, Marika. The All has given you talents most silth would commit the thousand crimes to possess. You have learned to evade the consequences of the Jiana complex. I hope. Its aura does not hang so strongly upon you now. You have resurrected the Reugge from the ashes and have given them the potential to become one of the great sisterhoods of the future."

Kiljar coughed again, not so terribly. Marika waited in silence, knowing Kiljar was working hard to get said what she had to say.

"I suspect you now face an opportunity to do for the meth race what you have done for the Reugge. If you walk the stars in the proper frame of mind."

"Mistress?"

"I see three frames. Three great portraits sketched upon a canvas of time, perhaps overlapping one another, all forming a complete new life. The first is that of a pup. I forsee you dark-faring for the wonder, for the thrill of venturing where none have gone before. That is a thrill I knew well when I was young and first faring the void.

"A second frame surrounds your quest for revenge upon those who did you, the Reugge, and all silth so much evil. It is in your character to become fixed within that frame, and to lose the wonder and the grand potential of what could come of a successful stalk. You must carry with you always the knowledge that a successful hunt could define the entire future of our race. Have you thought at all about what might come of open intercourse between our world and that of these aliens the Serke discovered?"

"Only a little, mistress," Marika admitted. "My entire concentration has been devoted to the mirrors. But great evils or great benefits, surely."

"Indeed. One or the other, but nothing trivial. They will be very different, pup. Very different, indeed, from what I have been able to learn. You must realize that they will not all be magnificent and terrible weapons and technologies and whatnot that not even the brethren have begun to suspect. They will be modes of thought and slants of eye and ways of hearing that have not occurred even to our greatest thinkers. They will be the product of a distinct evolution, with all that implies in the way of millions of years of shaping minds as well as forms. They will infect us with ten thousand new ideas, new hopes, new fears—as, I am sure, we will infect them. Imagine the impact of the silth ideal upon a species that has no concept of that sort."

"I have seen the edges of such things, mistress, and I find them frightening."

"Indeed. And how much more frightening to silth who are narrower of mind? Who have known but one way since first rising to walk upon their legs alone? How threatening to them? There is great potential in this meeting of races, and its shaping for good or evil will lie strongly in the paws of the successor to Bestrei, for that successor will have the strength to determine anything she wishes in the void. You recall the frontier maxim you quoted to me so often. As strength goes."

"I understand, mistress."

"I hope you do, Marika. I pray you do. Truly. Like it or not, the future lies in your paws. You are the shaper. The eyes of all silth will be upon you after my passing. Your defeat of *Starstalker's* raid and your mirrors have made of you the best known of silth, though you sought no notoriety. The world over, meth will look to you first. It is a heavy responsibility. Can you be a Dra-Legit? A Charhein? A Singer Harden for our times?"

Had Kiljar not been so close to dying, Marika might have

become impatient. At the moment she could say only, "I will not disappoint you, mistress."

"Good. Good, pup. And do not disappoint yourself. Sit with me now. In silence. I believe I am ready. I have done all that I must do."

Kiljar closed her eyes. Marika felt her composing herself through the mental rituals. She continued to hold the old silth's paw.

The All was not long in claiming Kiljar, then. And for hours afterward Marika did not think of anything else, did not once calculate what Kiljar's passing might mean on the mundane level of what direction the Redoriad would now take. Even the importance of Kublin's escape did not penetrate her awareness till she had come to an accommodation of her loss.

In her grief she was reminded that even now, when she had acquired the power, she had not discharged a debt placed upon her when she was but ten years old. She had not seen to the Mourning of the Degnan pack. That was a thing that would have to be done. She would discuss it with Grauel and Barlog.

Kiljar gone. The world would not be the same.

Chapter Thirty-Three

I

Marika worked out her grief aboard her saddleship. She flew north, into the wilds below Skiljansrode, and spent three days in the hunt for Kublin. Three days during which few traces of the fugitive were found. He had planned well, her crafty little littermate. He traveled by night, in the dark of the moons, in snow storms, in high winds, seldom leaving a trail that could be seen from aloft the next day. Those who hunted him always knew where he had to be within a hundred square miles, but they could not pin him down more closely.

After three days Marika left the hunt, resigned. The All would will Kublin caught or not, according to its grand design. She had more pressing matters to attend.

She made daily pilgrimages into the void, studying the progress of the mirrors, learning the neighbor stars of her sun. Each of those, she discovered, had its unique flavor that she could identify instantly if she simply abandoned thought and opened to the All. Once she found the key the learning process accelerated till she could know a star in seconds.

All was well with the mirrors. Bagnel kept a firm paw on the project. She was not needed there looking over everyone's shoulder every moment.

She went out to Kim again and experimented there, and found she was able to learn the new, strange stars visible only from there in just a matter of hours.

Home again, after having intentionally stretched herself by not pausing to rest upon the planet. She returned to Ruhaack to catch up on the situation upon the homeworld.

Kublin had not been taken, though Bagnel had sent a squadron of dirigibles to help with the search. Their technological advantages had been of no value.

Marika began to suspect that her littermate had used the fartouch to call in help after all.

She learned that the new most senior of the Redoriad was a silth named Balbrach, who had been nominated by Kiljar before her passing. Balbrach had pledged to pursue her predecessor's policies, particularly in operating in concert with the Reugge. The alliance represented a concentration of power unseen for generations.

There had been a Serke courier incursion. The patrols hoping to jump the messenger had been insufficiently alert. The darkship had gotten past them and gotten down without betraying its landing site.

"We're still hunting for them," Bagnel told her. "We have traces picked up by satellite, but the optics just aren't what they should be. If our resources weren't so totally committed to the mirror project, we might develop an observation network. . . . "

"It isn't really that critical. What we have will do the job. It's just a matter of forging better communications between your radar operators and our huntresses."

Bagnel was amused. "Of course. Just plant a qualified fartoucher in each of our installations. Or put one of our radio operators aboard each of your darkships. Nothing to it. Assuming you can get around however many millennia of tradition."

"Of course," Marika said, with sarcasm equaling his.

"Nothing to it. There are times when I wonder how we meth have managed to survive."

Bagnel had come down from the Hammer soon after learning of her return. He had called her from the brethren legation at Ruhaack and they had flown together into the wastes to that remote base from which the Reugge cloister at Maksche had been attacked. The brethren still maintained a small establishment there, rebuilt after Marika destroyed the base, as a way station at the intersection of dirigible lines. Marika had gone out upon her saddleship, flying off the wing of Bagnel's increasingly venerable Sting fighter. Now they were aloft in the Sting, putting it through its paces.

"I hear you've been promoted again," Marika said.

"Yes. As always, the factors reward incompetence. The leading mirror is now all mine to demolish."

Marika was amused. He was so persistently negative about his own abilities. "I will be going away soon, Bagnel. As soon as modifications to my darkship are completed and I have trained a group of new bath." She had asked for the four strongest upcoming bath the Reugge and Redoriad could provide. The extra would be a reserve, would allow rest and rotation during extended interstellar passages. And she had a further experiment in mind that would require the presence of an extra silth. "I have the darkship at the dome on Biter being fitted to carry a detachable pod in which we can haul stores."

"Then you plan to be gone a long time."

"I'll be back in plenty of time to celebrate the triumphant completion of the first mirror."

"I see little enough of you now. If you disappear for years again . . ."

"I seriously doubt I will be gone that long. I was teasing."

"You're going after the Serke, aren't you?"

"That's the main reason. But also to see what's out there. Just to see it."

"Then the Serke are as much excuse as they are reason."

"Of course they are. I'm really going because that is what

I've wanted to do from the moment we pups first heard stories of meth who went to the stars."

"I wish I could see . . ."

"You could. One more wouldn't make much difference. You might decrease our range, but not enough to concern me."

"I wish . . . I have too many responsibilities, Marika. We have reached a point where the mirrors definitely look practical. No, I couldn't. Yes, I would like to see the stars. Maybe later. After this is done, and the warm is falling. After you have done what you have to do. And that frightens me."

"Why?"

"I am frightened by what you may find. What you have been doing cannot remain a secret. Those here who are still in contact with your enemies will hear about what you are doing. And they will relay the news. It will find the Serke before you do. And because you are Marika, and can do what other silth cannot, they will be afraid. They will prepare for you. They'll be waiting."

Marika had thought of that, and it was of concern to her. She did not know how to prevent it. "You'll just have to do better preventing contact. That's all I can say."

"You know I'll try. But do not forget that that is not my specific responsibility. I can only nudge and urge and appeal and beg and suggest. Others, perhaps with less concern for your welfare, will be in control."

"I have faith in you, Bagnel. Fear not. We will fly together again, in this same box of rusty bolts, over this same barren landscape. Let's hope it's on a day when fewer dooms shadow the world."

"That can't help but be, I think. Though the dooms breed."

Marika's eyes narrowed. "You are trying to tell me something."

"Perhaps . . . Being out at the mirror or the Hammer most of the time, I have little opportunity to keep track of what those who look for rogues are doing. But before I joined you a friend came to me with the latest rumor they had tapped."

"Yes?"

"The warlock is back."

Marika took a minute to get herself under control. Then she took another. "That is impossible. He perished when I destroyed those who had ravaged Maksche."

"I report only hearsay."

"The warlock?"

"The same one. The one who was the rogues' great hope a few years ago."

"I suppose it had to be," Marika murmured. "And I blinded myself."

"What?"

'I have done the unforgivable, Bagnel. I have made the same mistake twice. That is never forgiven."

But who could believe Kublin in the role of the warlock? A whimpering coward?

"What is it, Marika?"

"Nothing crucial. Let's fly a bit more, in silence, then take our leave."

There was something Marika had to do before departing, before pursuing her stalk among the stars, and she was afraid.

II

Marika brought the darkship out of the Up-and-Over virtually on top of the darkness that lurked at the edge of her home system. That blackness reeked to the touch, stinking of wickedness and death, of gnawed bones and ripped flesh and corrupt corpses and hatred unconstrained. If the void had a heart of evil, this ghost was its animate form.

This ghost was like no other she had encountered, and she had identified hundreds of different kinds. This ghost was, in a way, an absence. Most others seemed bright, flighty, sometimes curious, sometimes afraid, but always colorful and seldom inimical unless under silth direction.

This was an absence of color moved by its own grand malice. It was a thing that did not need direction to be inimical. It would strike out at the unwary. Only because it could not move as swiftly as lesser voidghosts, and because the silth had learned to appease and baffle and, rarely, to control it, did it not strike every darkship that tried to leave the system.

Control. That was Marika's goal. The highest or darkest of dark-sider sorceries, managed only by a dozen silth before her . . .

It moved toward her, almost as swiftly as thought. She squeezed the ghosts that carried her darkship, fleeing, pulling it along after her, staying out of its reach while she explored it with her touch.

She let it catch up.

Three times she recoiled from its cold, malignant vibration before she found sufficient courage to reach farther, to strive to control it.

Control came far more easily than she had expected. In some way she could not fathom her dark side spoke to its, and meshed with it, and, in moments, the great monster became an extension of her will, a force she could hurl as simply as tossing a pebble with a flick of her wrist. She threw it at a piece of cometary debris. It struck savagely, compressed, caused gases to boil, to explode. A short-lived flare illuminated space.

Marika turned loose and backed away, awed. So much power! No wonder Bestrei was feared.

She reached again, lightly, and found the darkness possessed of a fearful respect for her, a vague, almost thoughtless admiration for her dark power. It acknowledged her its mistress after those few moments.

She backed away again. And now, at last, she began to see and understand what it was so many silth had seen in her, and had feared.

She reviewed the strongest silth she knew, and knew none

of them could have done what she had. Few could have taken control of the ghost at all, let alone so swiftly, so easily, so thoroughly.

And she knew, then, what it was she had sensed about Bestrei that time when their trails had crossed. Bestrei could take a great dark ghost easily too—though hopefully without imagination, or cunning, or any especial ability to direct it with her intellect. Bestrei, too, was slanted far toward the dark side.

Marika turned and drove toward the homeworld, toward the dome upon Biter where her venture was being prepared, but she watched over her shoulder, considering a region about thirty degrees to one side of the Manestar. *Bestrei,* she sent, in a hopeless long touch. *I am coming, The long wait of the meth is nearly done. Soon we will meet.*

It was from that region that the Serke had come each time they had struck at the mirrors. Somewhere in that area she would cross their trail.

"Marika, you look terrible," Graul said when she returned. "What did you do?"

And Barlog said, "She has that look of doom about her again."

"That is it. Isn't it? It's been absent for years. What did you do out there, Marika?"

Marika refused to explain. They would learn soon enough.

Grauel kept after her, but Barlog said little more. She looked terrified of what was to come, for she and Grauel, as always, would walk Marika's path with her.

Marika spent a busy few days contacting silth all across the world, silth with whom she had worked in her rogue-hunting days. She left suggestions and instructions, for there had been no further trace of Kublin. He had escaped for certain, though. The warlock rumor had begun to grow.

How could she have been so blind? The thought that he might be the one had never occurred to her.

Everyone who had investigated the destruction of Maksche, silth or brethren, agreed that that whole city had died because of the warlock's determination to kill her. And she had spared him twice.

Why did he hate her so? She had given him no cause, ever, that she knew.

He would not escape again. If he persisted, she would destroy him as surely as she would anyone else who rebelled against silth power.

The waiting was not a happy time.

III

Marika's first venture through the Up-and-Over was the most ambitious she had yet tried, three times the length of the journey to Kim. The magnitude of it overcame her.

She lost her nerve and turned loose before she should have, not maintaining the courage to follow what her talent told her was right. The star she sought still lay ahead, brighter now, but still far away. She searched the broad night, locating her home star and all the stars she already knew, then noted all those that she had not seen before. There in the heart of the dust cloud those were few, and she was able to inventory them in her mind with no trouble at all.

She dithered awhile, reveling in the glory of the void, till Grauel and Barlog began to disturb her with their increasing nervousness. Then she went down through her loophole again, gathered ghosts—which were scarce in the deep— and went on, pulling the darkship in close to the target sun.

It was not an inhabited or even habitable system. Marika had known before she jumped that it could be little more than a landmark on the trail the Serke walked, both because the system had been investigated often and because all logic said the Serke would have taken up residence in a system capable of sustaining life. Perhaps they shared it with the aliens or had taken control of the aliens' homeworld, as they wished to do with the homeworld of the meth.

In any case it did not seem plausible that two races of apparently similar needs would stumble into one another in the neighborhood of a giant or dwarf. Each would be seeking worlds of potential value, and those circled only certain types of stars. Only a small percentage of stars fit. Marika meant to concentrate upon those and use other types only as stellar landmarks.

Of course, all that had been reasoned and done before, in the hot, furious days after the bombing of TelleRai, when the might of all the dark-faring sisterhoods had been flung into the hunt. But Marika meant to carry the search far afield, avoiding stars already claimed or visited. The surviving Serke documents suggested that that sisterhood had been much more daring than any other, and that they had visited scores of starworlds to which they had laid no formal claim. That, unlike the other orders, they had kept exploring long after it had come to be deemed counterproductive.

It would be among those unnamed and unclaimed worlds that she would find her enemies.

She drifted near that first target star, a red giant, devouring its vast glory, extending her touch through its space in search of watchers, feeling for new or unusual ghosts or one of the great blacks, and found nothing of interest but the giant star itself. She scanned the night, learning the new stars she saw, then looked for and found her next target. This was another star on an almost straight line out from her homeworld. This one lay at the edge of explored space and would place her outside the dust cloud when she reached it. She would see the universe as she never had from home.

She faced that with trepidation, for the few silth who had been that far out had been unable to relate the marvel they had felt when they had been able to see the cloud and the galaxy from beyond the mask of dust.

Too, she was frightened because once she reached that star she would no longer be able to see her home sun. She would be cut off. The way home would rely upon memories impressed upon a few chemicals within her fragile brain.

She almost abandoned the quest then.

But she went on, defying fear, and those-who-dwell bore her well and quickly, and this time she did not allow her self-confidence to flag during the course of the jump.

She returned to the natural universe close to a white dwarf so brilliant she dared not look in its direction. It radiated so powerfully in the electromagnetic range that it threatened to disrupt her grip upon her talent. She did not stay long, though she did take in one awe-inspiring glimpse of a cloud of stars upon one paw and a vast darkness upon the other, only lightly speckled with points of light.

Grauel and Barlog practically whined with fear. The bath were unafraid, but stricken with awe.

Onward. And this time with care, for the next target was a wobbling star that, even from so far away, could be heard screaming as it died. A sister who had been there had told Marika that that star had an invisible companion that had to be treated with great respect, for it was a cannibal star, devouring the stuff of its visible sister the way some insects devoured the stuff of others.

The electromagnetic fog around that third target was more furious than anything Marika could have imagined. For minutes she remained disoriented, unable to select her next target, her last. It was hard to find. It was a normal little star much like her own sun, and it defined the outer known limits of exploration in this direction. It lay against the flank of the dust cloud.

Marika battled the numbness creeping over her. She recalled the most furious thunderstorms of her puphood in the Ponath. This was a hundred times more terrible.

She clung to her ghosts mostly by instinct and urged the darkship away, gaining velocity as the impact of the star lessened. In time she was able to think clearly enough to locate her target star. With head aching, she commanded her ghosts and pulled into the Up-and-Over.

The headache passed. Soon she found herself letting go

almost automatically, almost without conscious calculation. The darkship fell into normal space, drifting toward her target.

This star boasted a world that could be used as a way station. It was a friendly world, the record said, but it was nothing like home. It was uninhabited. It would be a fair place to rest. A place where Grauel and Barlog could get solid ground beneath their boots once more.

She located the world and guided the darkship into orbit, released the massive stores pod after Grauel and Barlog and the extra bath had removed what might be needed below, then descended.

It was a hot, humid world with an atmospheric pressure much higher than that at home. Having descended to the level of discomfort, Marika cast about till she found a tall mountain. There she made her landing.

She had gone to the very bounds.

Soon the hunt would begin.

Chapter Thirty-Four

I

"Marika!"

Grauel's tone startled Marika. She threw a hasty touch toward the huntress, fearing she had encountered something deadly. But it was not danger, just something she had found. Something that had her excited. Marika hastened to join her.

This was at least the hundredth habitable world and thousandth star they had visited since leaving home. The number of stars inside the radius Marika considered logically limiting, worth investigating, seemed infinite. She had lost track of time.

Time had little meaning when all worlds were different and each begged to be explored. She had thought the film Bagnel had given her, in rolls upon hundreds of rolls, was a ridiculous oversupply. But now most of it was gone, exposed, sealed, ready to be returned to those who would be avid to search it for the new, the weird, the terrible. The universe seemed capable of producing an infinitude of wonders.

More than three years had passed. None of Marika's

original bath were with her anymore, having one by one proved out the value of her experiment or simply having grown homesick and opted to return on the Redoriad voidship *High Night Rider,* which resupplied Marika's base every few months.

Marika scrambled across a decomposed rock face where striations glistened unsettlingly alien blues, perched a hundred feet above a patch of tableland where Grauel crouched, studying something. "What have you got, Grauel?"

"A campfire site," the huntress called back. "Come down and see. Your talent might find something I cannot."

Marika's heartbeat picked up. Campfire site! There was no intelligent life on this world. And it had not been visited by any meth before, unless by the Serke. Maybe after all this time, chance had brought her to a warm trail.

She had discarded the world as a possible Serke hiding place only seconds after making orbit. The presence of silth would not have been hard to detect. These years among the stars, reaching out to find an enemy never there, had stretched her far-touching talent till it would have shamed the most talented of fartouchers back home. She did not believe anyone with the talent could hide from her long.

Aliens of the sort she sought should not have been hard to detect either, if only by the talent vacuum the brethren suspected should exist around them. She had grounded only because they all needed to rest, needed to feel a planet beneath their feet.

She was very strong now, able to make venture after venture without pause. She was not the least uncomfortable with the void or the Up-and-Over. It was as if she had been born to stalk the stars. But her bath reached their limits after six or seven passages and needed several days to recuperate. Grauel and Barlog never became comfortable with star-faring. She had taken them all to their limits this time. This site she had chosen only because it looked safe and comfortable.

Talus bounded around her boots as she slipped and slid down the slope, thanking Grauel's increased propensity for wandering while they were down, thanking the All for interesting the huntress in the oddities produced by the worlds they visited. It had paid a dividend.

Maybe.

Grauel remained crouched over a circle of stones blackened on one side. The circle lay away from the foot of the cliff, but was still sheltered from the prevailing winds. A glance told Marika it was an old site, barely recognizable for what it was.

Grauel glanced up. "It was not like this when I found it. I had to reconstruct it. I noticed some stones that looked smoked on one side scattered around. Then just a hint of a smell of smoke still in the ground here. Once I started looking around I found more stones. It all came together fairly easily."

Marika nodded. "What can you tell me about it?" Grauel was the huntress. This was her area of expertise.

"Very little, except that it's here. And it shouldn't be. But it did seem that this ledge would be a good place to ground a darkship."

"How far afield did you go?"

"Not far."

"Let's snoop around, see what we can find."

Careful visual search turned up nothing more.

"If they were here, they must have had a latrine and some place to dump their garbage," Grauel said.

"They may have had huntresses with them," Marika chided. Grauel and Barlog, treating the search as they would a hunt in their native Ponath, left every resting place pristine, naked of evidence that anyone had visited. Both huntresses believed the Serke were hunting for them in turn.

"One doubts it. No skilled huntress would have left a fire site so obvious to the eye. My thought was that you might use your talent to look where the eye cannot see."

"You are right, of course." Marika went down through her loophole and caught a suitable ghost, then searched the area again, using the altered perspective of the otherworld. She found what Grauel wanted in a crack to one side of the ledge. She returned to flesh. "You were right. Over here. Whoever they were, it looks like they used one natural hole for a garbage pit and a latrine both."

"Grab yourself a stick," Grauel said.

"A stick?"

"Do you want to stir through it with your paws?"

"Of course. All right." Marika collected pieces of dead wood. Grauel used one to dig at soil that had been used to cover the wastes.

"Been a while for sure," the huntress said. "It has all decayed away to nothing. It must not rain or snow much here, for the black on the rocks to have remained noticeable. But we're wasting our time. There's nothing. . . . Hello!" Grauel dropped onto her belly and reached into the hole. She wriggled forward, bent at the waist, got hold of something, wriggled back and sat up. She held a lump to the light. Marika saw nothing special till Grauel spat upon it and cleaned it on her sleeve.

"A button." It was a tarnished metal button with a few fibers of thread still attached. It was embossed. Grauel passed it to her. Marika studied it, then compared it to the five upon the left wrist of her jacket. "That is a Serke witch sign on it, Grauel. We're on the trail. They've been here. I have a premonition. We are within a few passages through the Up-and-Over of catching up with them."

"That's what you've been saying since we established our first base."

"This time I am right. I can feel it. I am convinced."

"I hope you are." Grauel sounded sour.

"Grauel?"

"I do not want to die out here, Marika. How would the All find me?"

"What?" This was a surprise.

"In fact, if I had my choice, I would spend my final days in the upper Ponath, at the packstead that gave me life."

Marika was baffled. What had brought this on?

"I am getting old, Marika. In the Ponath I might already be one of the Wise. Likewise Barlog. The witchery and medicine of the silth have kept us young beyond our time, but time never stops gnawing. Lately I find I cannot help remembering that we are the last of the Degnan pack, and that our pack lies beneath the northern ice still unMourned."

"Yes. I know all that. You are indeed old for the Ponath, but not old by standards of the silth. There will be time, Grauel. We will see to the Mourning. But we can't go now. We're finally making some headway out here. We've finally found something besides a place where they aren't and haven't ever been. Maybe this world is a regular stop. Maybe if we just sat here and waited. . . . I know what I'll do. I'll make this world our new base. We'll continue the hunt from here."

"Which means a whole new globe of space to search," Grauel countered, showing no excitement. "It will be like starting from the beginning."

"Think positively, Grauel. Think lucky. Let's go tell the others."

"What I think is I wish I had not called you down here."

That evening Marika climbed a peak while the others rested. She stood staring at the stars. There were few to be seen, for the dust cloud spanned the heavens of that world. She selected the next half dozen stars that should be investigated. Into the cloud itself this time? Yes. What better place to hide?

For the most part she had avoided going into the cloud during her search. She was much less comfortable operating there because there were so few landmark stars. She had reasoned that the Serke explorers would have suffered the same reluctance. But perhaps one of their more daring Mistresses of the Ship, possibly a Bestrei, might have dared the darkness and have found the aliens.

What lay beyond the cloud? No one knew. No one had tried to reach its nether side. Maybe no one but the Serke had had any contact with the aliens because they were over there and they too were reluctant to enter the dust.

The dust cloud it would be, for a time.

II

Marika's bath had again been rotated. Grauel and Barlog had begun to show gray and even lose a little fur. Marika herself had begun to feel age in her bones when she rose some mornings. And there were moments when the homeworld called so strongly that her resolve almost broke. There were moments when she was tempted to go home just to discover what had happened in her absence. Sometimes, during the on-planet resting pauses, she lay awake when she was supposed to be sleeping, wondering about Bagnel, longing for his company, and wondering about the progress of the mirrors she had imagined into reality, and even about the warlock, her littermate, Kublin.

She knew very little about what had happened since her departure. But for the regular visit of *High Night Rider,* and the occasional appearance of a Mistress of the Ship with an adventurous spirit, a desire to visit the strange worlds Marika had reported, and a knack for assembling bath of like temperament, she had no ties with home.

Grauel and Barlog had recognized the process at work and had ceased their importunities for abandoning the quest, fearing their petitions would harden her resolve.

She was finding it increasingly difficult to convince herself that the hunt was worthwhile. There was no end to the universe, even within the dust cloud. There was always another star. And, inevitably, always another disappointment.

It was time for *High Night Rider* to come again. She felt she had reached a time of decision. If the news from home were bad, she would return.

The mirrors, insofar as she knew, were coming along well. A brief note half a year earlier, written by Bagnel, had told her the mirror in the leading trojan was well ahead of schedule. So much for his doubts about his management skills.

But he had mentioned trouble down on the homeworld's surface. The old rogue male trouble had begun to reassert itself. The Communities seemed unable to stem it. This time the outlaws seemed to be working independent of the brethren, under the dominance of their wehrlen, but there were those, according to Bagnel, who did not believe the warlock was the true source of their witchcraft. Silth did not want to believe a male could be so strong, so felt the rogues had to be getting aid and encouragement from silth smuggled in by the Serke.

On its last visit *High Night Rider* had brought word that the rogues were sabotaging the brethren as well as silth, that assassination had become their primary weapon. They were using their talent-suppressing device again, and the sisterhoods could not cope.

Marika suspected they could not cope because they did not feel motivated enough. Even now, after all the disaster they had wrought, it was difficult to get silth to take males seriously as a threat.

Marika did not want to take up that task again, but it seemed she might have to, if the vague reports she received indicated the way things were actually moving. If the Communities themselves would not spend the effort and energy to defend themselves adequately.

A wave of undirected touch passed over her. She looked at the sky as one of her bath called out, "Mistress, *High Night Rider* has come."

A blob of light moved across the sky, visible even in daylight. It slowed, maneuvered, fell into orbit. Marika rose and stalked through the camp, which today housed nearly a score of meth. Two other darkships were operating from her base, not participating in the hunt, but examining more closely the most interesting of the worlds that Marika had discovered. Their Mistresses were young ones, filled with a desire to expand the frontiers, and they had found themselves teams of bath willing to join their ventures.

Marika's reports home had had one effect: They had somewhat revivified the old spirit of exploration. Once she had blazed a trail others were eager to devote closer attention to what she had found.

She suspected Bagnel was irked. That meant darkships scattered about the void contributing nothing to the mirror project. She suspected the tedium of construction work was what had encouraged these younger Mistresses and bath to come out to the edge of beyond.

The explorers could do little to truly expand meth knowledge. There were more curiosities among the starworlds than could have been cataloged by ten thousand darkship crews in ten thousand lifetimes.

Of late even Marika had been spending more time looking at those curiosities than she had been being driven by her need to overhaul the Serke.

"Darkships coming down, mistress," someone called. "At least three of them. Maybe four."

That was to be expected. There were supplies to be delivered, and always there was another group of explorers who had saved themselves effort by scavenging a ride aboard the giant voidship.

Though the darkships would not ground for a long time yet, Marika went to the landing area with the others. They all stood around waiting, joining in speculation about what news would come from home.

The first darkship down carried a passenger.

"By the All! Bagnel!" Marika swore as the tradermale stepped down. He was shaking, numb with awe. "What are you doing here?" He did not hear her. Whether he was amazed to have arrived healthy, or overawed by having traveled so far, he was completely turned inside himself. She rushed over and repeated her question as meth yelled about clearing the area so the next darkship could ground.

Silth stared. A male! Out here!

Bagnel shuddered as though shaking water off, and said, "Marika." He looked her over. "You have changed."

"So have you. Is that gray I see there? Time gnaws, does it not? It must be fate. I was just thinking about you—and here you are. What are you doing here? Come with me.

Before that Mistress gets impatient and plops down on our heads."

"Are you all right? You look tired."

"I am tired, Bagnel. I have looked at more stars than you can imagine even exist. Though you must have seen how many there are when you spanned the reach outside the cloud. Come. Let's get something to eat. You must be starved."

"My stomach is too unsettled. That passage . . . It was too much for me, I fear. The Up-and-Over . . . I find myself dreading the return trip already."

"You still haven't told me what you're doing here. Has something happened?"

"No. Except that I have been stripped of my job and prerogatives. Whoa! It's only temporary. A cabal of senior factors and high silth ganged up on me and ordered me to take a vacation. They said I was pushing myself too hard, that I was on the edge of a breakdown because I was trying too hard to keep the project ahead of schedule. They stripped me of my powers so I would have no choice. Since they wouldn't let me do anything at all, and the Redoriad were willing when I approached them, I decided to come walk the stars while I had a chance. You invited me, you'll recall. I think I am sorry I did it."

"I recall. I believe I invited you to come after I caught the Serke."

"But you haven't. You've been out here forever. It begins to seem unlikely, doesn't it?"

"I am narrowing it down, Bagnel. Narrowing it down. I have a very good idea where they're not."

"You are still able to be amused at yourself."

"Not often. But I don't think it will be too much longer."

"You sound like you're trying to convince yourself."

Marika noted Grauel and Barlog hovering. They were polite enough to remain out of earshot, but they were there, eager to discover the meaning of Bagnel's appearance. Marika asked, "You're sure this isn't business? That someone didn't send you out to get me to come home?"

He looked surprised. "No. Why do you ask that?"

"We get very little reliable news out here. What we have gotten are rumors about increasingly bad rogue trouble. Trouble nobody seems able—or maybe just willing—to solve. I thought maybe someone sent you to get me to come back and deal with it."

"Marika . . . I might as well put it bluntly. The vast majority of silth are very happy that you are out here instead of at home. That's why you get the support you do. The farther away you are, the happier they are."

"Oh."

"The rogues have become a problem again, though, that's for sure. They're much better organized this time. They learned a lot."

"I believe I predicted that. I believe no one would listen to me."

"Right. It's no longer possible to use the tactics you developed. One cannot be taken and forced to betray scores more by subjecting him to a truthsaying. They have structured their organization so that few members know any of the others. And they are careful to keep the risks low whenever they choose to strike."

"That was predictable too."

"And even where the hunters know who they are looking for it has been hard to track a culprit down. Your Kublin, for example."

"Kublin?" Marika had done her best not to think of her littermate over the years. It had been her thought to destroy his hope by shattering the support lent by the Serke and their rogue companions. But the Serke remained unshattered.

"He is rumored to be the mastermind, the one they call the warlock. Not one hunter has been able to find a trace of him since his escape from you. Whenever someone does get a line on him he is found to be gone by the time the hunt closes in. There is still strong support for him and those who fled with the Serke among the bond meth and even our worker brethren."

"I can find Kublin."

"No doubt. You have always done whatever you set your mind to. I will mention that to anyone who is interested. My own opinion is, you should continue the search for the Serke. Step it up, even. It could be important."

"Ah? Is that it?"

"What?"

"The true reason you put yourself through what it takes for a meth unfamiliar with the Up-and-Over to come out here?"

"I came for a vacation, Marika. I came where I could see a friend who has been missing from my life for far too long. I'm just trying to tell you what is happening at home. If you care to interpret that as an attempt at manipulation . . ."

"I'm sorry. Go ahead. Tell me the news."

"Last month we finally caught a courier from the rogues trying to sneak in. Two of them, actually. Both brethren who had gone into exile aboard *Starstalker*. I was brought in for their questioning because they had things to say about the project."

"And? Did you get any hints as to where they are hiding?"

"Just one. Inside the dust cloud. Which you suspect already. Naturally, they would not have been risked had they known more. I wish we could have taken the Mistress of the Ship who brought them in."

"Of course. What did they have to say otherwise?"

"We learned a lot about what they've been doing, which is mostly marking time and hoping the aliens find them before you do. They are no longer so confident of Bestrei."

"What?"

"It turns out that our estimates of the Serke situation were not quite right. They have no direct contact with the alien. What they have is a very large alien ship orbiting a planet. They have been studying it and appropriating from it, while they wait for its builders to come looking for it."

"But . . ."

"Give me a chance, Marika. There is a story. I'd better tell it so you know what I'm talking about."

"I think you'd better. Starting from the beginning."

"All right. Here it is. Way back, a venturesome Serke Mistress of the Ship . . ."

"Kher-Thar Prevallin?"

"Exactly. That most famous of the farwanderers. A legend of our own times. But if you keep interrupting you will never hear the story."

"Sorry."

"Way back, Kher-Thar decided she wanted to see what lay on the far side of the dust cloud. While she was passing through she decided to rest her bath at a particular world. An almost optimally friendly one, by all accounts. After several days down she had just reached orbital distance departing when the alien ship appeared, I take it out of the Up-and-Over. The way I was told, it was not there one moment, and there the next. It detected the darkship and gave chase. Out of curiosity, apparently."

Marika grumbled beneath her breath. He was stretching it.

"No. There was no evidence the creatures aboard were hostile. But Kher-Thar, you will recall, was not known for her cool head. She panicked. Thinking she was being attacked, she attacked first. The aliens were unable to deal with her, though she was not known for the strength of her talent for the dark side. The aliens abandoned the chase. Kher-Thar scrambled into the Up-and-Over and scurried home, nearly killing her bath."

"I always thought she was overrated. She was a total misfit, which is why the Serke put up with her wandering in the first place. They wanted her out of their fur."

"You would understand that better than I."

"Vicious, Bagnel. Tell your story."

"Let me."

"Well?"

"The aliens who survived Kher-Thar's attack managed to get their ship into a stable orbit around the planet, but could not save themselves. When Kher-Thar returned, accompanied by a horde of Serke investigators, they were all dead. The investigators knew the importance of their find, but could make no sense of it. After long and often savage debate their ruling council voted to ask the dark-faring brethren bonds for help. Ever since, for more than twenty years, they have been studying the alien ship, appropriating equipment and technology, and waiting for another ship to come looking for the first."

"Why do they think one will come? We seldom send anyone to look for a lost darkship."

"I am not certain. But they are convinced one will. Perhaps because of the investment such a vessel would represent. The prisoners said it is huge. That for us to build it would take an effort on the scale of the mirror project."

"Then everything they did to us in the Ponath was purely on speculation? They might have gotten nothing at all for their trouble?"

"Apparently. Even under truthsaying the prisoners insist that no meth has ever met one of the aliens alive."

"Idiots."

"Maybe. You don't know how you would have reacted in identical circumstances. One like your Gradwohl, obsessed with making the Reugge Community into a power, might have done the same. Or worse. You dare not fault the Serke without faulting all silth. They were being silth."

"I will not argue that. I will only say they behaved in the most stupid fashion possible in being silth. And they continue in their stupidity. All those years and no ship has come? And they have not given up?"

"How long have you been looking for them?"

"More years than some care to count. Grauel and Barlog are not happy with me."

"It is the only hope they have left, Marika. If the aliens do not come, sooner or later you will. And, as I said, they are afraid Bestrei is no longer what she was.

"Suppose that ship was an explorer, the same as Kher-Thar's? With no more fixed a routine than hers? Suppose she had been lost instead? How long have you looked, knowing the place existed?"

"Even so . . . I suppose I understand."

"So I think you should go on looking, though I am sure the search is wearing. You have to be getting closer, if only by the process of elimination. But so must the aliens. I wouldn't like to guess what might happen if the Serke were to make common cause with them."

"The weapons that destroyed TelleRai."

"Not to mention those mounted on the ships the rogues used. We have studied those endlessly, from fragments we captured, and we can make no sense of them. I fear we are just too far away in knowledge and technology. They might as well be your witchcraft. Nevertheless, brethren in the sciences believe larger weapons of the same sort could be used against planetary targets."

"I will admit I have been tempted to give up the hunt."

"I thought so when I saw you, Marika. You look tired. As if you're ready to accept defeat. But enough of that. I really did not come here on business. I'm dedicated to carrying out my orders, which are to spend a few months without worrying."

"How is the project coming?"

"Seventy percent completion on the leading mirror. Forty on the trailing. The orbitals for making fine and local adjustments are in place. We're getting almost forty percent of peak output. I understand that they have begun to have an effect. There was no measurable advance of the permafrost line this past winter."

"How far did it get?"

"Almost to the tropics. Well past Ruhaack. But it should begin to fall back soon. If the dust gets no thicker. And the probes we have run in the direction the sun is moving show no increase in density along the path to be followed for the next five hundred years. I think we will win the battle against the long winter. And, though you have spent very little time on it since you got it going, you will be remembered as the dam of the project."

"I am not much concerned about how the future recalls me, so long as there is a future. And I am still battling for it out here. In a hunt that, I am sure, will not be in vain, and that will not last much longer."

Bagnel bowed his head as if to mask his expression.

"Well, tradermale. Adventurer. Want to make it a working holiday? I can squeeze another body onto my darkship. You could be the first male ever to see new worlds."

III

Bagnel stepped down off the darkship and surveyed the encampment with the look of one returning home. "I'll confess this, Marika. I never once worried about the project."

Marika lifted a lip in amusement. "It could not have been that bad. It wasn't the same as traveling in *High Night Rider?*"

"No. It was not the same. As you know perfectly well. It was more like falling forever. It was more unnerving than riding a darkship at home. There is something under your feet there, even if it is several thousand feet down. Still . . ."

"What is that look in your eye?" Marika kept one eye on her bath and Grauel and Barlog, making sure *they* made sure the darkship was being readied for its next journey. She ruled the base strictly. She insisted all darkships be ready to lift at a moment's notice. The Serke could strike at any time. Would strike, she suspected, if they knew where to find her. She was stuck to their trail like the stubbornest hunting arft.

"Wonder, I suppose. I have to admit that, harrowing as it was, the experience touched something in me. I could develop a taste for exploration."

"Give up the mirrors, then. I am here. The darkship is here."

He looked at her narrowly, startled and tempted. "I think not, Marika. Your sisters would not understand."

"I suppose not. It was just a thought. Maybe someday. When the project is complete. When the Serke have been disposed of. When the aliens have been found and some sort of accommodation with them has been reached. Wouldn't it be in the grand tradition for us to fly away and never be seen again?"

He picked it up as a game. "Yes. We could just go on exploring, skipping from star to star, forever. We might be touched occasionally, in the far distance, and rumors would rise about a ghost darkship flitting out on the edge of the void. Young, fresh Mistresses would bring their darkships out to hunt the legend."

"But it couldn't be. We couldn't carry enough stores. And where would I find willing bath?"

"Oh, well."

"Tomorrow we will go out again. There is no end of stars in this sector—though those really worth investigating are running short."

But Marika returned to space much sooner.

The night was just hours old when a sudden, sharp, panicky touch smote Marika. *Darkship! Starting down. Not from home.*

Marika rushed from her hut. The base began coming to life around her. Darkship crews rushed to their ships. The touch came again. *Serke! Oh. They have detected us. They are starting back up. They are fleeing. They are very frightened. The otherworld reeks of their fear. Hurry!*

"Grauel! Barlog! Will you come on? We're going up!"

Sleepy-eyed, the untouched huntresses had come out to learn the cause of the commotion.

Marika's bath raced toward the wooden darkship, preflight rites forgotten. Marika tossed her rifle across her shoulder and dashed after them, shouting, "Come, you two. The Serke."

Grauel and Barlog raced for the darkship after snatching their weapons.

One voidship was off the ground already, rising swiftly. Marika's eyes were fiery as she glared at her senior bath, who was not hustling the silver bowl around fast enough to suit her.

"Wait!"

Bagnel wobbled toward them, trying to keep his trousers from tripping him by holding them up with one paw.

"No," Marika said. "This is the real thing, Bagnel. There are Serke up there."

Bagnel played deaf. He lined up for his turn at the silver bowl. The bath muttered something unappreciative, let him sip. Grauel extracted another flask of liquid from the locker under the axis platform and dumped it into the bowl. Then she dug out a spare rifle and forced it upon him. "One I owe you, male."

"I see you still carry the one I gave you at Akard."

"It has been a faithful tool. Like me, though, it is getting old and cranky."

Marika swore. The other darkship was aloft now. The first had dwindled to a speck, its Mistress driving it hard. And she had not yet gathered her ghosts. "You meth strap down good," she said. "Everyone strap down. This is going to be the ride of your lives."

Bagnel was strapped already. He began disassembling the weapon Grauel had given him. The huntress nodded with approval. Seated, she and Barlog did likewise with their own weapons.

Marika snatched the bowl from the senior bath, gulped its contents, then bounced to her place at the tip of the wooden dagger. She went down through her loophole and snagged ghosts, lifted off, and continued gathering ghosts as she rose, dropping smaller specimens as she snatched ever bigger, stronger denizens of the otherworld. She pressed mercilessly.

She overhauled one darkship at fifty thousand feet and the other before it made orbital altitude. All the while she caressed the void with the touch, tracking the Serke darkship as it fled toward where it could clamber into the Upand-Over. She soon had its line of retreat clearly defined in her mind.

It pointed toward a section of cloud she had not yet explored. She sketched an imaginary circle around that line, finding only four stars within it. She discarded the one farthest off center.

She reached with the touch and told the other two Mistressess of the Ship, *We will pursue. There are three stars close to their line of flight. I will take this one.* She sent a picture of the stars and indicated which she had chosen for herself, then assigned each of them one of the two remaining. *Push yourselves. Try to arrive before they do.*

That was unlikely, she thought. Even for her, with her advantages. Though time lapses in the Up-and-Over depended on the strength and talent of the individual Mistress of the Ship, the Serke Mistress had a long start and death raving behind her to motivate her.

Marika began pushing down her chosen course before she reached orbital altitude and began gathering ghosts for the Up-and-Over long before she reached the traditional jumping distance. She grabbed at the Up-and-Over only minutes behind the Serke—long before she should have. Echoes of silent terror came from her bath, whom she had pushed near hysteria already with her demands.

Blackness, twisting. A sensation of infinite nothing. A hint of a deep space ghost, a great black ghost, startled by the voidship's passage.

Then light again. The target star lay nearby. Marika struggled to gain her bearings, groggy from the violence of her plunge through the Up-and-Over.

The bath recovered more slowly than she. While she waited on them Marika reached into the surrounding void, searching for the Serke darkship.

Mentally righted, the senior bath left her station to prepare another silver bowl.

Marika's probe revealed that the star had no planets. It

might have had at one time, but something had happened. Perhaps too close a brush with another star. The surrounding void teemed with rocky fragments, some of them bigger than the moon Biter back home. None were big enough to retain an atmosphere, and nowhere could Marika sense the betraying glow of life.

There were no Serke bases here.

And no Serke darkship.

She stalked up the blade of the wooden dagger to see how Grauel, Barlog, and Bagnel had fared. She had drawn upon them as well as upon the bath, though the strength they had to lend was feeble.

Bagnel looked sick, like he might vomit any second. He was down, clutching the framework with his eyes sealed. Grauel and Barlog looked strained and a little stunned by the savagery of the passage, but they had been with her long enough and had been through enough to be accustomed to the occasional violent passage. Though this had outdone everything that had gone before.

Marika touched Bagnel briefly, gently, encouragingly. The one silth ability for which she had very little talent was healing, but she tried to let well-being flow from her to him. He nodded. He was all right. He was just shaken.

She suspected, in her more dark moments, that she was a poor healer because she was not sufficiently whole and at peace within herself.

She started back toward her station.

Plop!

It had the feel of the sound of a pebble falling into water as heard from beneath the surface, only it fell upon the silth part of her mind.

The Serke darkship.

Where?

She searched, found a line, drove toward the enemy darkship. If she could strike before they recovered. . . .

They sensed her coming, turned, gained velocity rapidly. Marika swept into their wake, skidding like an aircraft in a tight turn, began gaining, began snapping up stellar

landmarks as she went. Those were few indeed. This deep in
the cloud only a dozen stars were visible in any direction.

The Serke ship vanished. Marika fixed its line of flight
and a target star and grabbed for the Up-and-Over herself.

She did not press as hard this time. She guessed she need
not strain so to arrive first.

Correct.

From that second system, in the dense heartstream of the
dust, only three stars were visible. One was that from which
Marika had come.

There was no life in that system. Nor had there ever been
any, for the star was a dwarf of a type never associated with
planets. Marika scanned star and system only casually.
Then she concentrated upon those two farther stars.

One was a red giant.

The other was a yellow, like the meth home sun.

Elation filled her.

She had sniffed out a hot trail at last.

She gathered everyone at the axis and had the senior bath
pass the silver bowl again. Once everyone had sipped and
taken a few moments to relax, she pulled the darkship into
the Up-and-Over again and returned the way she had come.
Back to the base world.

Let the Serke think they had eluded her.

Chapter Thirty-Five

I

Bagnel left the wooden darkship at the Hammer. Marika scanned the surrounding void. The Hammer was just one of a dozen huge orbital stations now, and far from the largest. Near space seemed almost uncomfortably crowded. There had been many changes during the years she had been gone. Some she had heard about, of course, but the seeing was nothing like the hearing.

She wanted to make a pass by the leading trojan, to see her brainchild, but responded to the anxieties of Grauel and Barlog. They had not set foot on the homeworld in nearly seven years. It was time to be attentive to their needs. Time to take the darkship down. The mirror would be there forever.

Too, the huntresses wanted to move fast, lest some unpleasant welcome be arranged.

Marika did not arrive ahead of the news of her coming. Bagnel had not been able to keep her return quiet simply because there were meth who had known he was with her. Random touches, mostly unfamiliar, brushed her, curious.

She descended toward Ruhaack, ignoring the touches, sending only one of her own ahead, to warn the Reugge cloister that she was coming in.

Most Senior Bel-Keneke herself came out to meet Marika. Marika fixed her gaze upon the Reugge first chair, ignoring the amused silth studying her wooden darkship and the firearms that she and her companions bore. She tried to read Bel-Keneke.

She had been gone so long. This would be a changed world, perhaps a different world. . . .

Assuredly a different world. She could feel the difference. There were new smells in the air, smells of heavy industry, such as had plagued Maksche when the air was still. But Ruhaack was far from any industry. The smell must be everywhere.

Had it become a world remade in the image of a brethren dream? Had it become what she had battled to avoid, simply because that was what had to be to escape the grasp of the grauken winter?

She glanced up. The mirror in the leading trojan stood high in the sky, almost too bright for her eyes. Yet the air seemed colder than she remembered.

Snow lay everywhere. It looked very deep.

She could not recall what the season should be. She suspected the snow would be there no matter which. Bagnel had said the permafrost line had moved far south of Ruhaack before it halted.

The silth awaiting her looked thin and haggard. They had not been eating well. So, too, the bonds waiting to handle the darkship. So. How much worse for the run of meth?

Marika let the darkship drop the last few inches, formally reuniting her with her homeworld. When she stepped down she nearly collapsed. She had pushed herself too hard making the long journey homeward.

Bel-Keneke greeted her with elaborate honors. Marika returned the greeting formulas, pleased that her stature had not suffered in her absence.

"Welcome home, far-fared," Bel-Keneke said, now speak-

ing for herself rather than as the voice of the Community.
"We wondered if we would ever see you again. There have
been repeated rumors that you had perished in the dark
gulf, that you lived on only in legend, that the Redoriad
were only pretending you were still alive to keep the warlock
and his ilk afraid."

"I have gone farther afield than any silth before me, Bel-
Keneke. I have seen ten thousand stars and marveled at ten
thousand wonders. I can tell ten thousand stories that no one
would believe. So. I have come back to the world of ice. I
have come home."

"You have abandoned the hunt? You have given up? We
surely can use your help here."

"No, I have not given up. Not exactly. Why would you
need my help?"

"Rogues."

"Ah. And my friend Bagnel was convinced no one would
want me around, poking my nose into that business. That
everyone would be happier were I to stay a legend among
the stars."

"No doubt there are a great many high silth who would
feel that way. Your return is sure to be the topic of discussion in every cloister. It will be searched and researched
endlessly for meaning. But I speak only for myself and the
Reugge. We are glad to have you here, and we will welcome
your help."

"Tell me."

"That can wait. We are standing in the weather. You have
just set foot to earth. You need rest more than you need
news."

"This is true. Are there quarters for me?"

"The same as always. They are being cleaned and the
heat let in."

"Good. Will you attend me there at your earliest conve-
nience? Would that be too much of an imposition?"

Bel-Keneke blinked, glanced at Grauel, Barlog, and
Marika's bath, none of whom had departed for bath

quarters. "I think not." She was feeling around, trying to recall how one dealt with the wild silth Marika.

Marika, too, was trying to remember. Seven years she had done without the artificial protocol and ceremonial of homeworld silthdom. Seven years since she had seen Bel-Keneke. Perhaps the most senior no longer felt indebted.

Marika nodded. "Please do not speculate. To anyone, or even within yourself. I am here. That is enough for now. Let other sisterhoods drive themselves silly trying to figure out what I am about."

"Yes." Bel-Keneke seemed amused. "Will you need anything? Other than your quarters, and food?"

"A roster of all the current most seniors and ruling councils of all the dark-faring sisterhoods. Eventually, I suppose, the interesting and relevant data on the rogue problem. Though I may not be inclined to help those who have not helped themselves."

"I will see to it." Bel-Keneke blinked some more. "Welcome home, Marika." She hurried away.

Marika watched her go, a little puzzled. She had not been able to read Bel-Keneke well. Had she lost the touch while away? Perhaps because she had been with so few meth for so long, and all of them well known?

Bel-Keneke vanished through a doorway. "Come." Marika gestured. Grauel, Barlog, and the bath followed her, trying to ignore the stares of the meth in the landing court. That the bath did not go to the bath dormitories would fuel wild speculation, Marika knew. But she doubted anyone would strike on the truth, and to allow them a chance to let that slip seemed a greater risk.

It was a strain, keeping her eyes open till Bel-Keneke arrived. The others she sent to rest as soon as they had eaten and the workers had been chased from the still frigid apartment. She tossed more wood on the fire, paced before it awhile. She had been on warmer worlds too long.

Pausing to gaze out the window, she watched a small brethren dirigible drift down and begin unloading firewood and what probably were food stores. Perhaps she had been unwise to take the old Serke cloister as the new Reugge main cloister. Maybe she should have chosen a site nearer the equator.

She had to give up. Her eyes refused to remain open. She put still more wood on the fire, then slouched in a chair before it.

Bel-Keneke's scratch at the door did not waken her. But the squeak of hinges as she let herself in did. Marika sprang up, rifle swinging to cover the most senior.

"Oh. I am sorry, mistress," she apologized. "I dozed, and out there we are accustomed to . . ."

"No matter," Bel-Keneke replied, regaining her composure. "I believe I understand. May I?" She indicated another chair.

"Of course. Come close. Singe your fur. It is very cold here. Is it winter, or has the weather turned this bad? Or have I just forgotten how bad it was?"

"It is the heart of winter. The coldest time. But these days the summers are little better. You could have forgotten. I do not recall the winters having been much more harsh when you left. And the mirror meth tell us that from orbit you can see that the project is beginning to have an effect."

"My friend Bagnel told me the permafrost line has been halted."

"So they say. The energy from the mirrors falls day and night. When both are finished there will be no more night. What will we silth do if we do not have the dark?" She twitched her ears to signify that that was a joke. "I have hopes of seeing another summer before I join my foredams in the embrace of the All."

"The project continues well? Asking Bagnel did me no good. He is as determined a pessimist as ever."

"Very well. It remains ahead of schedule, more or less. The sisterhoods and brethren remain unified and determined, much to my amazement. If you had asked me when we began I would have said there was no chance there would be any enthusiasm left at this time. But there is. I suppose because those with the training can see positive results. There is, however, that element I mentioned before."

"Yes. It is just possible I may have a cure for that. I have come home to . . ." Marika paused. Some great reluctance held her tongue. It was almost as if some part of her did not want an era to end.

Bel-Keneke waited expectantly.

Marika forced it. "I have found them."

"The rogues?"

"The rogues and Serke. Yes."

"Why are you here? You have dispatched them?"

"I have not. It is not something I wish to hazard alone. For many reasons. No. I have come home to ask for a convention. For this I want to gather all the voidfaring darkships of all the Communities."

"I was certain you would . . ."

"Go after them myself? Perhaps the Serke think the same. I hope so. It will keep them confident that they have not been found out. But I would not try it alone. I am not that wild novice from the Ponath anymore, Bel-Keneke. I have learned to regard consequences. And our enemies are not the Serke of yore. They are not true silth at all anymore."

Bel-Keneke did not care to comment. She just sat there toasting her boots, face composed in a mask of neutrality, waiting.

"Were I to go in alone, and challenge Bestrei alone, and were I to defeat her, still nothing would change. They would not accept the failure. They would destroy me and keep on. They put the old ways, the traditions, the laws, aside long ago, the day TelleRai died. Would the meth who cast down the fire upon TelleRai . . ."

"I understand. I do not like it, but I understand. They have backed themselves into a position where they must do what they must to survive."

"Then you understand why they must be approached with all the force that can be mustered."

"I see it, but I do not think you will win much support.

Many of the old starfarers have retired now. They are content working the mirror project. They may be content letting the Serke lie. Those who do venture to the starworlds now are younger. They are not motivated by the hunt. For them, come from here, the grauken is a danger more to be feared than the legendary Serke. I believe times have changed. Though I could be wrong. Certainly there are those of us who do remember, and who still hurt."

"We shall see. What I would like, if possible, is a quiet gathering of the most seniors of the dark-faring silth. Those who do remember and who have the power to order done what needs doing. If we move quickly, we can strike before the news reaches the rogues."

"You are sure they do not know you have found them?"

"Only one meth outside my crew knows. And the crew only suspect. And them I intend to keep here in the apartment till decisions are made and action begun."

"Who is that one?"

"You, mistress."

Bel-Keneke gave her a strained glance.

"The story is a simple one. For the past several years I have made my base on a world where we stumbled across evidence that the Serke had once rested a darkship crew. Just recently a Serke darkship, possibly headed here, appeared. We pursued it and it pointed the way, though I allowed the Serke Mistress to believe she had lost me. She was not as strong as I."

"They will have defenses, Marika. They know you are hunting."

"Of course. That is another reason I do not care to undertake the final move alone. If I am lost, nothing is gained for anyone else."

"I will contact the most seniors immediately. I fear I cannot promise much, but I will do my best." Bel-Keneke passed Marika a large envelope. "These are my comments upon the various most seniors. As you asked. I think, though, that you should rest before you do anything else. You do not look ready to challenge the universe."

"I do not feel ready. You are right. I have driven myself hard for a long time. I will rest before I begin studying them. Thank you."

"Good. I will return tomorrow, then. I should have a response from the most seniors. I will tell them as little as I can, and what I do tell I will bind with oaths."

"Yes. That you must. Though the news will escape soon enough."

Bel-Keneke rose and moved toward the door. A few feet short of the exit she halted, turned, looked at Marika oddly.

"Yes?" Marika asked.

"A random thought. About how you have become a huntress despite having become silth."

"I have had similar thoughts often enough. But what game I stalk. Eh?"

"Yes. Tomorrow, then."

"Tomorrow."

II

Marika wakened in the night, cold but somehow more comfortable than she had been in years. She had missed being enfolded in the homeworld's unconscious background of touch. Even the base, with its population of transients, had not become comfortable.

She entered the room where Grauel and Barlog were sleeping and found them resting peacefully. She studied them in the light cast by the coals in their fireplace, wondering that they had remained with her so long, through so much. She knew they would continue till the All reclaimed them, though it was past time they moved on into the role of the Wise. Both had gone gray. Barlog had lost more spots of fur.

She considered ordering them to remain behind when she returned to the void. But she knew she would not. She could not, for they would be hurt beyond measure. They were her pack. They were her only true sisterhood. Her loyalties beyond those two attenuated very quickly. And they had none but to her and to a dream of yesterday.

She went back to the fireplace in the main room, added firewood, settled in her chair. She opened Bel-Keneke's envelope.

Few of the names had changed. Death had not been busy during her absence. She wondered what time had done to change those old silth. Attitudes were most important. Had they lost their desire to finish the question of the Serke?

Attitudes could not be gotten from pieces of paper. Those she would not know till she had faced the meth themselves. . . . She became restless.

She missed Bagnel.

Already? She mocked herself. It had been but hours since their parting.

For how long this time? Years again? Somehow, that seemed insupportable.

She went to the window and stared at endless vistas of white, skeletal in the moonlight. Biter grinned down like a skull, Chaser like something hungry in close pursuit. That was a change, if noticeable only to one who had been gone a long time. There was no permanent overcast.

She looked past the moons, and all the roving dots of light that had not been there before, in the direction whence she had come. She would be going out there again, soon. And this time she might not come back. Win *or* lose.

"How old are you, Bestrei?" she whispered. "Too old? Or still young enough?" Her restlessness increased. Finally she could stand it no more.

She went to the cabinet where she had stored her saddle-ship in times long gone, times that seemed to belong to another's past. Who had that been, that pup-silth who had drawn a bloody paw across the face of the world?

The saddleship was there still, ready for assembly. It had not been touched. She brushed dust from her personal witch signs.

She considered only a moment more.

The outside air was more bitter than she remembered. She ignored the chill, drifting above the rooftops of Ruhaack, between pillars of smoke, looking longingly on winter-bound streets where nothing moved.

An occasional curious touch brushed her and departed satisfied. Her presence was accepted. She was home.

She was pleased. They were alert, for all that they could not be seen.

Where was Kublin now? What was he thinking? He must have had word of her return by this time. Could he guess its significance? Would his rogues react?

She should let it be whispered that she had come home to break their backs again. They would believe it. Kublin the warlock would believe it. He was mad. He feared her. Feared her as he feared nothing else, for he knew that he had strained her mercy beyond endurance.

They all feared her. For them she was the grauken, the stalker of the night without mercy, without pity. She was the hunger that would devour them all.

The rogue problem had been of great concern to Bagnel. She ought to examine it while she was here. Ought to get back into touch with it. Perhaps she could again find a fresh approach that would give these earthbound silth a novel way to defend themselves while she hunted down the ultimate authors of the dissatisfaction that produced the rogues.

She looked to the stars.

After Bestrei, perhaps. After a probe to the far face of the dust cloud, to look for the aliens. Then a short time home, to eliminate Kublin and secure her bridgeheads behind her.

This time she must. This time the world would be watching. This time there could be no mercy even were she so inclined.

She had slain Gradwohl, her mentor, rather than be thwarted. Why not Kublin? In terms of her own wild frontier culture, let alone that of the silth, a male meant less. Even a littermate. Even a male who was the last surviving male of the Degnan pack.

Soon sunlight set the eastern sky aglow. It was time to

return, to catch a nap before Bel-Keneke brought the results of her contacts with the most seniors. Below, meth had begun moving through the snowy streets. An occasional startled eye or paw of greeting rose when her shadow passed.

She considered the soft silver brightness of the mirror in the trailing trojan, which had risen before the sun. Unlike the mirror in the leading trojan, it did not yet appear impressive.

The smaller mirrors in geocentric orbit formed a necklace across the morning. Where they doing any real good? Was the project all wishful thinking, despite Bagnel's positive reports?

She drifted in through her window and, after dismantling her saddleship, stoked up the fire and sat before it, warming her paws. A glance around at ancient stone, piled into a structure by Serke bonds and engineers thousands of years before her birth. It was a fortress haunted by time. A long way from a Ponath loghouse, she thought. A long, long way.

She knew she was aging. She had not been very reflective when she was younger.

Much to Marika's surprise, Bel-Keneke arrived before anyone else stirred. Marika responded to her scratch, let her in, then returned to her place before the fire. "You are up and about early, mistress."

After hesitating Bel-Keneke took the other chair. "I have been up awhile. I heard you were out on your saddleship. I thought if you were up and around already we might as well get started. I have spoken to all the appropriate most seniors. It took rather less time than I anticipated. None of them were surprised. They had their decisions made."

"Yes?" Marika was surprised, if the several dark-faring most seniors were not.

"They had heard of your return and suspected its import. From those who were more talkative I gathered that it has long been an article of faith that Marika the Huntress would not return till she had sniffed out her quarry's den. You will be pleased to hear that, without exception, they have issued orders to their star-faring Mistresses of the Ship to assemble at your base world."

Marika faced Bel-Keneke. "I honestly did not expect such a quick, affirmative response. Certainly not a unanimous one. From what Bagnel had to say I gathered that my return would not be greeted with unreserved joy. I expected to have to argue and threaten for weeks."

"Some decisions have been debated on the quiet for years, Marika. I think every most senior knew in her heart what she would say when the time came. Too, as some mentioned, a formal convention would cost valuable time and would draw unwanted attention. So the thing was done entirely informally, quietly, and the darkships will join you as quickly as they can be redirected."

"I have missed something, I suspect. All this without debate. Without consulting me to see if I might have been touched by the All and gone raving mad? I have a feeling I must do some reflecting."

"It is a thing that needs doing, Marika. That is long overdue to be done. We cannot survive if this shadow persists. The rogue problem is about to go out of control. Defeat of the Serke and those brethren rebels who fled with them would deal the warlock's followers a crippling emotional blow. Suddenly they would stand alone, with no hope of gaining the technology they believe will give them victory. Their only weapon would be the sorcery of the warlock—the very thing they are fighting to destroy."

Marika nodded and waited. The rogue problem did deserve more examination before she departed.

Bel-Keneke continued, "All are agreed. Destroy the Serke and break the back of rogue hope. As for debate, what have we been doing? Everything has been debated a thousand times in your absence. Every nuance has been brought forward and laid open and the entrails read. Every most senior has had ample opportunity to examine her heart and determine where she must stand. And stand for this we must."

"It seems—almost disappointing. From the moment I

turned homeward I have been steeling myself for a grand battle. All that worry wasted."

"The fact is, they think they know you, Marika. As I said, you coming home meant you had found the Serke. And they were confident that you would, one day. So some policy had to be established. Perhaps you could have had your big battle four, or even three, years ago. There are ancient enmities to be gotten around. Some cannot, even now, consult directly with others. Tacit agreement formed, and eventually solidified into fixed policy. If there was any way to manage it, every sisterhood would be there when the final confrontation came."

Marika had begun to catch a glimmer. "To make certain that the Reugge do not take up what the Serke began?"

"Probably. In part. You see some of it now, I think. There is always more to everything than meets the eye. You must set aside the simplicities of your life over the past seven years and recall the complexities of life on this world. All unity is born of fear. Have a care that you do not move before you are politically ready, able to do the thing backed by a mix of sisters that is above reproach."

"I understand."

"I am told that some voidships are headed out already. How soon will you leave to guide them?"

"Ah-ha," Marika murmured. "Glad to see you, so sad you have to leave."

"What?"

"I get the feeling that, whatever else it may signify, there is not great joy at Marika's return."

"To be honest, there is very little. As I have said, you have become a legend in your absence. And that legend is not entirely a positive one. Your great violences are the things that are remembered. As the legend grows, so grows the fear of what you may do next."

"I see." Marika reflected for a moment. "I will be staying a few days for sure. My huntresses and bath need to get into touch with the homeworld once more. I need to do that myself. When you return from so long out there you are almost stricken by the realization that something has been missing." She thought a moment more. "When I leave, it will be by night, secretly. Do not tell anyone that I have gone. Meantime, have bonds begin whispering that I have come home to silence the rogue menace."

"Are you sure?"

"They will hear of it quickly. The warlock will respond one of two ways. He will attack wildly, in which case you will decimate his followers, or he will go into hiding, taking his vermin with him, in which case you will have a breathing space in which to regain your balance. Further, if the world believes that I am here to hunt, it will not concern itself with other possibilities. It will not watch for me to slip off to the stars. Perhaps, even with the delay for assembly at my base, I can strike before the Serke learn that they have been found."

"Perhaps you should have remained most senior. You have the twisted bent of mind, like Gradwohl before you. You go at things no more directly than did she."

"I am happier being Marika. I never wanted first chair."

"For which I remain in your debt. Will I see you again?"

"Again?"

"Will you come back after you have subdued the Serke?"

"I expect to. There are the rogues. There is the warlock, with whom I have an especial grievance. He has been allowed to make free with his villainies for far too long."

Bel-Keneke did not seem pleased. Marika was surprised. After all this time she still did not feel secure in first chair?

She might be wise to watch her back once the Serke threat ceased to be. "Come to morning ceremonies with me," Marika suggested. "It has been half a generation since I celebrated them properly. It seems an appropriate time to petition the indulgence of the All."

"Very well," Bel-Keneke replied. Reluctantly. "I am behind in my own obligations."

They slipped out of the apartment quietly. But not so quietly that their departure went unremarked. Grauel took up a revolver and trailed them through the cloister halls.

III

Marika stood before the window, contemplating falling snow. Huge, slowly drifting flakes. Chill drifted in around the window frame and lapped across her toes. There were no real thoughts in her mind except that, out there somewhere, there was a pup whom she had loved more than any other creature. Her littermate. Her only ally when she was small. And now her most deadly, most intractable enemy.

And she did not understand.

What had happened in his life to make him change so? To shape him to such iron hatred?

For all she had sworn to herself, so many times, to forget, she still recalled the pup that was. That was the Kublin she knew, not this incredible monster called the warlock. This male *thing* with the skills of a silth and a mind so far askew that . . .

Some would say she was his mirror image. That she was mad too. So who knew? . . .

A feather of touch brushed her. It was time.

She retreated to the chair before the fire. The fire had died to coals barely putting out heat. She slipped her boots on, donned her coats, collected her personal arsenal, extended her touch to see if anyone was in the hallway.

All clear.

When first they had come among silth, Grauel and Barlog had been terrified of sisters who, they believed, could move about invisibly. This was not possible in reality. But a talented and cunning silth could use the touch below a conscious level to direct the gaze of others away, so that she might walk unnoticed except by those she did not notice herself. Marika extended that low level of touch as she passed through the cloister to the landing court.

It was the heart of night. Her precaution was unnecessary. No one was stirring.

Grauel and Barlog had the darkship prepared. The bath

were ready. She strode to her place at the tip of the dagger. The senior bath touched her, asked about the bowl.

It will not be necessary this time. She had not told anyone anything about the flight. *We will not be going off planet.* The cloister would rise in the morning to find her gone, with nothing save a brief note saying she would return soon.

She surveyed the others. The snow was falling faster. The bath at the hilt of the dagger was the vaguest of dark shapes. They were ready. She secured herself with her straps. Seldom would she do without anymore, unlike the rash Marika who had dared fate every flight when first she had learned the darkships.

Up. Away. Low, over the steep slate rooftops. Here and there a brush of startled touch as some silth sensed a darkship passing. She brushed them aside, gained speed.

Her initial flight took her southwest, till she was beyond touch from the cloister, then she turned north and drove as hard as she dared into the fangs of the wind. It was as vicious as ever it had been.

The wooden darkship settled into the courtyard of Skiljansrode. Nothing seemed changed there, except that the surrounding snows were deeper and the old fortress harder to pinpoint. To the west there was a wall of ice, a massive glacial finger, forerunning the even more massive accumulations to the north. How much longer would the silth of Skiljansrode hang on? Till the ice groaned against the roots of the wall? Was secrecy worth so much?

The darkship touched down. As Marika stepped from the dagger there was one sharp touch from one of the bath: *Watch out!*

What had appeared to be banked snow exploded. Heavily armed voctors stepped forward, weapons ready. *Careful*, Marika sent, especially to Grauel and Barlog. She allowed herself to be disarmed, feeling little trepidation. It was impossible to disarm her truly without killing her. The others accepted disarmament with less grace.

A sleepy-eyed Edzeka appeared from the doorway leading to the inner fortress, way below the ice and earth. "Some greeting for your patron," Marika chided.

"You should have sent warning," Edzeka said without a hint of apology. "The visitors we get are seldom friendly. You are lucky the voctors gave you time to be recognized. Come. Cferemojt, return their weapons."

After the chill of the flight from Ruhaack Skiljansrode's interior seemed stiflingly hot. "That bears a little elucidation," Marika said. "That you seldom get friendly visitors. Do you get unfriendly ones?"

"Only the enemy knows where to find us. Three times he has sent forces against us. Three times we have devoured them, leaving none to take him their woe. But he will try again, because this place means much to him. It is more than just a place where he was held in bondage. This is a place that defies his technology. I believe he has been shocked. His talent suppressors have meant nothing here. We do not need the talent to obliterate his brigands. Intelligence is adequate. That must frighten him. That must make him suspect his doom may spring from this place."

"His doom will spring from *here*," Marika said, tapping her skull. "He is the reason I have come. Skiljansrode, though isolated, is the best place to begin taking those steps necessary to eliminate the rogue threat—assuming you have continued in the fashion set when I dwelt here myself."

"We go on. We seldom change."

Marika noted and ignored the continued disdain of ceremony and formality. Her own fault, of course. Gradwohl had created Skiljansrode, but she had shaped it, and she had had little use for ceremony or formality in those days. Or even now, most times, though sometimes a part of her insisted that it was her due. Was she not—though she never felt it herself—the preeminent silth of her generation?

"The intercept section is still in place?"

"It is. Though reduced. There is very little on which to eavesdrop these days. The brethren have changed their codes and signals since they now know we eavesdrop, but we have kept up with their honest side. Only the rogues themselves give us much trouble. But their traffic is seldom significant. *He* knows we are listening. He must have his important messages paw-delivered."

"Very well. I will be spending most of my time in communications and intercept, arranging some unpleasantries for him."

"How long may we expect to share your company?"

"You will not have to endure me long. Perhaps two days. Three at the most. How long depends on how quickly I make my contacts and how cooperative I find those who have not seen or heard from me in ages."

Edzeka understood that well enough. "And it is true, what they are saying?"

"Is what true? What are they saying?"

"That you have found the Serke."

"Where did you get that idea?"

"Off intercept. It is the topic of the day. Did Marika return to the homeworld because she has found the Serke at last? Has she destroyed them? Has she not? In either case, if they have indeed been found, what will that mean to silth, to rogues, to the honest brethren, to meth in general? Will the Reugge arrogate to themselves the technology of the aliens, as they arrogated the Serke starworlds?"

"What? We received three poor planets and a begrudged right to venture beyond the homeworld's atmosphere. Hardly an arrogation, considering what we suffered at the paws of the Serke and their allies. We should have gotten it all. We would have taken it all had I been then what I am now. There would have been no negotiation, no convention, no nothing but the obliteration of the Serke and their allies."

"Calm yourself, mistress. I merely repeat what I have overheard. Those Communities that have been in the void for generations naturally resent the intrusion of the Reugge. They make accusations, take positions. Would they be silth if they did otherwise?"

"True. Of course. Posturing. Always posturing." But there was food for thought in what Edzeka had said. The solution of the Serke problem would raise new troubles possibly as dangerous. She had refused to face that before. It was time she invested in some reflection.

Marika had set herself a task. And for the first time she feared she had found one she could not handle. A simple job: Contact those silth who had worked with her in her days as the Reugge charged with bringing the rogue under control. Enlist them in a new and similar effort, gathering intelligence against her return from the meeting with the Serke.

But it was not simple. Many years had passed. All those silth had moved around, been promoted, passed into the embrace of the All, changed their names. Many were impossible to trace. Silth were not strong on keeping records.

Of those she did find, few were interested in helping. New duties, new responsibilities, new perquisites. Older and more sedentary, in some cases. Plain laziness in others. And complacency. The curse of most silth, complacency. How could anyone remain complacent after the events of recent decades?

The internal workings of the Reugge were more orderly than those of most Communities. Marika had less trouble finding old allies and agents. But even there she had trouble recruiting. Many did not wish to be identified with her anymore. She was not in power and not upon the pathway to power. She had abdicated.

Yet she did locate a few score old accomplices willing to strive for the communal defense, who recalled the old hard ways and who were willing to seek and implement new hard ways of excising the cancer surrounding the warlock. Probably most of those thought they saw a chance to improve their places.

"The world changes," Marika told Grauel. "But silth do not. Not in any way that matters. I think we may be living in the last years, at the end of time, as silth history goes. And those fools do not begin to suspect." She leaned back in a chair. Grauel and Barlog watched with faces of stone. "They cannot see anything in the mirror of the world. They cannot foresee with the simple intellect the All has given them. In one way it does not matter if the warlock is eliminated. I can obliterate him and everyone who serves him, to the last rogue meth, and still what he symbolizes will live on, just as strong. It is a poison in the heart of the race. Why do I even bother?"

Barlog said, "Because you must. Because you are what you are."

"Profound, I think, Barlog. You are saying more than you think you say. Because I must. Yes. And perhaps all those dead silth who declared me a Jiana were also saying something they did not know they said. Maybe I will, in a way they could not imagine, preside over the downfall of silthdom. I think I may be the doomstalker, but not so much the cause as the product of the event."

Grauel and Barlog had no further remarks. Marika didn't need to read their minds to know they did not doubt that the fall of the silth would be a universal benefice. Most of the world felt that way. In battling to preserve what she herself did not love she was battling the very tides of time.

This world had seen that there were other ways.

And that *could* be her fault. *She* had put those artificial suns up there where even the most remote savage could see that mystery and magic were not all the answers. Could see that they were not even the best answers. Could sense that they were not answers in which any but the very privileged few could share. . . .

It could be that she had written the doom of silthdom in an effort to save the race on whose backs silthdom rested.

"I am grateful for your aid and cooperation," Marika told Edzeka. "I believe these few days may have made it possible for us to concoct a few unpleasant surprises for the warlock once I return."

"Now you go to meet Brestrei, eh?"

Marika did not answer that. She asked, "All the world is convinced that it has come to that?"

"That is the message of the intercepts. The Serke have

been found, and Marika is going out to meet their champion."

"Then the warlock may believe it too. He will be considering moves. Beware, Edzeka. You are right about his attitude toward this place. Skiljansrode does much valuable work, and most of it hurts him. Do not let me hear that you have been called into the embrace of the All before your time."

"If I am lost, many rogues will light my path into the darkness, Marika. You have a care where you are going. The race can ill afford to lose you, little as many value you. You are probably the only silth who could deal with these aliens reasonably."

"I will be most careful. I am nearing the end of the list of those things I must do for others. I am on the brink of freedom. I have no intention of wasting that. Grauel, is the darkship prepared?"

"We are waiting on your pleasure."

"Very well. Edzeka, fare you well."

"Where to, Marika?" Barlog asked as she and Marika approached the darkship. Night held the world in shroud.

"Ruhaack, where we will reappear as we disappeared. Without announcement or ceremony."

"And then?"

Marika pointed upward. "And then we go out there again. The dark-faring Communities have begun assembling their strength. I will lead it in the final run of the long hunt."

"And then?"

"Kublin, I suppose."

"And then?"

Irked, Marika snapped, "That is enough! Until the time comes. Let be, Barlog. Let be."

"As you command, mistress. As you command."

That night Marika took the darkship into the high cold and rode with the wind, without strapping down, letting the freedom and risk of flight leech away the uncertainty and anger.

Chapter Thirty-Six

I

There were nineteen voidships waiting at Marika's baseworld when she arrived. A challenge greeted her the instant she came out of the Up-and-Over. Several of those ships were in the deep, patrolling. The others, on the ground, were so packed together that they could not have lifted off in any hurry. There was little room to bring more down. Few voidships could be dismantled or folded the way on-planet darkships could.

High Night Rider was in orbit. Kiljar's successor, Balbrach, was aboard. In fact, Marika soon discovered that Bel-Keneke was among the pawful of most seniors of darkfaring Communities who had chosen not to appear.

She was surprised. So much interest by so many who stood so high.

Nineteen darkships. And a twentieth arrived before Marika had completed her descent to the surface. Nearly all the dark-faring sisterhoods were represented, including several with which Marika had had no prior contact. She was impressed. In both scale and scope the gathering was more than she had hoped it would be.

With the exception of the Redoriad, the most seniors were down on the surface, awaiting her. She was surprised and pleased to find that they treated her as the most senior of the baseworld. She had anticipated having to face down several too arrogant to accept that.

Once Marika had eaten and rested and refreshed herself she led her high visitors down to the place where Grauel had discovered the old fire site. There was nothing to see, but it was a good, isolated place where leaders could talk, free of the watchful eyes of those they ruled. And it had symbolic significance as the first step upon a long trail.

Another two darkships arrived. The newcomers had to ground where they could. There was no more room at the main site.

Marika carried her weapons and wore her most barbarous garb. She and Grauel and Barlog wore bloodfeud dyes. With the most seniors assembled, Marika said, "What we are about to attempt will not be easy. Our enemies have had a decade to prepare for our coming. Much as we might wish tradition to hold, they will not be satisfied to have the matter settled by the outcome of a meeting between Bestrei and myself—if their champion fails them. We may expect to face alien weapons. We may have to face the talent suppressor we have seen used by rogues at home. We may expect almost anything—including the fact that some of us are going to die."

She marched back and forth, trying to look fierce, and something in Grauel's eye gave her pause. Then she realized what it was. Grauel was seeing yesterday. Just this way had her dam, Skiljan, paced in the hours of decision before the nomad had come down upon the Degnan packstead. This was the tone, the tenor, Skiljan had used on speaking to her huntresses before leading them out of the packstead to attack a nomad gathering below Machen Cave.

She gave Grauel a slight bow to indicate that she knew what the old huntress was thinking. She growled, "If you are not prepared to die, are not prepared to face the worst you can imagine, you may go now. But hear my spoken word. My blood pledge. She who does not partake of the risk will not partake of the profit. There will be no caviling of carrion eaters over the corpse as there was when the Serke properties were divided. We go to hunt, sisters! Those who will not hunt will not feast afterward. This is spoken by Marika of the Reugge. Is there one here who would argue?"

She was in a fine, ferocious mood. No one would have argued with her had she told the most outrageous lie. "Good. There was a saying in my home province, 'As strength goes.' I have never been one to brag. I will remind you this once. I am the strength. I am in my prime. When this has ended there will be no more Bestrei. I will have replaced her. My will shall rule that new starworld, as it does this one. And I will decide how we share in what we take from the rogues."

Now they did respond, and the response was bitter and protracted. Once Grauel took her weapon off her shoulder. That quieted the silth somewhat. Marika said, "I told you, I am the strength. But if you wish to dispute me, you may. Now or later. Ah? What? No takers? That is what I thought."

She continued, "Listen. I have grown weary of the way the sisterhoods feud with one another. I am not going to permit that out there. Bury your secret ambitions in the soil of this sad world. No one sisterhood is going to oust the Serke and leave the rest facing an unchanged situation. I say I will decide who shares what. What I mean is, I am going to hold that starworld in trust for all meth. With the exception of those who side with or do not help suppress the rogues."

She paced awhile, letting them bicker among themselves, then interrupted. "You may save your arguing and scheming for later. For now I only want to hammer upon one theme: that this is not going to be the simple bloodduel some expect. It is going to be darkwar, sisters, and darkwar as has never been seen in all the history of silthdom. The prize will be the future of the race. There will be many deaths. I hope most of those will be among our enemies. That is all I have to tell you now. Go. Prepare your hearts and minds. We will begin when we have twenty-five voidships rested and ready and willing."

She turned her back upon them and stood staring out across the hills of the world everyone but she accepted as hers.

Marika delayed till there were thirty darkships ready. And there was the promise of more to come. During the wait she visited *High Night Rider* and the Redoriad most senior, and arranged for a special role for the great voidship.

The day came when she felt she was stalling. She took her fears by the throat. Next morning, before dawn, the darkships began lifting, unhurriedly, and in some cases reluctantly. Perhaps she had waited too long. Too many of the silth had had time to reflect on what they might face. The fever of the hunt had begun to fade. Many were going on now only because they did not wish their orders to be cut out of the plunder.

Marika went up last—counting daggers.

The attack force numbered twenty-five ships, including her own and the Redoriad *High Night Rider.* The others would form a second wave, a reserve. *High Night Rider* would return for them and any who joined them too late for the first wave.

The darkships assembled around *High Night Rider,* forming the greatest concentration of voidships ever seen. That fact alone awed the silth. Only the mirror project had ever drawn more, and those were never gathered in a single drop of space. Marika peered at them, so many titanium daggers glistening in the light of a foreign sun, and she was awed herself. Once again she faced the fact that she was remarkable. Who else, with a word, could have drawn so many here? And so many of the mighty, at that?

Who was working the mirror project?

That could be set back years if the Serke had the perfect trap set at the far end of the Up-and-Over.

Marika closed her eyes, shunned all doubts, opened to the All, reached with a general touch, felt other minds grow aware. She opened her eyes again and fixed her gaze upon the first milestar of their journey. *See with me. This is our first target star. I will lead off. Come you behind me one by one. We will assemble again before continuing.*

She felt a murmur of assent, like the soft rush of water over sand. They, too, had put all doubts and reservations aside.

I am going.

She gathered her ghosts and went.

Blackness. Then the reality of stars again. She was drifting down toward the heart of the system. She felt for a foreign presence and found none. *Good.*

A darkship came through. So long, she thought. Were they really that slow? She touched the Mistress of the Ship to let her know where she was, and that the system was clear and safe. She repeated that over and over while the others gathered, till *High Night Rider* had come through.

The ships finally completed reassembly. Nearly four hours had passed since her own arrival. That was not good. It meant an erratic appearance at the business end of the quest too.

There was a way for darkships to travel in concert, though it was used seldom, and never had been tried with so many voidships. Still, she was tempted to try. If they exited the Up-and-Over in no more orderly a manner next passage, she would, third time.

She repeated the general touch, picturing the next target star and went, and came out well ahead, and again had satisfied herself that the system was untenanted before the next ship appeared.

Again it took four hours to gather them preparatory to the final jump, and this time yet another hour for each of the senior baths to pass fresh draughts of the golden fluid. She wanted no crew to arrive in need.

We face the final leg, Marika sent. *This time, to avoid the disorder we have suffered thus far, I will mesh all Mistresses in a general touch before we go into the Up-and-Over. We will go it together, as a lot, traveling with the slowest. Open to me, and to the All. It is time to go.*

There were protests. Marika ignored them, *Open to me,* she sent. And *Prepare your souls. It is time for the final jump.* She reached out and collected ghosts, waiting for others to do the same. She was amazed that they should be so slow, should have to labor so hard. For her it was a task done almost without thought.

At last they were ready. At last even the most reluctant surrendered to control. She gathered them in a tight formation, nearly touching, surrounding her, and sent, *Here we go.*

She fired one last arrow of touch at the Mistress of *High Night Rider,* and went.

Behind her, *High Night Rider* also disappeared, but bound back to the base world, to assemble and guide the second wave.

II

It was a dragging passage, making the pace of the weakest Mistress. Marika became restless. It gave her too long to become concerned about what might await her.

She began to question her conviction that she stalked the sun of the world where the Serke were hiding. She had no concrete proof that her target was the Serke star. Suppose she had been set upon a false trail? How discredited would she be if the star proved to be just another blank milestar on the secret pathway?

And there was Bestrei. Always in her thoughts there was Bestrei. She was not eager to meet the Serke champion, old as she must be now. Bestrei was three times victorious in darkwar over the strongest challengers of her time.

And there were all those surprises desperate meth might prepare. . . . But the Serke could not expect a raid in such strength. Could they? Would they not expect her to come alone, thinking she, as most silth would, would want to claim the prize for herself?

She found a part of her counting the time, flashing away too swiftly for all it ran so slowly. She crouched, as though to offer a smaller target.

Time ran down. Ran out. Her will wavered as the last second approached. . . . She let go.

A star flared into being. The disorientation was strong because she caught echoes of that suffered by other Mistresses of the Ships. She wrenched herself out of touch, got a grip on herself, gasped in awe the moment she had herself fixed in space and time.

They had come out of the Up-and-Over within spitting distance of a world, a greenish-blue planet shrouded in cloud. . . . There! Rising.

I have it! she sent. *Coming over the horizon. I sense silth. Let us move.* She pushed her darkship forward. Others followed as they regained their composure. The formation stretched and became ragged.

She felt the alarm rise ahead, the terror spread as lashes of touch whipped from her target to the world below, and into the depths of the system. She followed those touches and learned that she had come out of the Up-and-Over well inside a picket maintained by two darkships. Down on the world itself she detected a huge base beside a river. Already meth had begun evacuating farms and factories in panic.

The Serke had done well, Marika thought. Their courier flights must have been collecting meth on the homeworld. How else to explain the numbers she sensed? They could not have bred their workers here.

She faced the approaching object, which had to be the alien ship.

And she recoiled in awe.

Nothing made ought to be that huge.

It was a great ripped and rent thing half a mile long. A hundred *High Night Riders* would fit inside it.

Touch brushed Marika. She responded, *I have come, rogues. It is time for you to pay your debts.*

Who?

Marika. Of the Reugge.

Panic redoubled.

Something flashed on the great ship. Marika sensed rather than saw the beam, She began flying an erratic course, projecting that undercurrent of touch that might make her invisible to some silth minds.

She touched her companions as well, detailed five Mistresses to meet the two darkships rushing in from picket duty, ordered five more to go down to the planet, and another five to stand off and intercept any darkships that came up. The remaining darkships she led toward the alien vessel.

More beams crisped the darkness, never quite touching their target.

Something was wrong. She could detect no darkships save the two out on patrol. At least a dozen had escaped, of which only three were known to have been lost. With the brethren to help, they could have built more had they the sisters to crew them. And *Starstalker* was nowhere in evidence.

Give it up, she sent. *Let us not waste any more lives. Your situation is hopeless. Surrender to the inevitable.*

Beams flared around her.

Pinpoints of light winked around the alien ship. Marika grabbed ghosts and flung them forward to investigate, found the void aswarm with tiny ships. They had machine minds and carried explosives.

She detonated two score in rapid succession and drove her darkship through a cloud of expanding gases. But she stopped only those missiles directed toward her. Others slipped past. A scream tortured the otherworld as a darkship died.

Marika hurled ghosts toward the alien vessel, found

tradermales working the weapons there, and began neutralizing them. She sensed others following her example.

Something ripped near her, jiggling her grip on her ghosts. Talent suppressor. Behind her another silth crew screamed and died. She regained her self-control and ghosts and hunted for the operators of the suppressor. She found several weapons and crews.

She received a broken touch from the atmosphere, where another silth crew had lost their darkship. The rogues had suppressors down there too. She withdrew, left that problem to those who had to face it, and pushed her own ship up to the hull of the alien.

She set the wooden darkship down upon a flat area, out of danger from the ship's armaments, and sent ghosts ravening through its innards, dispatching tradermale after tradermale, and a few Serke as well. There were not many silth.

Still, there was something wrong. There were males in there who were immune to her ghosts. They wore space suits similar to those used by workers on the mirror project. Each radiated a suppressor field.

She sensed many more suits of that kind. The dead males had not had time to don them. She sabotaged all she could find while they remained inactive.

She felt another darkship die and grew afraid that the rogues were too thoroughly prepared.

But no. Surprise had been hers. The alien ship could no longer fire upon its attackers. Its weapons had been disarmed. Inside, those who did not wear the suppressor suits were dying. The task was not complete, but the anchor of rogue strength had been neutralized.

Marika reached for the planet, where the darkships had scattered and were descending amid a welter of beams. No darkships rose to meet them. The darkships Marika had detailed to support them had elected to join the descent, to help stifle the defense. She touched her surviving companions and ordered all but one darkship to join her. The remaining darkship she detailed to stand off the alien to thwart any escape attempt.

The screams of perishing silth filled the otherworld. It took Marika a moment to realize that she had sensed several crews perishing at once. She reached. . . . And was astonished by the nothingness she found.

All five ships she had sent to intercept the patrol! All gone in an instant!

Something cold and dark and hungry lurked behind the inward-bound Serke, death on a tether.

She found an aura she recalled from long ago. From her first flight aboard a dark-faring darkship.

Bestrei.

Bestrei was aboard one of the picket ships. She was coming in.

Fear filled Marika.

Bestrei. The undefeated Champion. Arrowing toward the world. Dragging the heart of the deep behind her.

Marika murmured mantras, calming herself. The inevitable had come upon her, as she had known it must. It was time to face it.

She unslung her rifle and gripped it tightly, swung the wooden dagger toward the Serke champion. She touched Grauel, Barlog, and her bath. *We go to meet Bestrei. I must have your best.*

III

Marika turned her conscious mind off, opened to the All, maneuvered without calculation.

She gathered ghosts, climbed into the Up-and-Over, let go an instant later, raced toward the Serke. She sent a strong ghost whirling ahead.

She had to release the ghost and bounce into the Up-and-Over to evade the pounce of Bestrei's great black. She came out again. The great black surged toward her, trailing her by just a few seconds. She barely had time to recover her equilibrium.

It was to be hammers, then, and no finesse. Strength against strength.

Of course. Raw power was Bestrei's strength.

Marika touched the black ghost, grabbed at it, tried to wrest it away from Bestrei. The great black was the most real of ghosts, the most responsive to stimuli. This one screamed in touch, radiating cold rage and frustration. Bestrei had it on an unbreakable chain, and now it was being torn another way.

Marika darted closer, sweeping around the vacancy where the great black lurked. Vaguely, her eyes caught the glimmer of sunlight skipping off titanium darkships. Bestrei moved, too, remaining opposite her beyond the great black, leaking a bit of touch that betrayed her amazement. She could not believe she had encountered one so strong.

Where had she been this past generation? Did she not know that the Reugge had raised up a champion against her?

Marika could not take control of the ghost. She felt she was stronger than Bestrei, but the great black was attuned to the Serke champion and remained inclined to serve her interest. Perhaps Bestrei better suited its bleak, dark taste.

The ghost drew in upon itself as it recoiled from the demands placed upon it. The Serke were not three hundred yards from Marika, beyond the ghost. Her wooden darkship rocked and jerked. Grauel and Barlog were firing, using vacuum ammunition Bagnel had given them. Their fire did little but distract Marika. They seemed unable to calculate the ballistics between moving darkships.

Marika recalled the Serke she had bested in the Ponath, during the fighting at the ruins of Critza. She squeezed the great black viciously, then broke away to fling a burst of her own Bestrei's way. Her tracers flew so wide one ricocheted off the second Serke voidship.

Marika's senior bath touched her with an appeal. The

second Serke ship was trying to harm her while she was preoccupied with Bestrei.

Suns, stars, planet wheeled as darkships danced around the sullen great black, locked in a stalemate. Marika found the duel somehow anticlimactic. All those years anticipating this encounter. It did not seem as dramatic as it should. But such was life. Anticipation, then disappointment or anticlimax.

What was the story? Bestrei was a sport, overpoweringly strong. She, the upstart, was strong, too, but she supposedly had a brain as well. Why was she not using it? Why had she locked herself into a reactionary role? Was it her fear? Or a misplaced respect for the great?

She *was* afraid. Terribly afraid. And that *had* crippled her ability to reason and plan.

She turned the tip of the wooden dagger toward Bestrei and pushed forward, trying to drive through the great black, trying to part it as if it were some dark, noisome fog.

She failed. Bestrei forced her back, though she had to strain to her limits. Marika sensed Bestrei's growing concern. Never before had the Serke champion encountered an opponent she could not overpower immediately.

Marika allowed Bestrei to force her back. She withdrew from the contest of strength gradually and devoted her freed strength to gathering ghosts for a jump into the Up-and-Over.

That took more effort than she had anticipated. Lesser ghosts were scarce where the great black prowled.

Marika gathered enough. She sighted on the nearest neighboring star and climbed into the Up-and-Over, drove with all her strength. A tendril of victory touch from the Serke trailed her.

Only seconds passed. She reached her destination, regained her equilibrium, felt the void.

There. It was very far out, but it was there. Another great black. She scrambled into the Up-and-Over again, and came out near it, grasping desperately for balance before it pounced. For a moment she feared she would lose the gamble. Cold hunger, dark hatred engulfed her. Then she found the place to touch, to grab, to command, and took control.

Marika rotated her darkship and sighted upon the Serke star. She fixed Bestrei's darkship in her mind, then climbed into the Up-and-Over.

Her bath projected a whining complaint about the load she imposed upon them, She was drawing upon them heavily, conserving her own stength.

She dragged the black along with her. It went with great reluctance.

Out of the Up-and-Over again. Closer to the planet now. The otherworld was astenchful with fear. Those who had come with Marika were in flight from the Serke champion.

Marika rushed the Serke, flinging her great black ahead.

Bestrei wavered, then turned back.

Marika's darkship and Bestrei's hurtled toward one another. A silth scream filled the otherworld as Marika dispatched Bestrei's companion, then fended the Serke's great black.

If anything, the ambience was colder, more dark and hate-filled with the second black added. The two great ghosts slid around one another like slippery water creatures never touching, though those who wielded them tried to use them like swords.

For a time Marika and Bestrei traded blows like fighting huntresses standing toe to toe, hammering one another with doubled paws. Neither could harm the other.

Brains, Marika reminded herself. The reason silth feared her more than Bestrei. Supposedly because she had brains. She should use her head as well as her hatred.

She used the reluctance of the blacks to touch to force Bestrei's monster to one side. Those demons of the void twisted around one another, well out of the way. Bestrei concentrated upon that struggle, for that was what she had been taught and that was her great strength. Marika nudged her darkship nearer Bestrei's, letting it drift, keeping most of her strength with the great black. She let the Serke think she was winning the test of strength slowly.

Fifty yards separated the darkships. Then twenty-five. Marika lifted her ship slightly relative to the other. In seconds she would be over Bestrei, just yards from the Serke. Ten yards away.

Bestrei finally sensed her danger. She tried to pull out.

Marika leaned and fired short, rapid bursts that raked the titanium cross, sent sparks scattering into the void. She emptied her magazine. Graul and Barlog laced the night with tracers.

Bestrei pulled away. Marika slapped another magazine into her weapon and pushed after the Serke, firing down the length of her darkship.

Bestrei almost got her with a surprise strike from her black. Marika turned the blow, but barely, and had to abandon the chase. Bestrei withdrew several miles.

Then she turned and started back, accelerating—straight toward Marika. Marika watched with her eyes and silth senses, dumbfounded. What was Bestrei doing? It seemed she meant to collide with her, taking them both out in one magnificent crash.

Then she understood.

A bullet had found one of Bestrei's bath, and another Bestrei herself. Neither wound was mortal or incapacitating, but they had weakened and distracted the Serke, and she was no longer confident of victory.

She *did* mean to go out in a glorious suicide, taking her Reugge opponent with her.

It was an act worthy of a legend. Worthy of the noble silth Bestrei was supposed to be.

Kalerhag.

The only hope for the Serke who had fled the homeworld.

Marika wrenched her darkship away. The Serke dagger passed within inches, Bestrei trying to roll it so an arm would tangle with one on Marika's ship. Marika rolled too. Bestrei missed.

Tracers streaked around her.

Bestrei's black struck. Marika pushed it away. By the time she freed her attention the Serke was coming at her again, a silvery streak driving toward her heart.

She dodged.

But this time Bestrei made it even closer.

Marika emptied her rifle as the titanium cross ripped past. Grauel and Barlog did likewise. This time it was the recoil that saved the wooden darkship, for it skewed away, twisting, barely sliding beneath the sweep of Bestrei's voidship.

Somebody got lucky. The storm of bullets tore one of Bestrei's bath apart. The performance of the Serke darkship declined immediately.

Marika stabilized her ship, faced Bestrei, waited. Bestrei waited too.

This is hardly traditional darkwar, Marika thought. We cheat on our silthdom. Especially I. Bestrei must be scandalized.

She felt for the great blacks. Hers had fled into the void. Bestrei's was going. The Serke champion seemed too weak to recall it.

Bestrei seemed to have strength enough only to guide her darkship toward the planet.

Marika reached for Bestrei's great black.

It did not want to be ruled again. And she was not at her strongest. She needed another draught of the golden drink. But she did take the great ghost, and brought it back, and drove it toward the Serke.

Bestrei tried to force it back. But wounded herself, with one bath wounded and another dead, she could not withstand Marika's greater strength.

Silth screams filled the otherworld.

Before long the Serke voidship was a fiery meteor plunging toward the surface of the planet.

The song of Bestrei was sung.

BOOK SIX
STARSHIPS

Chapter Thirty-Seven

I

Marika neither mourned the Serke champion nor waited for her dying to end. She gripped Bestrei's great black ghost tightly and drove it at the alien starship.

The suppressor suits worn by the brethren were powerful, but they could not withstand the great black. Images of insects in campfire coals crossed Marika's mind as she listened to dying cries haunting the otherworld.

She reached out to her allies—those who had not yet vanished into the Up-and-Over—and summoned them back to the struggle. *Bestrei is no more, cowards! Come! Let us put an end to this tale.*

Marika directed her darkship to orbit, following Bestrei, watching as the Serke's titanium voidship heated white hot and began to burn. She felt those on the planet below pause, watch the glow streak across their sky, and realize what it meant. She reached, pulled the great black toward her.

Could she force it down there, to the surface itself, to complete the conquest of the brethren? She tried, but the black's resistance was too much for her. She did not have the strength to overcome its will to avoid large masses. But she believed she could force it down if she were fresh.

She released it with a stroke of gratitude. It flashed away across the void to resume its place on the edge of the system.

Marika sent her allies down to complete the subjugation of the planet. She drifted across to the alien starship and forced her way inside. The last minutes before she succeeded were desperate ones, for she had no strength left and was beyond help from the senior bath and her golden fluid—even had the bath had strength enough to leave her station. Had she tried to descend to the planet's surface she would have followed Bestrei as a shooting star.

She led her huntresses and bath into halls filled with breathable air. The moment they were safe she sat down, her back against metal, and sighed. "That was close. As close as ever I want to get."

It was very strange in there. Very spartan and spare, all metal and cold and electronic lighting and the hollow sound of feet shuffling on deckplates. Her curiosity was intense but she hadn't the strength to pursue it. "Grauel. Barlog," she whispered. "I *must* rest. Stand watch. Please."

The bath, except their senior, had collapsed into sleep already.

Grauel and Barlog shared their remaining ammunition and stood guard, though they themselves were near collapse from exhaustion. Marika had drawn upon them as well as her bath.

Marika wakened ten hours later, feeling little better than when she had closed her eyes. Barlog was snoring. Grauel had the watch. The bath were all still asleep. "Any trouble?" Marika asked.

"None yet," Grauel replied. "Not a sign of life. But this place makes me nervous. It vibrates all the time, and makes sounds you cannot hear unless you listen. It makes me think of putting my ear against someone's stomach and listening to what is going on inside. It makes me feel as if I am inside the belly of some mythological monster."

When Marika listened she could hear and feel what Grauel meant. It was disconcerting. She opened to the All, seeking those who had come to the system with her.

Dead ships were adrift everywhere. A disaster? She counted carefully. There were only ten derelict or missing. Not as bad as she had feared. But *only* ten? Was that not disaster enough? That was almost half the force she had brought. A massive loss of dark-faring silth. Virtually every void-faring Community would be plunged into Mourning.

And the expense of victory did not stop totally with a count of darkships lost. The survivors down below, upon the planet's surface, resting and inventorying what had been taken, numbered only enough to cobble together crews for seven or eight darkships. The fall of the Serke might mark the end of an era in more ways than one.

"Is there anything to eat?" Marika asked. "Did anyone think to bring anything in? I'm ravenous." The struggle had consumed her body's energy reserves.

"There is cold meat," Grauel replied. "The bath remembered to bring it in, but I have found no way to cook it."

Marika was amused by a vision of nomads cooking over a dung fire in the middle of the floor of an electric kitchen. Neither she nor any of those with her had any idea what anything aboard the alien might do.

"Did we take any captives who know anything about the ship?"

Grauel shrugged. "I'm not silth, Marika. I can't communicate with those below."

"Of course. It was foolish of me to ask. Get some rest now. I'm going exploring."

"Marika . . .

"Give me your ammunition. I'll be fine."

Grauel did not argue, which indicated just how far she and Grauel had extended themselves. Marika moved the ammunition from Grauel's weapon to her own, then settled down to gnaw on cold, half-cooked preserved meat. Her stomach rumbled a greeting as sustenance finally arrived.

Having eaten, she reached out to the planet and tracked down a Mistress who was alert enough to be touched. She sent a series of queries and learned that only a pawful of Serke had been taken captive. Few of the rogue brethren had survived either. There had been a lot of anger in the struggle down there, and each death scream of another allied darkship had heightened the fury of the attackers. The majority of the prisoners were bonds. They would know little or nothing.

Some who had been interviewed were unaware that they were not still upon the meth homeworld.

But we did capture the records of the investigation of the alien ship, apparently intact.

That is wonderful, Marika responded. *I will come down to examine them as soon as my bath are rested enough to make the descent. We will want hot food, and lots of it, when we arrive.* She broke touch and began to wander through the dead ship.

She found dead brethren everywhere. Those who had not gotten themselves into their suppressor suits had begun to bloat, to stink. The first order of business would be to get rid of them before they polluted the environment permanently. She stepped over and around them, ignoring them, as she examined alien hardware.

The ship was a Jiana, she reflected. Or, if not a doomstalker, certainly accursed. Twice those it sustained had been slaughtered by enemies from without. She sped an admonitory prayer to the All, suggesting that that not be made a tradition.

The starship was a tradermale's dream. It recalled the wonder she had felt the first time she had entered the control cabin of a dirigible, now so long ago the moment seemed excised from another life. The line of descent from that crude array to this was obvious at the control stations.

Much of what she saw was recognizable in terms of function, if not of actual operation. She saw several places where tradermales had made repairs and brought parts of the starship back to life.

The subliminal throb of the vessel continued, almost unnoticed, like her own heartbeat. The ship was crippled but far from dead. She wondered how much the rogue brethren had hoped to restore it. There had to be limits to what they could comprehend.

How broad those limits, though? They had had more than two decades to study it.

She wandered for more than two hours, growing ever more awed by the ship's size. In that time she was unable to see everything that had been restored, and that part of the vessel represented but a fraction of the whole. She could duck through her loophole, capture a ghost, and sail through vast sections still unreclaimed, seeing ten thousand wonders that were absolute mysteries.

Wouldn't Bagnel love it?

A worthy next project for him and his loyal brethren? There must be studies enough here to occupy generations.

Something touched her. She had a vague, general sense of something having gone wrong. She opened to the All.

A darkship had arrived.

She probed more closely. It was *High Night Rider*, at last come from the baseworld with the second wave.... No. When she scanned the surrounding void she found the Redoriad voidship alone, and limping discernibly.

II

Feeble touch brushed the starship. Marika thought she recognized its flavor. *Balbrach. Are you there? Is that you? What is wrong? Where are the other darkships?*

The weak touch focused. *I am here, Marika.* Balbrach's touch did not become much stronger. *We jumped into an ambush. The Serke were attacking your base when we arrived. They had destroyed everyone caught on the ground and were dueling two darkships. We tried to help and nearly were destroyed ourselves. We lost bath. We managed to shake them returning here. But they could appear at any time. Our very direction of flight would unnerve them.*

Do they know we have found them?

I do not know. It is likely they will learn, if they do not guess from the way we fled. We did learn that they were trying to destroy you with their attack. They were disappointed because you were not on your baseworld. My impression was that they planned to remain there till you returned. But if they guess that you have come here they will bring all their strength back. Come help us, Marika. We may not have the strength to make orbit.

I will be there as soon as I can. How many darkships did they have?

Five still functional when we fled.

Hold on. I am going to collect my bath now.

Marika withdrew into herself and hurried to rejoin her crew. But soon she learned that she was lost in the corridors. She had to go down through her loophole and catch a ghost and ride it through the starship, scouting a pathway.

She touched her senior bath. *We have to go out.* High Night Rider *has arrived after skirmishing with the missing Serke darkships. They lost bath and are in trouble. We are the only ones able to get there. Get your sisters up and ready.*

The senior bath grumbled to herself, but prepared.

Marika debated having her let Grauel and Barlog lie where they were, but decided against it. They needed the rest, but they might waken, find themselves alone, and think that they had been abandoned.

Marika joined them as the senior bath passed the silver bowl and led the way through the airlock to the darkship. While she waited for the bath to untie and push away, Marika reached down and touched a Mistress on the planet to relay Balbrach's news.

We could have unfriendly visitors at any time. All darkships must lift off immediately, lest they be caught on the surface. Assemble near the starship.

The response below was not one of great joy, but the silth

down there sorted themselves out and got seven darkships off the ground. Marika was not pleased. Only seven surviving. She touched the silth who remained, telling them to keep a firm paw on their captives.

Her senior bath touched her. *We are clear, Mistress. You may drive when you will.*

Marika marked the location of *High Night Rider* and surged away from the alien. She gathered more ghosts and did the unthinkable: skipped through the Up-and-Over. She matched courses with the voidship, took her darkship inside, and loaned one of her bath to the senior Redoriad bath. Then she put her head together with Balbrach's.

The Serke darkships materialized only hours after *High Night Rider* made orbit in the starship's shadow. Marika and the others were waiting. They rushed in. The struggle was fierce, bitter, and without mercy asked or given. Though they were tired, the Serke showed well. They destroyed another three darkships. Marika had to summon the great black to end it.

The survivors limped back to the alien starship. Marika found Balbrach wandering the cold metal passageways of the ship. Balbrach greeted her by gesturing, saying, "This reminds me of the ice in a brethren factor's heart. There is nothing here but function. Is this species a race without a soul?"

"I do not know, mistress. I have not had time to learn. Come with me. I can show you what they look like."

"You have one of them?"

"No. An image."

As they walked, Balbrach asked, "And what will you do now?"

"We have broken the Serke threat at last," Marika replied, scarcely able to believe that the long hunt had come to an end. "Now we go on to . . ."

"You have fulfilled the role for which you were shaped by Gradwohl. Where will you go from there?"

Marika temporized. "I think nowhere. I will return to the homeworld, briefly, to gather meth to study the starship. Maybe I will come back here and stay here, awaiting the advent of the creatures who built this ship—if ever they come seeking their brethren."

"Brethren?"

"Most seem to have been males, though their crew was mixed. Actually more like bonds at work than silth or brethren. Or I may hunt some rogues. There is one in particular with whom I have a grievance."

"For a long time there have been close ties between Marika and the Redoriad first chair," Balbrach observed. Her body language suggested that she was imparting an important secret. In a softer voice, she continued, "I suggest that you not spend much time at home, Marika. That you be very careful and abnormally alert if you do visit."

"Why?"

"There are many sisters who feel that we should not have to endure the continuous threat represented by one silth who is able to impose her will upon anyone. Bestrei was tolerated because she did not interfere. She enforced the Serke will in the void, but according to a rigid and ancient noble code. They will see the silth who defeated Bestrei as more flexible, less predictable, and more likely to interfere in areas considered none of her business."

"I see. You fear someone might try to eliminate that unpredictable silth."

"Certainly the rogues would make that effort. The warlock will have been planning your fate from the moment he heard a rumor that his stellar allies had been found. And if he failed, then those sisters would take up the blade."

"And?"

"And another thought strikes me now. This ship has proven to be a treasure that inspires madness. And you have made statements already sure to arouse the enmity of the greedy."

"I see what you mean. I also sense that you speak not on

the impulse of the moment, and that you do so without guessing. That you know whereof you speak."

"Perhaps. I am sure there were Mistresses who came out here with orders to close the legend of Marika the savage if that was possible. The Serke ended their tales instead in this great slaughter. That in itself is going to cause considerable dismay. A useful villain has vanished. A third of all void-ships in existence have been lost, and with them the most seniors of many dark-faring sisterhoods. There will be chaos when the news reaches home."

Marika reflected. "Yes. Not only within the Communities bereft, too. If he has prepared as you suggest, and recognizes it, that would be a great moment for the warlock to strike."

"So I have thought."

"Then I shall race the news homeward. I shall arrive before he hears and complete my business there before the Communities can recover sufficiently to turn upon me."

Looking within herself, Marika found her ties to her homeworld attenuated. But for wanting to see Bagnel again, and hoping to encounter Kublin, she had little desire to return. She hardly missed the enfolding subconscious touch of the planet. In fact, if she could convince Bagnel to come out to help unlock the secrets of the alien ship, she would be content to spend the rest of her life there, perhaps using it as a base from which to continue her explorations and to fare beyond the dust cloud in search of the creatures who had built the starship.

If she could fulfill her responsibilities toward Grauel and Barlog . . . She was stricken by an old guilt. "Whatever else I may do, Balbrach, there is one task I am compelled to undertake upon the homeworld. In one sense, now that the Serke have been overcome, I no longer have any excuse for delaying."

The Redoriad most senior awarded her a baffled look, confused by her body language. Marika had ceased to be silth. She had lapsed into the upper Ponath savage she had been as a pup. Balbrach said, "I sense that some old haunt has recalled itself to you."

"You know my background. You know I never completely rejected it. Nor have my two voctors, my packmates, who have been with me since we escaped the nomads the Serke sent down upon our homeland. It has taken us all our lives to avenge our packmates. But with that done, we still owe them one obligation. And we cannot complete that without returning to the place where they died." She tried to explain a Mourning to Balbrach. The Redoriad could not encompass the savage practice. It was unlike anything in the silth experience. But she managed better than most because of her own rural background. Most silth would have mocked the notion of rites for a band of savages.

"I wish you could engineer it so you did not have to do this thing, Marika. I wish you could stay here and never again venture homeward. But I cannot presume to tell you what to do. I can only warn you of the dangers to your person."

Marika nodded. "Here we are. This is the place from which the vessel was controlled. Where their equivalent of the Mistress of the Ship was posted."

The chamber was large. It had three separate levels, with seating for forty beings. Most of the chairs faced screens similar to those meth used for communications. Balbrach said, "It looks like an oversize comm center."

"Look here." Marika touched a switch. One of the screens assumed life. A creature peered out at them. Balbrach made a startled sound when it began talking. The sounds it made were more liquid and round than any that could be formed by the meth mouth and tongue.

"That is one ugly beast," Balbrach said in an attempt at humor. "Such a flat face. Like someone smashed it in with a frying pan. And no fur, except on top. It looks like a badly deformed pup. Look at those ears. They are ears, are they not?"

"I suspect so. They are taller than we are, in the main, judging from the size of their chairs and doorways. That one seems to be male. The one in the background behind him, though, may be female."

"Do you have any idea what he is saying?"

"No. At a guess, this is a recorded report to whoever finds the ship. This is the reason the Serke were certain someone would come. As it progresses you will see what appears to be a report about what crippled the ship, followed by regular reports on the fates of individual crew members as they perished."

"You could tell all that?"

"Some things do not need words. A picture says more."

"True." Balbrach turned from the screen. "So. What *are* your plans?"

"As I said. I will go home briefly. I will assemble a team to study the ship. I will close out my life there. I think it will be my last visit, unless I go home to die. I will leave soon, to arrive before anyone who slips off with the news. Can *High Night Rider* carry darkships and Mistresses who have had to loan their bath?"

"If necessary. That leaves me with only one question, Marika. Perhaps the most important question of all."

"Yes?"

"What about *Starstalker*?"

It was a question Marika had been avoiding, even within her mind. *Starstalker* had not been among the Serke void-ships destroyed. "What about *Starstalker*? I do not know. I think that will have to answer itself. Possibly at a time and place of their choosing."

III

The first rest stop on the path home came at the former baseworld. Marika drifted in through space scattered with broken voidships and dead silth. One third of all voidfaring silth lost. One third of the best and brightest of all silth. And the warlock had not had to lift a paw.

What would the disaster mean to the mirror project?

She took the wooden darkship down to her old camp. And there she found more of the same, twisted darkships and decomposing corpses. The Serke had been thorough. She walked with her memories of her years there, rested as best she could with haunted dreams, then climbed to the stars again, running out hours ahead of *High Night Rider* and the survivors of the struggle.

Her thoughts kept turning to *Starstalker*. What had become of *High Night Rider*'s littermate and the one or two ordinary Serke darkships that remained unaccounted for? Nothing could be found of them at the baseworld, and they had not participated in the counterattack upon the system of their exile.

Were they on the run again, that last dozen or so? Had they another hiding place still? Would *Starstalker*'s survival leave a hope where she wanted all hope slain?

Marika felt very old when her home sun materialized and she saw her birthworld again. Very old and very useless. Yet she was convinced that she was far from playing out the role that had been decreed for her by the All. Beyond the few remaining tasks imposed upon her by circumstance lay her own life. She might yet have something for herself, if she was not still a tool of fate.

She directed her darkship toward the Hammer.

Bagnel met her in the airlock. He directed brethren to care for her companions. The moment they were alone, he said, "The news is spreading already. You have destroyed the rogues."

Baffled, she asked, "How can that be? I *must* be the first ship back."

"You came back. That was evidence enough. It was on every radio network within minutes of your coming out of the Up-and-Over. At least that speculation. So. Did you do it?"

"We destroyed most of them. But it was very expensive. There will be little joy of it. I am exhausted, trying to beat the news home. And I'm depressed, old friend. Yet I am elated too. For once and all I have refuted the Jiana accusation. I have led the race out of its darkest hour."

"Have you?"

"What?"

"I don't like the look of you, Marika. There is a new darkness behind your eyes. It is the darkness I saw there when you were young."

Marika was not pleased. "It must be the darkness that comes of battle, Bagnel. It will be a long time before I can shake my memories of my meeting with Bestrei. There was darkness incarnate, for all her nobility."

"There is an old saying among the meth with whom I spent my puphood. It goes, 'We become that which we would destroy.'"

"I've heard it before. It's not always true. I will not become a new Bestrei."

"You're much more. You're a thing that cannot be understood. There has been much discussion of you in your absence. Undertaken in complete confidence that you would succeed in doing what you have done. That discussion has been underlaid by fear of Marika, the wild silth, the dark-walking sister with no allegiance and no limit to her power. I know you will do what you will do and nothing I can say will shift your course an inch. So I will only beg of you, be careful. The frightened do desperate things."

"So I have been warned already. Yet I have been given no specifics."

"There are no specifics to be had. At least by those of us who might be tempted to relate them to their target. Only rumors."

"What of Kublin and the rogues?"

"They have been quiet. Surprisingly so. Again, though, there have been rumors. That they have been preparing for your return, come you in triumph or defeat. It is said that they are convinced that by killing you they can start a scramble for control of the alien ship that will so embroil the attentions of the dark-faring silth that they will be left with a free paw here at home. I have a feeling their estimate is close to the truth. The rumor mill also has much to say about undercover planning in various Communities for an effort to seize and exploit the alien."

Marika folded a lip in sardonic amusement. "So I have no friends at all. Not that I ever had. And my death would serve everyone's purpose. I think we belong to a sad race, Bagnel."

"I could have told you that truth the day we first faced one another on Akard's wall."

"Does the project continue well?"

"As well as might be expected, considering that we have had to do without the voidships that accompanied you and the fact that so many meth have become distracted by other matters. We brethren persevere."

"Has it reached a stage where it could survive without you?"

"Everything can survive without me. I am wholly disposable."

"A matter I would debate strongly, with you or anyone else. Would you like a new challenge? A challenge greater than putting new suns in the sky?"

"You intrigue me, Marika. If anyone but you made a statement like that ... What is it?"

"How would you like to unravel the secrets of the alien starship?"

He examined her intently. "What are you saying?"

"One of the reasons I've come home is to recruit replacements for the rogue scientists who were studying the starship. I want you to be in charge."

"You found it? You have it? It wasn't just speculation?"

"It's very real. And very strange, in the way things are strange when they are similar." She began describing the ship.

"Ah."

She saw the marvel he tried to conceal. The eagerness. The excitement.

"If you want it, the job is yours. But it could be danger-ous. I have declared that the vessel is going to be mine, held in trust for all meth. As you suggested yourself, some Communities do not feel it should be that way. They feel they should have it for themselves, and I have been warned that more than one might try to seize it."

"Of course. No might about it. There will be efforts to grab it. Even with the lesson of the project before them, silth are unable to comprehend the notion of working together for the good of the species. They have trouble enough working together for the good of their orders."

"It may be a difficult thing, Bagnel. I am strong, but I stand alone out there. I will have to have support. Any team I put into the starship will be dependent upon my remaining on friendly terms with the Reugge and Redoriad. They will have to supply us. I cannot carry that load alone."

"Even them I would not count on completely were I you, Marika. But consider: How did the Serke and rogues sup-port themselves without supplies from the homeworld? Theirs may be the path you'll want to follow yourself. Sever the ties entirely. Go ahead and be what they have called you, a Community unto yourself."

"It may come to that, though I still refuse to believe that the silth can remain so narrow."

"Refuse if you like. I will refuse to believe that you have become so naive during your absence. Are you acting? To me? You know that the unity forged for the mirror project is a harbinger of nothing. That was and remains desperation, the only answer in a struggle for survival. It has come so far even the rogues would not dream of destroying them. But their very nature makes them vulnerable in other ways, to those who seek power and profit. Among all the other accusations thrown your way over the years the secret dreams of some have been betrayed by their canards about your intentions in regard to the mirrors."

"I have no intentions. My intentions were satisfied when I convinced everyone to build them."

"True. But still some whisper that you intend to seize

them when they are complete and use them to hold the race hostage."

"That's stupid. If I wanted to hold the race hostage I could do so right now, without mirrors. I am the greatest walker of the dark side this race has ever produced. If it was in me to extort something, I could scourge the population till everyone surrendered and there would not be a thing anyone could do."

Marika bit her lip, forcing herself to shut up. This was not something that needed to be said even to Bagnel.

"I know. You don't have to convince me. And I suspect that there is no point trying to convince others. They will believe what they want to believe, or, even knowing the truth, will say what they want to say to serve their own ends. Do what you have to do here, Marika, guarding yourself every second, then get out. Resign yourself to a life far from the homeworld. You may indeed be the strongest darksider ever to have lived, but you are not strong enough to survive here. I am not Degnan, nor even of the upper Ponath, but I would feel compelled to give you rituals of Mourning if you fell. And I don't know how."

"Enough. I appreciate your concern, as always. Will you go back with me once I finish my business here? Will you break all precedents and traditions and be second chair of my new star-roving Community?"

"I will."

"Then examine your brethren and pick out those you think will be most useful. Prepare to travel. I won't be long here."

Chapter Thirty-Eight

I

Marika surveyed Grauel, Barlog, and her bath as the wooden darkship tumbled over the edge of the world and plunged into atmosphere. They were as ragged a bunch of meth as ever she had seen. Worse-looking than any randomly assembled band of bonds. Worse-looking even than those desperate nomads who had driven her from the Ponath, all hide, bones, and tatters. This time she had to spend long enough down for them to flesh out, to acquire decent apparel, and to prove up their health. They were next to useless in their present state.

Touches reached for her. Some she recognized as those of skilled fartouchers with whom she had communicated before, from her own Reugge and the Redoriad Communities. She ignored them all. Let them wonder.

How was it that they could find her so easily, yet when a Serke courier came in they could see nothing? Did she cast so great a shadow? Or was it that they were just looking for her more seriously?

They stopped trying to communicate as she dropped

below one hundred thousand feet. She supposed they would be scurrying around at Ruhaack, getting ready for her. She could imagine Bel-Keneke's consternation when she did not appear as expected.

The world was an expanse of white that changed not at all as she descended. For all Bagnel's assurances, she found it difficult emotionally to believe the mirrors were doing any good. He said it was like trying to reheat a loghouse with one cooking fire. It was easier to maintain a temperature than it was to raise it once the loghouse had cooled off. You had to do more than warm just the air. The snows of the world and all that lay beneath were great reservoirs of cold that would take years to thaw. The cooling had not happened overnight. Neither could the warming. Unless she was unnaturally lucky she would not live long enough to see the ghost of normalcy restored.

Below fifty thousand feet Marika began pushing the darkship northward, toward Skiljansrode. She flung a touch ahead, to Edzeka, for she did not feel up to one of the fortress's welcomes.

Edzeka was in the landing court waiting, though Skiljansrode was besieged by a blizzard. Voctors ran to hold the darkship down and secure it, for the wind was fierce. Marika dismounted, strode toward Edzeka, and shouted against the wind, "Let us go somewhere where it is warm. I am not up to this weather."

"Is it not cold in the void?"

Grauel, Barlog, and the bath practically shoved them into the underground installation. They were starved for a decent meal. Bagnel had tried on the Hammer, but what the brethren served was no better than meals aboard the voidship.

"Yes. But it does not touch you. There is no wind out there. Not much of anything at all. I would appreciate it beyond measure if you would see that my meth are given the best food possible. We have gone and come a long way, and have barely set foot upon a world since our visit here before. They are starved for something hot and real. Their bellies are shrunken smaller than fists. They need to be reminded that they are live meth, not some ghostly denizens of the void."

Edzeka seemed mildly amused. "Indeed? Then you have come to the wrong side of the world. We survive on plain, spare rations here. As you and they know."

"As we know. But those rations are feast stuff compared to what we eat out there."

Edzeka led them directly to the cafeteria. She joined Marika at table. When the grauken in Marika's belly had been soothed, she asked, "Why did you come here first? The impression I got was that you wanted to arrive before the news of your victory. Which you have done, more or less, though speculation will disarm the value of your effort since you have chosen not to appear among the courts of the mighty."

"When I go among those courts I want to do so armed with the knowledge you have gleaned in my absence. About the rogue problem. I have a fixed public policy I wave like a banner, but I have no real strategy. That will be the great issue before us after I announce my success. I must have something to offer."

"If you were counting on me to arm you I fear I am going to send you off on the hunt naked. The sisters you recruited were quite imaginative in their search for information, but the warlock is obsessive in his quest for security. I wonder that his organization grows, he is so fearful of spies."

"I will examine what has been gathered."

Edzeka was right. There was nothing useful in the filed reports. Marika contacted those she had recruited in hopes they had learned things they had been reluctant to impart to anyone but herself. They had very little to say that was useful. Unanimously, they did warn her that the rogue apparently had wicked designs on her life. She told them to intensify their efforts, to keep a closer watch on anything or anyone even remotely suspect. Her return should instigate movement by the warlock. Something would happen, and that something might betray him.

In discussion with Edzeka later, Marika said, "I almost fear I have wasted my time. I could have gone directly to Ruhaack and been no more ignorant. Still, there was a chance. I had to know. I suppose the absence of information is information in itself. I know him. Something is moving beneath the dark waters. I would suggest you concentrate on producing darkships. There will be a demand for replacements if things go as I suspect they will."

Edzeka nodded curtly. "There are those that have not returned. . . . I wonder, Marika, how popular you will be when the extent of the disaster out there is known. An entire generation of dark-faring silth gone, to all practical purposes. Whatever the gain, there will be those who will not forgive you the price you paid." She strained to phrase herself politely. It was clear she preferred having Marika elsewhere.

"I will pluck myself out of your fur after one more good sleep, Edzeka. My rogue hunters will move their center of operations to Ruhaack. Your Community will be yours once more."

Edzeka neither thanked her nor acknowledged the implicit rebuke.

It was impossible to slip into the Reugge cloister unnoticed aboard a voidfaring darkship. Marika cursed that state of affairs. She would have preferred having the cloister rise one morning to find her reestablished in her quarters, come like a haunt or breath of conscience out of the darkness. But she had to arrive amid all the ceremony Bel-Keneke could lay on, with representatives of all the Ruhaack cloisters watching.

Practically before her feet left the tip of the dagger there were demands for her time and news. She made one general statement announcing the defeat of the Serke fugitives, the extermination of their rogue allies, and the taking of the alien starship on behalf of all meth. Then she retreated to her apartment, allowing only Bel-Keneke to accompany her. And her bath, at their request. She had given them permission to go to bath's quarters this time, but after considering the pressures and attentions they might face, they elected to remain with her, hiding within her fortress within the cloister.

Marika closed the door. "I have said it in public. Now it is known and sure. Now the excitement of the aftermath begins. I suggest you be more alert than ever before."

"How bad was it out there, Marika?"

"There are no words. Edzeka, perhaps, said it best. A generation of dark-faring silth spent to end the Serke terror. And possibly with very little actually gained. The starship, though, is impressive. I wish every meth alive could be taken to see it. It is going to change our lives as much as the age of ice has."

"And you intend keeping your pledge to hold it in trust for all meth?"

"I do. We may part somewhat on this. I do not know your exact attitude. But yes, I mean it. You will recall that I come of a region where my pack was held in primitive straits for the advantage of other meth. I resented that greatly when I learned it, and I do still, though now I am one of the other meth. I cannot allow one small group to seize this starship. It is too important to us all. How it is exploited may shape the entire race for ages to come. I do not want it to become the grauken of the age, dam of a tyranny to beggar that of the most vicious sisterhood. In the past we have allowed the land and oceans and even the stars to be seized for the advantage of the strongest few, but with this we cannot keep on in the same old way."

Bel-Keneke seated herself before the fireplace. She said, "I read in you a deep undercurrent of fear. Never before have I known you to be frightened of the future. Not in the way I sense it now."

"You are probably right. I would not call it that, but even the wisest of us sometimes lie to ourselves. Do we not?"

"Yes."

"These days I am often confused about who and what I am in the grand picture painted by the All. Sometimes it

seems I am the only silth alive willing to battle to preserve
our traditions. And at other times I feel I am exactly what
they accused me of being when I was younger, the new
Jiana who will preside over the collapse of silthdom.

"And still I do not feel stronger or different. I just feel as
if I am on the outside. . . . I talk too much. We face ever
more interesting and exciting times. But maybe we are over
the summit now, with the mirrors in place and the Serke
defeated. Perhaps a semblance of normalcy will reassert
itself after we dispose of the warlock."

"You might reflect on the fact that for most meth now
living, silth included, this *is* normalcy. They are not old
enough to recall anything else."

"I suppose you are right. Let me rest awhile. Let me
become attuned to where and when I am. Then I can get on
with trying to reshape my world in the image of its past.
Amusing, no? Me, trying to back into the future."

Bel-Keneke did not understand her words or mood.
Marika suspected that she did not understand them herself,
though she pretended otherwise. Maybe it was all just age
sneaking up on her.

II

Marika brought the darkship southward over the tops of
dead trees, barely high enough to clear the reaching
branches. She cleared the edge of the woods, then dropped
till the wooden cross hurtled along inches above the snow.
The landing struts sometimes dragged. The wind of her
passage whipped up and scattered loose powder snow behind
her.

She brought the darkship to a violent halt and dropped it
into the snow. She and Grauel and Barlog piled off, ran low
to the edge of a ravine, flopped.

Below, a dozen rogues were reloading a rocket launcher.
The females opened fire with their rifles. Bodies jerked and

spun. Two of the males got off shots of their own before they were hit, but did no damage. Some tried to flee. Marika seized a ghost and overtook them. Then she led the huntresses in a wild scramble down into the ravine, snow flying, to finish the wounded.

"This one is faking, Marika," Barlog said, yanking a youngster upright.

"Hold him. We'll take him with us." She examined the others. All dead or soon to die. She kicked the nearest rocket launcher. "A fine piece of machinery."

The first rocket had hit the Reugge cloister only moments before, wrecking the tower Marika customarily occupied. There had been no warning. Marika and her huntresses had been out almost by chance, down with the bath mapping a search sweep of rogue territory northeast of Ruhaack.

She had been airborne before the second rocket arrived.

"They look like the machines made by those aliens," Grauel said.

"Don't they, though? I wonder how much knowledge they spirited out over the years?"

"What shall I do with this pup?" She had the captive cringing at her feet.

"We'll truthsay him. For what that's worth." Marika did not expect to learn much.

She had been back to Ruhaack five days. This was the third attempt upon her life. One she had been unable to trace. She believed silth might have been behind it. The other had been brethren in inspiration, but her search for those behind it had dead-ended. Her enemies were careful to cover their trails these days.

"Here? Now?"

"Here is fine. We can leave him with his friends."

Truthsaying the youngster was easy. He had no resistance. And was almost an empty vessel where knowledge was concerned, though Marika nursed his entire rogue history from him.

"They are pulling them in young, now," she said. "He

was barely more than a pup when they enlisted him. That damned Kublin is insane."

Grauel looked at her expectantly.

"We'll backtrack him. At least he knew where he'd been. Somewhere there'll be a rogue who hasn't moved on. We'll grab him and hope he gives us another lead."

"The slow, hard way," Barlog said. "One villain at a time."

"That may be the only way."

"Kill him?" Grauel asked.

"Yes."

Grauel broke his neck. "I'm old," she said. "But the strength remains."

Marika replied, "Yes, you're still strong. But you *are* old. It's decision time."

"Marika?"

"I will be going back to the alien ship soon. Chances are that it will be many years before I return to the homeworld again. You have often expressed a desire to spend your last days as near the Ponath as can be."

Neither Grauel nor Barlog responded. Marika waited till the gawking bath had returned to the darkship to ask, "Have you nothing to say?"

"Is that what you wish? That we remain behind?"

"You know it isn't. We have been together for a lifetime. I don't know what I would do without you. You're my pack. But I don't want to stand in your way if you are ready to assume the mantle of the Wise. If I had any conscience I would, in fact, urge you to do so. The young voctors at the cloister are in desperate need of firm and intelligent guidance. By staying with me you'll only see more of the same, and probably come to no good end. Half the race wishes me dead, and half that half might try doing something about it."

"We will do as you command, Marika," Barlog said.

"No. No. No. You will do what you *want* to do. It's your future. Don't you understand?"

"Yes, mistress," Grauel said.

Marika favored her with a scowl. "You are baiting me. You are not as dense as you pretend. Come. We will discuss this later." She stalked toward the darkship.

She took the darkship up and turned out across the snowy wastes, toward the ruins of TelleRai. The rogues had come from there in a ground-effect vehicle still hidden among the dead trees of the woods.

The rogues who had sent them had moved out of their hiding place, but had not moved fast or far enough. Marika overtook them. She captured two, truthsaid them, and continued her hunt.

Before day's end the trail had taken her most of the way to the eastern seaboard. A dozen scatters of defeated rogues lay behind her. She found herself wondering why her sister silth had so much trouble suppressing them. They needed only to invest vigor and determination.

She took the darkship up and let her far touch roam the wilderness. Somewhere in those icy badlands there was a major rogue hiding place, one they had believed could not be traced back through the levels of their organization.

She sensed a place where many meth were gathered, deep beneath the surface. She captured a strong ghost, rode it through a long, twisting tunnel, and found herself inside a weapons manufactory. More than two hundred meth were at work there, including bond females. . . .

Females!

Marika considered them closely. They were not prisoners. Some even seemed to be supervisors.

Anger seized her. She set the ghost ravening.

The massacre lasted fifteen seconds. A screaming electromagnetic surge severed her connection with the ghost. She suffered a moment of disorientation. The darkship plunged fifty feet before she regained her equilibrium and control.

So. They had adapted a suppressor field so it would shield an entire installation. It was to be anticipated. They had adapted it so it would protect individuals upon the alien starship.

No matter. These meth were dead. Voctors would come to cleanse the place once she reported it.

She took her darkship up high and sent a general far touch roaming that face of the continent. *Kublin. The game is about to end. I am coming for you this time.*

She expected no response and received none, but was certain Kublin would receive the message if there were as many wehrlen among the rogues as some silth suspected.

She drifted away westward, to continue the hunt elsewhere.

III

"How long do you plan to stay this time?" Bel-Keneke asked from what had become her customary seat before the fireplace in Marika's quarters, though now those quarters had been shifted.

"Until I find the rogue I seek," Marika said. "A day or a decade." It had been a month since her return to Ruhaack. A dozen attempts on her life had failed. The cloister had suffered damage on several occasions. "Do not be distressed. Do not be frightened. I wish there were some way I could stem your fear that I intend to wrest the Reugge away from you."

Bel-Keneke was startled. "I do not . . ."

"Of course you do. Because your one weakness is insufficient imagination. If I have such wicked intentions, why have I not displaced you already? Do you doubt that I could in a test of strength? Entertain, for the sake of argument, the remote chance that I would not want to endure the responsibilities of being a most senior. Assume that I have a task to complete here and then I shall depart for the Serke starworld. I really would rather spend my time nursing secrets from the alien starship."

Bel-Keneke seemed mildly embarrassed.

"Shall we drop the matter and turn our attention to the rogue problem?"

That problem had become one silth dared not ignore. In the past month the rogues had become violently active, betraying a level of strength and organization unsuspected even by those few silth who had taken them seriously. Their weaponry was a shock, and they had made excellent tactical use of their talent suppressors. A lot of damage had been done and many silth had died.

It was, of course, all Marika's fault. So the word ran among those who refused to see their own failures.

"All right," Bel-Keneke said. "The rogues."

"They can be beaten. They can be wiped out. If the Communities would cease blinding themselves, pretending they are only a nuisance. The problem must be recognized for what it is and approached in the same cooperative spirit as the mirror project."

"That is a matter of survival, Marika."

"Stubborn folly. Stubborn folly. Things are not so because we wish them so. They have to be made so. *This* is a matter of survival, Bel-Keneke. Those rogues are determined to obliterate all silthdom. And they are going to manage it if someone does not wake up."

"They are but males."

"True. Absolutely true. Are you any less dead when a male puts a bullet through your brain?"

"Marika, you credit them too much. . . . "

"Ask yourself who unleashed the fire that consumed TelleRai. Mere males. They will not go away because we wish them away. They will not go away because we turn our backs and refuse to see them. Those are the very reasons they come back again and again. I smash them, then the rest of you pretend they do not exist after I have gone on to something else, and the disease reestablishes itself. It was not imagination that destroyed my tower."

Bel-Keneke looked like one patiently suffering the ravings of one touched by the All.

Irked, Marika continued, "They now have an unknown

number of hidden bases and manufactories. I have revealed several of those already. You have seen the things they were stockpiling. And you will still insist that they are just a nuisance? Must they kill you in order to gain your attention?"

Bel-Keneke shook her head.

"Try to imagine what they may be preparing in more remote places, safer from searchers."

Bel-Keneke showed no enthusiasm, even so. Marika was disturbed. Was all silthdom paralyzed by some mad suicidal urge? She feared she would have to call on the terror of her name to mobilize a real effort to overcome the rogues.

She was convinced that Kublin had built a movement so strong it no longer needed the support of the defeated Serke. It would attain its goals without it if silth continued to blind themselves to the threat.

Kublin, she was convinced, was not just the warlock; he was the driving force behind the rogue movement. She knew Kublin because she knew herself. Kublin might be cowardly at times, but he was very much like her. He was every bit as determined, if for reasons she could not fathom. In a way battling him, she battled her mirror image. She had acted, thus far, as though she *was* dueling herself, guessing what she would have done in Kublin's place before she made a move. And that had allowed her to deal this new crop of rogues numerous and frequent disasters.

The difference between Kublin and herself was that he was less willing to risk his person. In his place she would have come out to kill herself instead of sending assassins.

As a test she had tried an offer of rich rewards for information. She had had few takers. As she had expected. That revealed the real strength of the rogues. They were so strong and so feared that few ordinary meth would dare betray them.

"It is time to put the fear of silth back into the populace," Marika said.

Bel-Keneke looked startled.

"I do not want to press anyone, but I will if I must. I do

not tolerate willful blindness in myself and I will not tolerate it in anyone else. We will destroy the rogue if I have to *compel* the Communities to join in the hunt."

Bel-Keneke sighed. "There is a great deal of confusion yet, Marika. You know very well that many of the strongest Communities lost their most seniors during your adventure against the Serke. They have not yet stabilized into any fixed hierarchy. You cannot expect them to have formed policies."

"The lack of a certain meth in control should not rob a Community of direction at mundane levels. You . . . Never mind. Argument accomplishes nothing. As strength goes. I would appreciate it if you would contact those Communities that do have most seniors and tell them that I plan a major rogue hunt directed to the northeast. Tell them I want all the darkships that can be mustered. My intention is to mount a sweep that will cripple the rogue's offensive capacity. If in the course of the sweep I find the one rogue I am hunting myself, his loss will set his movement back so far the rogues will present no threat for years. You all will be rid of me, for I will disappear into the void once more. And you can all go back to your somnolent pretense."

Bel-Keneke refused to be angered. "Very well. As you wish. I will see that your fleet is assembled." Bel-Keneke's tone recalled that of Marika's dam Skiljan when she was discussing tribute that had to be paid to the silth at Akard. A little something yielded grudgingly so a greater power would leave one alone.

Damned blind fool. They were all damned blind fools. Maybe they deserved . . . "Thank you, mistress. I appreciate your efforts. I must go now. I have to visit the comm center." She left Bel-Keneke there, served and observed by Grauel and Barlog.

She stalked the hallways of the cloister, irked with herself. She was growing too intolerant and impatient, she feared. In younger days she would have tried to maneuver, to manipulate, to get what she wanted more slyly. These days the impulse was to turn to power at the first impediment.

From the comm center she contacted the Hammer, ostensibly to see how Bagnel's preparations were coming, actually to turn off her thoughts for a while while talking with someone who wanted nothing from her and from whom she wanted nothing. She left the conversation pleased. Bagnel had assembled a scientific team that, he assured her, was more than respectable in knowledge, ability, and reliability.

She began to feel anxious to move into deep space once again.

The homeworld was not home anymore.

If anywhere ever had been.

Chapter Thirty-Nine

I

Grauel returned from the window. "The sky is filled with darkships, Marika. They are grounded in the streets and on the open ground around the cloister. I never imagined there were so many."

"I am amazed," Marika admitted. She looked at Bel-Keneke. "What did you tell them?" In one week more than three hundred darkships, of the planet-bound sort, carrying as many as a half dozen voctors each, had gathered at Ruhaack.

"I told them what you told me to tell them." Bel-Keneke was not surprised at the response. "You are much feared, in more ways than you can imagine."

"Whatever moves them, I had better take them out before the spirit falters. Is there a place where they can be gathered so that I can speak to them all? Tomorrow I will lead them out against the rogue."

"I thought you would want to address them. I have made arrangements with the Redoriad. The west wall of their cloister overlooks open ground. Nearly half of them are grounded there anyway."

"Thank you."

Marika examined the weather auspices. It would be a clear night, and the major moons would be in near conjunction. She set her speechmaking for that hour.

She said nothing new or particularly inspiring, nor did she try to whip the assembly into a froth of hatred. She simply told the silth that they had a job of work to do, and if they carried it out properly they would end this rogue threat that had begun to seem like a reign of terror. An hour before dawn she raised her wooden darkship and led the airborne horde northeast, to that region she believed to be the heartland of Kublin's shadow empire.

She expected heavy action and she was not disappointed. In that region the rogues had invested heavily in time and labor and resources, and so felt compelled to resist instead of to run.

The Mistresses accompanying Marika learned quickly after several darkships had been downed by suppressor beams. Fear inspired cooperation. The moment a Mistress detected anything inimical she summoned aid. When superior strength had gathered the Mistresses grounded and sent in their voctors to do the killing, supporting them with their talents.

In the six hours following the first contact fourteen installations were captured and more than a thousand rogues slain.

Marika did not participate directly. She remained high above the hunt, probing the far distances with her touch, occasionally sending, *Kublin, I am coming for you.* She was certain he was out there, cowering in some secret command center, watching his fastnesses fall.

Grauel and Barlog watched her and became increasingly unsettled. They began to prowl the arms of the darkship, restless, watching her closely. They sensed a darkness growing in her.

The more stubborn the rogue resistance, the more angry

and hate-filled she became. Something had twisted inside her. She was no longer able to think of Kublin as the fragile, sweet littermate she had known as a pup. She could not remember him as the youngster she had saved in the Ponath at the risk of her entire future, nor as the adult she had spared by imprisonment and murder after his raid upon Maksche.

He would not learn. He would not recant. He would not cease his misdeeds. She had risked everything for him, and he had given nothing but pain in return. She had no more love for him. Not a spark. She wanted only to hurt him in return.

Splash the plains of snow with blood. If he did not join the dead, maybe he would read a message he would finally understand.

A squadron of latecomers arrived from Ruhaack. Marika touched them. They seemed eager to join the hunt, like pups racing after the panicky denizens exploding out of an opened leiter nest. She was pleased. Slow as silth were to start, she had no trouble inspiring them once they decided to move.

An eagerness for plunder animated many of the hunting crews. The rogues had betrayed several advanced technologies in their attempts to defend themselves—technologies that, locally, almost offset the overpowering silth sorcery.

Maybe that was the answer. Survival never had been much of a motivator when she had tried to get them to do something. But appeal to their greed and they swarmed.

She would never understand. But, then, she had been involved in a struggle for survival all her life.

She directed the newcomers to places in the sweep line, then turned her attention to a lone darkship at the limit of vision, rising and racing toward her. In a moment she recognized Balbrach's aura.

She flung a questioning touch. Balbrach was supposed to be aboard *High Night Rider,* in orbit, refitting after surviving the Serke.

Wait, Balbrach sent back, and continued her swift approach.

Marika waited, her nerves beginning to fray. Balbrach's tone intimated bad news.

The Redoriad darkship drifted close to her own till arms touched. Balbrach stepped aboard Marika's darkship and joined her at the tip of the dagger. "What news can be so bad that you have to meet me face to face up here?" Marika asked.

"Yes. You guess well. It is bad news, though not surprising."

"What is it?"

"A Chorada darkship has just arrived from the Serke starworld. They brought word that three voidships of the Groshega—their entire fleet, none of which joined us in the struggle out there—have seized the alien starship and claimed it for their Community."

"The fools. How stupid can meth be?"

"The universe is filled with fools, Marika."

"How do they expect to hold it? They must have support. I am here, and can cut them off . . ."

"I do not know. But something must be done."

"Must be done by me, you mean?"

"For two reasons, one being that no one will even begin to believe the noble motives of anyone but you. For all they may say otherwise, many silth at least grudgingly suspect you may actually mean it when you say you intend this find to benefit all meth."

"And the other reason?"

"The Groshega have a champion, Brodyphe, who was thought to be second to Bestrei before you proved that Bestrei was not first. No Community would dare challenge her. We Redoriad are strongest in the dark now in numbers, but I would not send all my Mistresses against her."

Silently, Marika appealed to the All. Why now? Was this a sign? Was she never to be allowed to extinguish the rogue plague?

"The dark-faring sisterhoods appeal to you to end this

usurpation, Marika. Before a precedent is set. You said you would hold the alien starship and its secrets in trust. Grudgingly, most of us have accepted that. But you are compelled to enforce that if you wish to maintain that acquiescence."

"I know. But I have a task here. It will not get done if I leave it."

"Have you not crippled the rogue enough?"

"No. Not enough. Far from enough to satisfy me. There is one I especially want to remove from the social equation. Without him the movement will become blind and halt."

"Can one male be so important?"

"This one can. He is very much like me. He is wehrlen, Balbrach. He is strong and smart and very dangerous. What is your hurry? Those Groshega will be there whenever I get to them."

"We dare not wait long. Any significant delay will give some meth the idea you have accepted the fiat. That would dissolve whatever unanimity of thought exists. . . ."

"Is *High Night Rider* ready?"

"Yes. I contacted your male Bagnel and directed him to begin sending his scientific team aboard. I intend to leave, with all the voidships I can gather, as soon as I return to the cloister and make arrangements for another extended absence."

"All right. Let it be known that your movements have my full approval and are my first move against the Groshega. Do not rush, but move with deliberation. I will continue here for a few days more, then will overtake you along the starpaths." Marika looked to the sky and silently asked the All what it wanted of her.

Balbrach nodded curtly. "That should appease the majority."

"This land should never have been abandoned," Marika said. "We Reugge never pulled out of our territories. We still have our outposts. Leaving the land unwatched only encouraged the rogues . . ." She was talking to empty air. Balbrach had returned to her darkship. It separated, turned, hurried toward Ruhaack.

Marika checked the progress of the sweep. Another rogue installation had been located. The darkships were settling in the snows and the killers were gathering. It was a large base and would be stoutly defended. But it was not the base she sought, the one where Kublin the warlock sat at the heart of his villainous web.

She did not waste time on anger or frustration when she did not find that one. It seemed fated that the worst would happen.

In the end, after taking three more days, during which her hunting teams exterminated another four thousand rogues, she gave up and hurried back to Ruhaack and her wooden voidship. She left the hunt in care of a sister she had known in the days when she had battled the rogue out of Maksche, a silth almost as stubborn and determined as she. But she did not expect the campaign to retain its momentum long after her departure. The Communities would convince themselves that they had struck a mortal blow and no longer need be concerned. They would begin withdrawing their darkships.

II

Marika came out of the Up-and-Over well away from the alien starship. She waited and probed the dark till *High Night Rider* and its escort of five Redoriad voidships materialized. She gave the Groshega sisters time to think about the advent of the force. Then she sent, *Brodyphe. I am here. If you do not leave peaceably, I will have to send you down the dark path after Bestrei. Go. There has been too much death here already.*

There was no response from the silth aboard the starship.

Marika had not expected one, really, though she had hoped that an attack of sense would smite the Groshega once they knew she was there to evict them. She drifted closer. The Redoriad darkships spread out. She glanced back at Grauel and Barlog, who had refused to be left behind, no matter their dreams of ending their days at home.

Go! she sent.

Three Redoriad darkships darted toward the alien starship.

Beams and rockets leaped to meet them. They pranced away, unharmed.

Marika scanned the surrounding space. The great black still lurked at the system's fringe, but it was not under control, not moving. It seemed disinterested in what was happening down near the sun.

Did the Groshega intend to maintain their claim with technical weapons?

Marika vacillated. There was something wrong with the whole situation. How could the Groshega hope to best her with alien armaments? They could not have the use of the suppressor suits and weapons developed by the rogue scientists. She had had those removed to the surface of the planet before departing. They were in the care of one of Balbrach's most trusted Mistresses . . .

She hardly thought about what she did. She grabbed ghosts and clambered into the Up-and-Over, bringing herself out beside the great black.

Was she mad? Had she begun seeing plots where none could exist?

Or had she been guided gently into a trap?

The Groshega had a strong champion. The Redoriad had numbers. They were silth, as subject to pestilential silth blindnesses and shortcomings as sisters of any other order. The Redoriad had been allies for years, but that did not guarantee an alliance forever.

And nobody loved Marika, who had the strength to thwart greed and crush schemes.

She took the great black under control almost without direct thought and leaped back to the heart of the system.

She dropped into an atmosphere of confusion. They did not know where she had gone, or why. Marika sent,

Balbrach, I want you to take High Night Rider *and your darkships back to the last milestar. Wait there three hours, then return.*

Why, Marika? Balbrach could not disguise the disappointment in her touch.

This is an uncomfortable situation. It has some very unpredictable aspects. To avoid potential problems arising from the uncertainties I have decided to handle it alone. I believe I can accomplish our ends more quickly that way, and with fewer silth killed.

Balbrach understood the message behind the message. She sensed the great black roiling around Marika, angry at being disturbed, eager to rip and slay. She sent, *As you wish, Marika.*

Marika did not move until the Redoriad had vanished.

Now she must move quickly, lest they not do as she had ordered, and try to surprise her.

Brodyphe. Are you coming out? Must I come after you? You have no chance against me.

She nudged her darkship toward the alien. No beams or rockets greeted her. After ten minutes two darkships left the derelict.

There should be another. Hurry. I am impatient. Come to me here.

Another darkship left the alien. Marika eased closer. She sent a lesser ghost into the starship and detected no Groshega silth.

The Groshega voidships floated toward her, into visual range. She sent, *Who were your allies in this venture?*

They did not respond.

She touched the great black.

Aboard Brodyphe's darkship silth screamed into the otherworld. Their bodies twisted, tore apart. The golden glow faded around them. Blood crystals and flesh fragments scattered.

Marika touched the Mistresses of the remaining ships. *Who were your allies in this venture?*

They confirmed her worst suspicion.

She touched the great black again, then turned away before it was over. Down to the alien starship she went, sending before her small ghosts to locate and disarm booby traps. Then she went aboard.

The moment they could talk, Grauel demanded, "Did you have to kill them?"

"Are you getting soft, Grauel? They intended to kill us." Huntresses were not wont to mourn enemies, nor to give them a second chance.

"No. It just did not seem necessary."

"It was, Grauel. I struck a blow at an idea when I eliminated them."

"What idea?"

"The idea that one sisterhood or a cabal of Communities can seize this ship for the purpose of limiting its benefits."

Grauel nodded, but was not entirely mollified. Marika reminded herself that in some ways the Wise were more tolerant than were younger females, who had to face danger more directly.

Barlog asked, "Are you sure you were not more interested in crushing any doubts about your own invincibility?"

Marika scowled at her and turned away. She stalked through the alien ship to the control area. She did not relax her hold upon the great black, which she moved far enough away that its presence would not be immediately obvious. She replayed the final message from the alien crew, again studying their smooth-faced strangeness, their methlike yet alien forms. How well had the brethren unraveled their language with the times and clues they had had available?

She settled into an alien chair and wondered what the rogues really had hoped to accomplish, wondered what had become of the few Serke who remained unaccounted for. *Starstalker* and one or two darkships. Where had they gone?

She sensed the return of *High Night Rider* and its escort and sighed. She did not look forward to the next few hours.

Balbrach. Come to the alien. I must speak with you.

III

High Night Rider departed the system unaccompanied, without Balbrach aboard. It carried Marika's message to the most seniors of all the dark-faring silth. It had left behind the brethren scientists and the darkship crews who had accompanied it out. Marika touched the great black, told it to let the voidship pass.

She had made that monster her creature entirely, a deadly sentinel guarding her system.

She told the Redoriad crews that they could not leave the system, that the great black would devour them if they tried to go. They would be released in time if they behaved. In the interim they must do ferry duty between the starship and the planet, where former Serke bonds continued farming and manufacturing, their lives little touched by changes in ruling Communities.

Marika made her home in the starship's control section. The brethren she assigned to the quarters that had been occupied by their rogue predecessors.

The very typical bit of silth treachery that had brought her back to the alien ship sent her into a depression that lasted for weeks. Her homeworld, and her deadly littermate with his bloodthirsty movement filled with hatred, slipped from her thoughts entirely. When she recovered she found she had very little interest in her roots.

She did not leave the starship for a year, not until she was convinced that her control would not be disputed by any element of the meth race.

During that year she mourned Balbrach often, for theirs had been a good partnership while it had lasted. At times it had approached the friendship she had had with Kiljar. But Balbrach had not had Kiljar's mental scope or character and had not been able, in the end, to resist typical silth greed. She had made her move. She had lost. Though it hurt

still, Marika had had to demand that she pay the price of
failure.

Darkships came and went, their movements carefully
monitored by Marika's tame great black. The dark-faring
sisterhoods were keeping a sharp watch upon her. After that
year, though, even the most suspicious and paranoid of
Communities had become convinced that she did indeed
mean the starship to benefit all meth. The watchers came
less frequently, but their visits lasted longer, and they joined
in the unraveling of alien secrets. Each departing darkship
carried a full report of everything that had been learned
about the starship and the aliens who had built it. Which
was not that much, considering the time and effort that had
gone into opening it up.

One day Marika went looking for Bagnel, whom she
seemed to see no more than when they had not been living
on the same ship. "Hello, stranger."

"Me? I am not the one whose thoughts cannot remain
where I am, who is always wandering somewhere else."

"Somewhere else? I have not been out of this ship . . ."

"Your heart has been."

"Have you reached any major conclusions yet?"

"Not really. Unless you do not know that this vessel was
built by creatures who do not think like meth."

"You've had more than a year."

"Most of which we have spent relearning what the rogues
learned."

"And?"

"They did find out more than anyone suspected, Marika.
If the Communities did not follow through on the hunt you
initiated at home last year they are going to be in for some
very nasty surprises."

"I am sure they did not. Oh, Dhervhil will have tried. Is
still trying, no doubt. They accused her of being as rogue-
obsessed as Marika. But the Communities refuse to learn.
Without some overpowering personality there to drive them,
they will just go on being the same petty backstabbers
trying to steal a moment's advantage. How soon can you

start some really original research work? And how has the repair work been going?" Most of the planetary industrial base developed by the Serke had been created for the purpose of refurbishing the starship.

"Sometime within the next few months I expect to okay a couple of projects my meth have proposed. Mostly attempts at getting to information stored in the ship's systems. The repairs go forward, but they are all gross things like sealing broken hull plates. The more subtle things are waiting for us to get into the information banks. The drive system, for example, is something I am not going to let anyone near until we have drawn out, examined, and come to understand every morsel of information available. By tinkering with it we might smash it beyond hope."

Marika thought a moment. "Bagnel, you were right. My heart is not here. Its feet have been wandering for a long time. I've decided to surrender to it. I'm going to sneak away and do something I have been promising myself to do for a long time. I don't think you'll have any trouble while I'm away."

"Yes?"

"Yes, what?"

"Where are you going? Or is that a secret?"

"To look at the far side of the cloud."

"That is a long passage. Are you sure . . . You're convinced we won't be troubled?" He was afraid. He had become important among meth, but he would remain important only so long as he enjoyed her protection.

"It'll be all right. Don't let on that I've gone. If somebody wants me, tell them I'm being moody again and won't see anyone. They're used to me. And I don't intend to be away long."

"You never do. But . . . All right. Be careful."

"I will. Indeed I will. There is much I want to see before I rejoin the All."

Marika's first exploration was a four-star voyage rapidly taken. It did not lead her out of the dust. She did not find a

world suitable for resting her bath. She returned to the
starship with her crew strained to their limits.

She found that her absence had gone unnoticed.

She tried another route a month later, with no more
success. The dust was deep and the stars in that direction
unfriendly.

Not until her sixth venture outward, late in the second
year after she had reclaimed the alien ship from the
Groshega, did she establish an advance base and begin
preparations for venturing beyond it. By then it was common knowledge that she slipped away occasionally, but she
kept her comings and goings unpredictable. She did so
mainly out of habit, for she no longer feared trouble from
the dark-faring silth. Her hold on the system had been
accepted because she had fulfilled her promises.

Midway into her third year of ruling the alien ship she
finally broke out of the far side of the cloud and caught her
first glimpse of skies ablaze with stars numerous beyond any
imagining, great reefs of starlight that beggared anything
she had seen on the nether side. Her awe remained undimin-
ished when she returned to the alien ship.

Bagnel was impressed by the film she brought back.
"Incredible," he breathed. "Absolutely incredible. Who
would have guessed?"

"Bagnel, you have to *see* it. I don't care what you have
going here. I don't care what you have to do. Come see it.
This will make your life. Remember how we talked about
flying off into eternity when we retired? Come. See this. It
will make you lust to do that now."

Bagnel looked at the film again, and he quivered all over.
But he was the most responsible of meth, bound by his
notions of duty. It took her a week to pry him away from his
work.

He had become enamored of the alien mysteries. But pry
him away she did, and get him aboard her fey darkship she
did, and carry him through the cloud she did. And his
response to those shoals of stars was all she expected. He
could find no words to describe his feelings when he saw

them, even months after he had returned to his mundane work.

For months after that venture Marika stifled herself and did not go out again, though those stars called to her incessantly. She concentrated on making her presence felt among visitors from the homeworld, who were becoming more numerous now that the starship had begun to yield some of its secrets.

She anticipated being away a long time on her next voyage.

Chapter Forty

I

"I do not think this journey is wise, Marika," Bagnel said. "Still, if you *must* go, take me with you."

"Not this time. This is going to be a far journey. Every pound of weight will have to be useful."

Grauel and Barlog were startled. Barlog asked, "Does that mean you are leaving us behind too?"

"I'm sorry. This time, yes. I must go without you. I will be taking extra bath and supplies instead. Do not look at me that way. I will behave and be careful."

She had no trouble finding herself a double set of bath. Bath from all the dark-faring sisterhoods journeyed to the starship in hopes of spending some time on her darkship. Bath who had served with Marika were much in demand. Somehow she opened hidden channels in their minds, and strengthened them immensely, so that many became immune to the weaknesses plaguing most bath, and a few even found that with her guidance they could grow enough to become Mistresses of the Ship themselves.

There were times when Marika had to resist pressures to

185

become a teacher and trainer of dark-faring silth. "Can you imagine me an instructress?" she complained to Bagnel. "Spending the rest of my life developing crews for the Communities?"

The notion had amused him.

Pursued by his displeasure and the unhappiness of Grauel and Barlog, Marika left the starship on her first far flight of exploration.

Double-crewed, she could make vastly extended flights, hopping as many as twelve stars before having to take a rest landing. She needed that capability if she was to venture beyond the dust cloud into that vastness on the other side, to satisfy the exploration bug that had been tormenting her since she had discovered those endless shoals of stars.

It was to be a voyage of terrible moment.

She was in the seventh hop of her second twelve-star run out from the edge of the dust. For this venture distance was her principal concern. She wanted to see how far she could travel before conscience and dwindling stores compelled her to turn back. A fever of excitement rolled along with the darkship. The bath were animated by the emotions surrounding the doing of a thing never before tried. Instead of becoming increasingly uneasy as they ventured even farther from home, the opposite was true. Every hop outward raised the level of excitement.

The darkship dropped out of the Up-and-Over, and even before Marika regained her equilibrium she knew that they had made an enormous discovery. *Listen!*

Awe gripped the bath.

The void reeked with electromagnetic radiation. It was not natural. In moments Marika detected a world in the star's life zone. A satellite network surrounded it. The space of that system sported moving objects that could be nothing but ships. Closed ships of the sort built by tradermales and others who did not have the talent. She nudged the darkship inward, caught ghosts and sent them ahead.

The creatures of the system were the creatures of the alien starship.

Marika turned toward the nearest ship, reaching with the touch. She could get no response. The creatures were deaf to the touch!

She considered climbing back into the Up-and-Over, to make a hop to planetary orbit.

The bath inundated her with a babble of touch, urging her to be more cautious in her thinking.

They were right. She knew little about these creatures. The one contact they had had with meth had proven disastrous. She continued to drift, probing with ghosts.

The world ahead was not the alien homeworld, that was evident immediately. It had all the roughness and wildness of a colony, like the world the crippled starship orbited. The aliens were numerous, but they occupied only limited areas—those apparently most hospitable to their species.

The colonies had the rough new look of settlements perhaps only a few decades old. Marika saw much that looked familiar, and as much more that she did not understand. She allowed the bath to ride the back of her thoughts to get their reactions to what she saw, but they were more baffled than she. They had not studied the information gained from the derelict and they had not lived on the frontier at home.

Everything supported Bagnel's conviction that the alien was not just deaf to the touch but ignorant of its existence, and equally ignorant of those-who-dwell, the otherworld, and what, for want of a better term, meth called the silth ideal.

They are a bunch of tradermales, Marika thought.

Males and females appeared to be equal in number and status, though that was difficult to determine while riding a ghost. They lived in simple structures easily understandable by meth, but the guts of the planet contained far more complex installations that recalled those of the rogue brethren she had seen during the last sweep. Those places were not places to live.

She had to communicate with the creatures. But how?

Fear grew down deep inside her, a knot that tightened yet swelled like a cancer, feeding on the fear already gnawing at the bath and tainting the aura of touch around them. The primitive in all of them wanted to flee from the monsters. It insisted that she forget she had found them. *Grauken, grauken, grauken,* it chanted.

This is silly, she sent. *Are we pups, to be terrified of the unknown? Are we going to whine at sounds in the dark? The dark is the time of the silth.*

Silth had contacted alien creatures many times before, on the starworlds claimed by the dark-faring orders. Nothing evil had come of those meetings.

The trouble was that these creatures were not savages, as all those others had been. These creatures represented a potentially real threat. They boasted weapons like none any meth had imagined before the Serke had encountered their starship.

She selected a ghost with great care. She tamed it well. Then she slipped it into the control section of the nearest alien ship, into the electronics there, commanded it to switch a comm screen on, then used the ghost to imagine herself appearing upon that screen. It was something Bagnel had postulated as possible in one of their rambling conversations, but something she had not tested for practicality.

She did not have the skill to do more, except to show her paws raised and empty of weapons. She clung to the picture for ten seconds, then had to let it go. The effort to hold it took too much attention from the darkship and her awareness of the surrounding void.

After resting, she sent another ghost, just to observe. She found the aliens extremely excited.

She was near their ship now, but they had not spotted her. Her wooden darkship was as invisible to their radar as it was to that of the brethren.

Her bath begged her to withdraw now. They had seen enough. They did not want to suffer the same fate the aliens of the starship had.

Marika ignored them. She swung in close to the alien ship and with half her mind kept a strong ghost in their control center, there to strike if they panicked and attacked her. They remained oblivious to its presence.

She took the darkship in so close they could not help but see her. When her ghost revealed that they had done so she waved politely and again showed them her empty paws. She wondered what they would make of the rifles she and the bath carried slung across their backs.

The aliens did not know what to make of her and the darkship. They babbled at one another. They pointed at screens where she appeared. They argued. Their vessel trailed spurts of electromagnetic energies.

Marika reached with the touch, searched mind after mind, found every one closed and deaf till she located a pup she guessed to be three or four years old. To that one she sent her message. *I am Marika. I come in peace. We have searched for you long and long, since we discovered one of your voidships years and years ago.* She tagged on a strong picture of the crippled starship, emphasizing the characters painted upon its exterior.

She did not expect the pup to understand her message, except that she was friendly, but she hoped those characters might attract attention. She tried to impress the pup with the importance of relating the fact of the touch to its elders.

She withdrew and watched. Aboard the ship, they went to their battle positions, but made no threatening move. She maintained her position beside them, being careful to do nothing to panic them. Once again she reached out to the confused pup.

In time it related its experience to its elders, who immediately discounted it. Marika gently prodded the pup to draw a picture.

It did not have the motor skills of a meth pup its own age. It was a long, hard job getting it to draw the alien starship with its hull characters plain enough to recognize. But, finally, it did create something recognizable. Marika prodded it to approach its elders again.

One who seemed to be Mistress of the Ship, despite being male, examined the picture. Marika judged that some part of her message had gotten through. She raised a paw again, gathered ghosts, and went into the Up-and-Over. She hurried homeward, pausing only when she had to rest her bath.

II

"You really found them?" Bagnel asked.

"Yes. It was a colony world like this one. Only more so, because they were moving in, actually making the world their home."

"It must have been far away. You were gone a long time. I worried. You tempted the All. There were those who visited who were tempted by your absence."

"They know better than to yield to that temptation. Bagnel, I am more excited than I have ever been."

"So I see." That very fact seemed to frighten him.

"They weren't hostile—just astonished. I don't know if they have encountered dark-faring races before, but they've surely never encountered anyone like us. They seemed unable to believe what they saw."

"You think they'll come here now?"

"I don't know. I left bait, but I don't know. Have you made any progress deciphering their language?"

"Some. On the simplest level. That tape you're so fond of, for example. We can translate most of what the creature says, but that doesn't tell us much. The tape is exactly what it appears to be, a report to anyone who finds the ship. It implies that there is a lot more information stored in the ship's data banks, but we can't get to them without the unlocking codes, and we don't have any idea how to decipher those. The books we've found, once we realized what they were, all proved to be technical manuals. They are valuable, but so far they have proven much more resistant to translation. It has been suggested that they are written in a language other than the one the creature spoke."

"Maybe they have castes with secret languages. Like the brethren."

"There is no evidence of that, Marika. Our principal difficulty is that we have no one trained for the kind of work we're having to do. The skills needed have to be found by trial and error. It is a slow business. And the language we are dealing with is not precise. We have found a number of words that, while identical in print, can possess multiple meanings. There are also words that, when spoken, sound the same, but appear differently in print. It isn't always possible to guess what they were trying to say."

"All right."

"Excitement running down?"

"No. Never, now. The gateway to the future is open. Before long we are going to be inundated with dark-faring sisters, all eager to pass through it."

"I know. And I don't look forward to that."

"Oh?"

"Silth will be silth, Marika."

"What do you mean?"

"It will be the same old story. Flocks of darkships will race out there and try to make first contact in order to lock up the benefits for their particular sisterhoods."

"Not this time. The All has decreed the impossibility. In order to reach these aliens one has to cross a desert of stars. There is no silth but I who has the strength to manage that crossing. The bath who accompanied me will attest to that. And even if one such did exist, no one but me knows the way. My bath didn't have the training to recall the sequence."

Bagnel appeared doubtful.

"Believe me. Call it chance or the will of the All. The alien's whereabouts is my secret. If the sisterhoods wish to participate in whatever comes of the contact, they had better try hard to keep me alive. You might let that drop occasionally, especially in your reports, just so the fact isn't overlooked or forgotten."

"Of course." He seemed amused. "You will play your games with the whole race, won't you?"

"With the most seniors, yes. There are times when I enjoy manipulating them. But don't you ever tell anyone I said that."

"I don't need to. They know already. Are you going there again? To that alien world?"

"Of course. But not right away. I'll let you know when. One thing I'll need from you is some simple messages prepared in their language."

"Why don't I go with you?"

"Who's getting bitten by the adventure bug at this stage in his life?"

Bagnel pretended to look around. "Who are you talking to?"

"Nobody here but me and thee, old-timer. Of course you can go. I hoped you would ask because I did not want to conscript you. It will be our grandest flight ever. Something they can write epics about."

"Epics are for silth. I don't care about epics. I want to see these aliens. I want to smell and touch them."

"You'd better find us some way to communicate."

"On the most basic level that may prove easier than you imagine. Assuming you can transport the equipment. Dare you trade bath for equipment?"

"Not really. The desert of stars is too wide."

"Suppose you spied out an alternate and easier route?"

"No. I won't do that. If only one is believed to exist, and that only within the confines of my mind, then my hold remains firm. Should it ever become necessary to transport large masses of equipment we'll have the Redoriad loan us *High Night Rider*."

"That would not make them happy."

"They haven't been happy with me for years. That doesn't concern me. They have earned their unhappiness. You will have to excuse me. I must go see Grauel and Barlog and smooth their ruffled fur. They are extremely displeased because I left them behind and they missed out on a memorable mission. Though they would have been just as displeased had I insisted they fly off with me on one of my mad exploratory jaunts. With those two I can't win."

"You should . . ."

"Don't even suggest it. They are my pack. Damn it, Bagnel, they are as good as my dams. I have known no other since before I first met you."

"Go. I will not pretend I understand the relationship between you three."

"We don't either. But it keeps us alive."

III

A year passed before Marika dared take the time to visit the alien world again.

Her discovery had excited the sisterhoods into a scramble. Till it waned she stood fast, guarding the treasure already in paw. She shook her head often that year, unable to believe grown silth could behave so, that they would so stubbornly cling to old values and ways in the face of a screaming need to adapt to altered realities.

Bagnel did not believe her when she informed him that she was ready for the trip. "I will pack my things when I see you step into the airlock."

"This is the real thing this time." There had been false alarms before, times when she had changed her mind at the last minute. "There are no schemes afoot, here or on the homeworld." Though it was difficult to manage from so far away, she had kept her small group of dedicated antirogue silth operating and had used them to acquire intelligence about other plots as well. "I am going this time."

He awarded her a doubtful look.

"Really," she said. "It's under control. Grauel and Barlog

can hold it down here. Everyone is preoccupied elsewhere. Do I have to make the trip without you?"

"You jest. Try it. You will find your darkship on a tether with me reeling it in."

Adding Bagnel and the equipment he needed made the journey much more difficult. Marika stretched herself farther than ever before—and was surprised to find that she could stretch that far.

She continued to develop endurance and strength. And those bath who remained with her did so too.

Even so, she entered the alien system uncertain she could manage the return.

They were alert this time, though so much time had passed. Perhaps they were watching for something else. Whatever, although she rode the wooden darkship, they soon detected her. Ships hurried to meet her. She sent a covey of ghosts ahead to probe their temper.

She was disturbed by what she saw. She sensed only nervousness and fear. As a precaution she gathered and held ghosts enough for a fast climb into the Up-and-Over.

She let the darkship drift directly toward the alien world. Starships took station around her, having some difficulty keeping position because they were not as maneuverable as a darkship. She pushed in and assumed a high orbit, then had the senior bath pass the bowl of golden fluid. She wanted to be ready to flee.

A return, though, would be far easier if she had a chance to rest her bath before departing.

Her discomfort increased as she examined the starships and cataloged the array of weapons trained upon her as she sensed the fear and disbelief filling the ships. She probed mind after mind and could not find one receptive to the touch. These creatures were all adult, and all voctor.

Throughout the system ships less heavily armed were scurrying toward cover.

Why? What could they fear from one darkship? Had

they had contact with silth before, to their dismay? Did they know what had become of the lost starship after all?

She reached back to the bounds of the system and, yes, there was a great black ghost patrolling the brink of the deep. It seemed there was a black wherever intelligence paused, one monster to a star system. She stroked that thing and sensitized it to herself so it would answer more quickly if she had to summon it.

She signaled Bagnel. It was time to try talking.

Bagnel fiddled with his communicator until she lost patience, ordered the strongest of her reserve bath to the tip of the dagger, had her take over as Mistress of the Ship. The bath had experience, but she did not want control while they faced a potential enemy. Marika had to insist.

She joined Bagnel. "What's the problem? Won't they respond?"

"I don't know if they are ignoring me or if I just can't find the right frequency. It should not be so difficult. I began with the range of frequencies used on the derelict."

Marika sent a ghost into the nearest ship. The creatures there were clustered around their communications screens. She returned. "You have their attention. Maybe they just don't want to answer. Keep with it."

Bagnel made a face. He was as frightened as any of the aliens. "Right now I think I made a mistake coming out here. This isn't the same as talking about it. Well, here's something." His tiny vision screen had come to life. A female alien looked out at him. The communication speaker squeaked.

Marika said, "Run your tape."

Bagnel snapped, "Marika, mistress the ship, will you? Let me alone. I know my task."

"I'm sorry." But apology did nothing to soothe her frayed nerves.

This could be the greatest moment of meth history. Its success or failure rested squarely upon her—and yet it might be entirely outside her control. The aliens might panic.

Bagnel had prepared a tape that began with a simple print message protesting the peaceful intent of those aboard the darkship. That looped ten times, then followed with a copy of the last message left by the folk of the derelict alien.

When that ran Marika was inside the nearest starship with a ghost, watching. The message stirred considerable response, but not of the sort she expected. Well, they *were* aliens. She had no cause to expect them to respond as meth might.

A message came back once Bagnel finished sending. It arrived too rapidly for him to follow. He used a tiny light stylus to letter a response on the screen of his communicator, asking them to go much slower. Then he requested permission to set the darkship down on the world below.

Again the response was too swift to yield any sense. Again Bagnel relayed his request for a slower information feed and permission to set down.

Permission came in the form of a map with a landing site indicated by a pulsing point of red light. Marika soon matched the map with the face of the world below. The site indicated was near the largest of the alien underground installations, in a barren area.

There was a grim, deadly feel to that region. The area hummed with modulated electromagnetic radiation. A rapid scout with a ghost revealed scores of weapons similar to those that had destroyed TelleRai, all mounted upon huge rockets.

Marika began to have doubts about making contact with these creatures.

But they had no grasp of the otherworld, no suspicion that it existed. If the worst happened she could call down the great black. She extended her touch to it again, shocked it, attuned it to herself more closely, until she was certain she could summon it if that became necessary. "Continue trying to get sense from them as we go down, Bagnel." She returned to the tip of the dagger, resumed control, dropped away from the alien ships.

They paced her to the edge of atmosphere, then turned away.

For a time Marika dropped alone, but when she reached 150,000 feet aircraft began arcing past her, and lower down they began circling. Bagnel observed them with awe. They were like no aircraft he knew. Their airframes were long and slim. Their long, narrow wings were rooted far back on the fuselage and angled forward, so that the craft looked almost like the head of a trident. They seemed to be rocket-powered.

Marika was impressed too. Nothing like them existed in the meth technical arsenal.

At fifty thousand feet she resumed exploring the assigned landing area. Already it was thick with aliens, all of them come up out of the ground and all of them armed. Again she wondered if she had stepped into something nasty.

At last the darkship touched down after she had floated a moment, seeing if the mob would rush her. The aliens surrounded the darkship, but kept their distance and held their weapons casually. She hoped that was a good sign. She touched the bath. *Keep your rifles slung. Do not unsettle them. I will guard us through the otherworld. But see you to assembling your own protective ghosts. Bagnel. Be circumspect in your communications. Do not give them something for nothing.*

Meth and alien eyed one another till an alien senior stepped forward. Marika was mildly surprised. This one was male. He presented a bare palm as he approached.

Marika replied by raising both paws, then indicated Bagnel. Bagnel put his communicator aside, produced pen and paper.

"How well have you learned their language?" Marika asked. Not well at all, she knew, but she had to say something to vent some of her nervousness.

"Not well. I don't know if it's the right one. What I'm hearing spoken here doesn't sound like what we've been hearing aboard the starship."

Marika fought to keep her ears from twitching, though she was sure the aliens could not read her body language.

The alien senior examined what Bagnel printed out so laboriously, frowned, summoned another alien. They chattered briskly. Then the second alien wrote something upon paper he carried. Bagnel studied it for a long time.

"Problems, Marika."

"What?"

"I am almost convinced that these creatures do not use this language. Or if they do, I am using it entirely wrong. But if I understand what this note says, then our starship belongs to their enemies."

"Trouble?"

He shrugged.

"Make it clear that we are enemies of no one. In fact, try to get across the notion that we do not quite understand what an enemy is. Also tell them that we never saw those starship folk alive."

"That is a lot to get across at a reading-primer level."

"You're a genius."

"I wish I had your faith in me."

"You can do it."

"I'll try. That's all I can promise."

"And tell them that all that deadly hardware makes me nervous. Tell them who I am."

"You expect them to understand or care?"

"No. But if you do it right they might be impressed."

"You expect too much of me." He resumed writing in curiously blocklike letters, passing small sheets of paper after each few sentences. "I'm telling them who I am too."

"Of course."

It was slow work. The strange-colored sun of that world moved. It, too, was slow, as the world moved more slowly than that which had given Marika birth. Not, she reflected, that she was much familiar with sunrises and sunsets anymore. How many of the homeworld's sunrises had she seen in the last twenty years?

The bath began to relax. Several stepped down from the

darkship and began prowling. Marika reached with the touch. *Remain alert. Do not allow any of these creatures to place themselves between you and the darkship.*

Their response did not go unnoticed. Bagnel said, "They're full of questions about us. Especially about how we can take a ship through the void while exposed to the breath of the All."

"We have questions about them too," Marika said. "Evade. Ask them about them. There's something not right here."

"I am. I'm not stupid, Marika. But neither are they. I am certain they intend to be evasive too."

Marika grunted. She was growing more unsettled by the minute. *Rest!* she sent to the bath. *We may need to get out of here at any moment.* There was a wrongness here that had little to do with these creatures' alienness.

She shrugged. Maybe she was imagining it. She climbed aboard the darkship while Bagnel struggled on, rummaged through a locker, and found the photographic equipment he had brought. She loaded a camera and began photographing the alien beings.

They became very agitated.

"Bagnel, what's the matter with them?" Some had begun shouting and shaking weapons.

"I'm trying to find out. Stop bothering me." After a minute he said, "They don't want you taking photographs."

"Why not? They've been photographing us."

Bagnel exchanged notes rapidly. It did seem to be getting easier for him. "They say this is a secret installation. They want no photographs to leave the system."

"Oh." Marika settled on the arm of the darkship and considered the implications for a moment. "Bagnel, what do you think of them?"

"I'm not sure. I have the feeling they're hiding more than we are. I have a growing feeling that they may be more trouble than they're worth. I am trying to be neutral but I find myself beginning to dislike them."

"Yes. There's something in the air here. An aura that

reminds me of those places where rogues hide. Did you ever get down into one of those underground . . . No. Of course not. We may have made a mistake, coming here without looking at them more closely first. But keep talking. See what comes of it."

"Stall?"

"Some. But learn whatever you can. I want time to rest the bath." She touched the silth again, ordered them to rest. They boarded the darkship, stretched out near their stations, performed rituals of relaxation, went to sleep. Marika pushed herself into a half sleep, leaving everything in Bagnel's paws.

The sun of that world eventually set. The aliens kept the landing site brightly illuminated. Some of the curious drifted away and were replaced by others. Always there were weapons in evidence. Marika went past half sleep into little naps several times. Bagnel continued valiantly, facing the same aliens who had come to the fore at the beginning. The speed of communication continued to improve.

Soon after the morning sun rose Marika asked, "Have we learned anything significant?"

"They're rogues of a sort. They have tried again and again to explain, but the situation is beyond my comprehension. It's something like what we would call bloodfeud, only every member of their society is a participant. Without choice. There are cognates with the Serke situation, in that one group is trying to take territory from another, but the motives make no sense."

"I did not expect to understand them that way. What else?"

"I have established that their society includes nothing like sisterhoods or brethren, or even our bond working castes. Their thinking vaguely resembles that of the brethren who joined the Serke in exile. It may have affected the thinking of those rogues back when they first entered the derelict."

"We suspected that."

"They have no consciousness of the All, the touch, nor any silth skills, except as the contrivance of fantasy. Their words. I have betrayed nothing by mentioning such skills because they refuse to believe they can exist. They call such skills superstition and directly accuse me of lying. They believe, and fear, that we are greatly advanced beyond them technically."

"What is their interest in the ship we found?"

"It belonged to their enemies. They suspect it was searching for their hiding places. They aren't interested, really. It vanished long ago by their standards. They're very interested in us, though. They have never met another dark-faring race. I suspect they would like to find a way to manipulate us into helping them in their struggle."

"No doubt. Just as the Serke would have enlisted them. But I have no interest in that. Especially if they're rogues. We're going to leave, Bagnel. I made a mistake. These are not creatures with whom I care to be associated. Our search will have to lead elsewhere. Did they tell you much about their enemies?"

"They're very reticent on the subject."

"That is understandable." She extended her touch, wakening those bath who remained asleep. She sent the strongest to their stations. The senior passed the bowl. Wearily, Bagnel continued his exchange. Marika said, "You will make certain you are soundly strapped down. You are exhausted and I may be forced into violent maneuvering."

"They want to know what we are doing, Marika."

"Express our regrets. Tell them we have decided that we made a mistake in pursuing this contact. Tell them we do not wish to become embroiled in the affairs of an embattled race. Tell them we are going home. Then get aboard and strap down." She passed the bowl to him, let him sip, then consumed what remained and took her station at the tip of the dagger. *Strap securely,* she sent to the bath.

Bagnel concluded his final note, passed it over, and climbed to his place at the axis. The aliens did not understand until Marika lifted the darkship.

They began shouting and running around and making threatening gestures.

Marika ignored them.

There were a few wild shots from handheld beamer weapons. They came nowhere near.

Marika took the darkship up fast.

She could not climb nearly as swiftly as the alien aircraft. A flight overtook her before she reached fifty thousand feet. She was in no mood to play. She sent ghosts to still their engines. They fell toward the surface. Their pilots eventually left the craft to float toward the ground on parachutes.

Rockets leaped up. Marika was prepared for them. She stopped them long before they neared her. After a dozen tries the aliens stopped sending them.

Above, voidships moved to intercept her. She did not want to make enemies needlessly, but they seemed determined to stop her, and that she would not permit.

She reached out to the fringe of the system and summoned the great black. It came to her struggling, wriggling, protesting, never having encountered silth before. She held it in abeyance, not loosing it till the starships fired upon her.

She silenced three ships in fifteen seconds, then shifted her course. Dimly, she sensed Bagnel laboring over his communicator, sending crude messages, trying to assure the aliens that the meth meant them no harm, that they wanted nothing but to return home and forget the whole thing.

The strike of the great black paralyzed the aliens' decision makers long enough for Marika to reach orbital altitude and gather ghosts for the Up-and-Over. Bagnel was apologizing for their having defended themselves when she climbed into it.

Chapter Forty-One

I

Trouble did not end with escape from the alien world.

The homeward journey became an epic of endurance and determination, and there were moments when even Marika doubted she would have strength enough to bring the darkship safely to the starship.

She succeeded—only to learn that her absence had been noted and someone had tried to take advantage.

She was barely able to stand when she came through the airlock, to be greeted by Grauel and Barlog, who had remained in a frenzy days after the event. They stumbled over each other explaining. "Someone tried to sneak in on us. We did not know what was happening till the killing started. We fired back, but if we had not gotten help from silth who were here, visiting . . . We managed to destroy them. Barely. At least fifty died here. We have not accounted for everyone yet."

"You did well," Marika said, leaning against a passageway wall. "But did you have to keep shooting till there wasn't a fragment of darkship left with identifiable witch

203

signs?" She had spied the debris during her approach and
had wondered about it.

The huntresses were not overcome with remorse. Grauel
said, "We know who it was. We saw their witch signs. They
were Serke."

"Serke? You must be mistaken. Or it was someone who
had assumed the guise of Serke? There aren't any
Serke . . ."

"Tell that to the dead brethren, silth, and voctors. They
were Serke, Marika."

"Or masquerading as Serke," Marika insisted. But who
would?

"It is a ruse that might make sense," Grauel admitted,
sounding as if she believed nothing of the sort. "But even
pretending to be Serke, what other sisterhood would unleash
such indiscriminate slaughter? Any other order would want
the starship for what it contained, and that has to include
the minds of those who have been unearthing its secrets. Not
so?"

"I suppose. I guess I just don't want that old haunt lifting
its head again."

How many Serke remained unaccounted for? *Starstalker*
and one, possibly two darkships. But it had been years. Even
she had forgotten them. They all had to be old, possibly on
the edge of becoming harmless. But if the attackers had
come from the dozen or so surviving Serke silth, then they
must have some contacts inside the meth civilization. Else
how had they known she was away?

"I should return to the homeworld," Marika mused.
"What I learned among and about the aliens is important
enough to be reported directly. And I really should see what
is happening with the rogues. I did not catch Kublin. He
must be up to something. But I dare not go, do I? This could
happen again."

Bagnel had been muttering with one of his associates.
Scarcely able to contain his grief, he said, "I fear we have
flown our last probe among alien stars, Marika. I have lost
thirty of my best meth. It might not have happened had I

remained here. I will not go out again. Not while meth remain meth and silth remain silth. It is ... What do you silth call ritual suicide? Kalerhag? It is an invitation to kalerhag. Exposing your back to the knife. I am too old to run through the snow with the grauken baying at my heels."

Marika nodded curtly. She drew herself together, willing her weariness away, and stalked off. She went into her quarters and isolated herself there, and opened to the All, and stayed opened longer than ever she had before. Despite her exhaustion, when she returned into herself she went looking for Grauel and Barlog.

"I have a mission for you two," she announced. "A tough one. Feel free to refuse it if you like."

They eyed her expectantly, without eagerness.

"I want you to accompany Bagnel to the homeworld. I want you to watch over him as you would me while he reports on our visit to the aliens and recruits brethren to replace those lost in this attack. I also want you to assess the situation there. Especially as regards the warlock."

Barlog remained as still as stone, not a ghost of expression touching her face. Grauel exposed her teeth slightly.

They were not happy.

"I know no one else I can trust. And I dare not send him unprotected."

"I see," Grauel said.

And Barlog said, "As you command, Marika."

"I command nothing. I ask. You can refuse if you wish."

"Can we? How? We are your voctors. We must go if that is what you want."

"I could wish for more enthusiasm and understanding, but I'll take what I can get. I'll assemble a crew and talk to Bagnel. I am certain he will be as thrilled as you are. But you must go soon. Quickness may be essential."

She spent a long time with Bagnel, wobbly with weariness, first convincing him—he was more stubborn than Grauel and Barlog—then detailing what she wanted said and what she wanted investigated.

"You will do fine," she said to his latest protest of ineptitude.

"Fine or not, I do not want to go. I have work to do here. Have you seen what they did to my meth?"

"I know, Bagnel. I know. And I think you will be better for recruiting replacements personally and bringing them out to undo what has been done. You've already agreed to go. Stop trying to change my mind."

"All right. All right. Will you get some rest now? Before they find you collapsed in a passageway somewhere?"

"Soon. Soon. I have one more thing to do."

She assembled the bath with whom she had ventured to the alien world. They were little more rested than she, though they had been sleeping. She told them what she needed, and told the strongest of the bath she now had her own darkship and a mission to fly it on as soon as she was ready.

All of the bath volunteered to accompany her, though a passage with a Mistress of the Ship who was not completely tested was risky. They all wanted to see the homeworld again. For several it had been years.

They bickered about who had the most right.

"All of you go," Marika said. "What's the difference? There are six of you and four will have to go to make a crew. What could I do with the two who are left?"

That settled, and everything she could do anything about done, she was able to rest at last.

It was a long time before she came out of her quarters again.

II

Marika became intolerable to those who remained aboard the starship and to those who came to visit, though visitors were not common. Few silth believed the attack had been delivered by the Serke who had survived Marika's capture of the derelict. The dark-faring Communities all eyed each other suspiciously and poked around in the shadows seeking those with guilty knowledge.

Bagnel did not return, and still did not return. She became more difficult after he became overdue, and the longer overdue he was, the more intolerable was she. More than once she caught herself on the brink of taking a darkship out alone, in a mad effort at limping through the homeward passage by herself. But that was impossible even for one of her strength.

She was strong enough to make a short passage, one star to another, on her own. But she would need long periods of rest between passages, and there were no resting places at many of the homeward milestars. Moreover, rests would consume too much time. Bagnel, Grauel, and Barlog, even with a weak Mistress, could make the journey several times over while she limped along.

A daring silth came to her quarters while she slept and wakened her. Marika did not so much as growl. Something dire had to be afoot if the female dared this. "What is it?"

"Darkship just came out of the Up-and-Over, mistress. Your darkship. It is in trouble."

Marika leaped up. "Send out . . ."

"Every darkship available is headed that way, mistress. We expect to save them, but it will be close. They came through with only two bath."

Marika settled her nerves carefully, turning to old rituals seldom used since her novitiate. She reached with the touch, lightly, for it would not do to rattle a novice Mistress in trouble.

She found the darkship drifting inward, unstable in flight, damaged. Bagnel was not aboard. Neither was Grauel. Three bath were indeed missing. Barlog was there, at the axis, lying down, apparently injured. The darkships rushing to help had skipped through the Up-and-Over and were closing in. Marika remained close till all four meth had been transferred to safety aboard other darkships.

Her ship. Her precious oddball wooden dark-faring ship. It had been crippled. The signs were unmistakable. Someone had attacked it.

She began stalking the passageways of the alien starship, boots hammering angrily. This was it. This was the end of all patience. She would not tolerate any more. Those responsible for this would pay. "I am the successor to Bestrei. Would they have dared this with her? No." She would make them remember. That fact would become painfully apparent to those responsible. The silth would change if she had to send half the sisterhoods into the dark. . . . Rage sapped by vigorous exercise began to fade into worry. Where was Bagnel? What had become of Grauel?

She was at the lock when they brought the survivors inside. She said nothing. She just stood there letting the healer sisters get on with their work, spurred by her dark, angry glare.

More and more meth gathered as the word spread. The atmosphere aboard the starship grew depressing. Marika sensed little anger. That fed her own rage. They were depressed because they knew she would avenge this. Because they knew this outrage meant the beginning of a new era of friction.

They were *not* outraged, and that angered her almost as much as the fact of the attack itself. All this time with her and they had given no loyalty to herself or to the project. Or maybe only to the project. They might not care who was in control so long as they could proceed with their studies undisturbed.

"Move them into the games room," she instructed the healer sisters. "Prepare sleeping arrangements for five. One of you will be there, on duty with them, at all times."

As she started away one of the healer sisters expressed her mystification with a simple, "Mistress?"

"I want them kept together, in one place. And I want to be there with them. I am going for a few things. Have them in the games room when I get there."

And she did move in with them, watching them every

instant, scarcely napping. If there was an enemy aboard the starship, he or she would not reach them.

There were moments when she marveled at her own paranoia, but they were far between. And even then she understood that paranoia was justified.

The bath she had made Mistress recovered first. She wakened and saw Marika hovering. Relief overcame her. Then embarrassment. Then silth training took hold and she began a formal report.

"Back up," Marika said. "Give it to me the way it happened—from the time you arrived on the homeworld."

"It is simple, mistress. Your male friend pursued his assignment with great vigor. He irritated many silth by his manner, and was tolerated only because he was your agent. But they are trying to forget you on the homeworld. They are angered by constant reminders of your power, though they have benefited much from what you have done. Already it can be seen where brethren have adapted knowledge we have gained here and have employed it to the benefit of all meth.

"But no one believed in our mission. Everyone believed we were spies sent to prepare the way for your return. No one would cooperate. Bagnel garnered what information he could by trading what we learned about the aliens for gossip. He worked long hours comparing what one order said to what others told him."

"Am I to assume that lack of cooperation was the reason you took so long?"

"Yes, mistress. That and the male's insistence on frequent visits to the mirrors. He learned more there than he did among those who have a logical interest in treating us honestly."

"Us. You keep saying us and we. Explain."

"We are not of the same Community, Marika, and that has stood between us. There have been moments of friction within our crew. But when we returned home we all found ourselves considered suspect by our seniors. None of our Communities welcomed us. We were all treated coolly and with suspicion, as though we were of an enemy order. Even your own most senior, Bel-Keneke, would have little to do with us."

"So what happened? Where are the others?"

"We were on a flight to Ruhaack from Khartyth, where we had spoken with the Frodharsch seniors, when we were attacked by rogue aircraft. They were much like the alien craft we saw when we visited that world. I amazed myself. I was able to gather those-who-dwell and strike at them. I had not been able to manipulate on the dark side before."

"Fear can inspire wonderful things. Rogue aircraft, eh? The Communities have let things go that far? Why do I bother trying to educate the fools?"

"Terrible things have happened, mistress. A fourth of the world is in rogue paws, mostly wilderness country, snow country, but held as firmly as any Community territory. More firmly, because it was from silth they took the land. The sisterhoods have ignored that, except for the few you organized to fight back. Many have become so frightened that they will not *try* to control the rogues. But you will find all that in Bagnel's reports. Let me continue.

"There were four rogue aircraft. I opened to the All and let it carry the struggle through me. I took the darkship down into rugged valleys where they could not follow, gathered and sent those-who-dwell. The rogue pilots were shielded by suppressor suits. But their aircraft were not protected. I downed three by damaging their control systems. The fourth fled. We sustained only minor damage.

"But as we neared Ruhaack we were hit by a suppressor beam. We were just two miles from the Redoriad cloister. I reached with the touch and appealed for help. None came. Rogues attacked on foot. There were at least a hundred of them, there in the shadow of that great cloister. It was a long, fierce fight. I slew many who were not protected by suppressor suits. But in the end we ran out of ammunition and they overwhelmed us.

"During the fighting I appealed repeatedly to both the Redoriad and Reugge cloisters. Finally the Reugge responded to my touch. Several darkships came out. They scattered the rogues and drove them off, but when they fled they took with them the voctor Grauel, the bath Silba, and the male Bagnel. The baths Rextab and Nigel were left dead. The rest of us were uninjured but in poor condition mentally."

The Mistress turned inward upon herself, remembering, radiating pain. Marika had to prod her. "Go on, please." She had a feeling there was more, and maybe worse, though her imagination had difficulty enough encompassing the disaster already set forth.

"Everyone refused to help us, then. We had been reduced to harmlessness, they thought, and that was enough for them. If they ignored us long enough, we would die eventually, I guess." A trace of sarcasm. "The threat of Marika's wrath would have no substance. She would be isolated in a far place. In time, I expect, messages would have gone out for all darkships to stay away from here, and recalling those few Mistresses who were with you. You would have been left to live out your life in exile."

Marika controlled the emotions boiling inside her. "I see. But?"

"I freely admit that some of us would have permitted that to happen had our own orders not treated us like bearers of pestilence. We suffered that for a few days only. Your voctor Barlog was enraged. She was also very determined to rectify the situation and to do something to recover our companions from the rogues—or at the very least to have vengeance. But as matters stood we were powerless. When even your own Community would do nothing . . . We argued long hours and decided we had to come for you. Still, we were short of crew. And still we could recruit no aid of any sort. Finally our anger and disgust grew so boundless we decided to attempt the passage, feeble though we thought our chances were. The voctor Barlog, with no talent at all, volunteered to risk herself completely by standing bath.

"But before we departed, she insisted we had to recover Bagnel's reports from the Reugge cloister. At that point, I think, she was in full command, though she was not silth. We bowed to her age, wisdom, and, most of all, her determination, which is not unlike your own when your mind is set."

Marika was mildly amused. It had been a long time since any junior had dared speak so frankly. She found she approved.

The Mistress continued, "We slipped in by darkship, hovered outside the window of our quarters there, and Barlog broke in. It took her several trips to bring all the reports aboard. During the last of those several Reugge sisters tried to compel us to return them. Barlog was out of patience with silth political nonsense. Her words. She gunned them down. Their voctors fired back before she finished them, too, and she was wounded. I then took the darkship up and headed here. There was no pursuit, probably because they expected us to perish. It was a difficult passage, but we made it."

"It was an heroic passage," Marika said. "If it does not spawn a legend it will be because of the fool nature of silth." Secretly, she was amazed that the Mistress had made it through—with almost no practical experience, only two bath, and a talent that was marginal at best. Her chances should have been nil. "There is a lesson in it that should not be lost. Determination counts for as much as any other factor. Where are Bagnel's reports?"

"Still aboard the darkship. In the carrier baskets."

"Thank you. This will not be forgotten. There will be great rewards and terrible reprisals because of what you have suffered. It has destroyed the last of my patience and mercy. You rest. You treat yourself well. I appoint you my deputy in my absence, with full powers to speak as I would speak."

"You are going back?"

"There are debts to be collected. There are friends in durance. This I will not tolerate." Within the hour Marika had conscripted a darkship crew and had had them ferry her out to her wooden voidship.

III

The homeworld of the meth swam before her. She drifted past the mirror in the leading trojan, noting that it was complete and in full operation. Afar, the second was so near completion it would be finished within a month.

Bagnel's report declared the long winter beaten. It was in retreat, though it would be a long time yet before it could be declared fully conquered.

The project was winding down. Briefly Marika wondered what impact that would have upon meth society. Perhaps the unity could be kept alive in projects designed to recover lands and resources the winter had given up.

She wondered for a moment about her place in history. It did mean something to her, despite her protests to the contrary. It concerned her a little because she had no friends among those who would do the remembering. She feared the silth would recall her for things that seemed to her of little real consequence, and others not for her accomplishments but her tyrannies.

She did not worry about it long. She was silth enough to have little attention to devote to far futures.

She drifted past Biter, past Chaser and the lesser moons, past the Hammer and all the stations and satellites that had been orbited during the erection of the mirrors. She moved into position above the New Continent, well inside geocentric orbit, but remaining stationary with respect to the planetary surface, a fraction of her mind devoted to controlling those-who-dwell, who maintained her position.

They did not know she had come, down there. They did not know out there on the edge of the void. She had come with the stealth of a huntress intent on counting coup upon a rival packstead. They were not watching, anyway. They did not expect her. How could they believe that one novice

Mistress with only two bath and a wounded voctor in support could run the long reach out to the alien starship?

She sent ghosts to explore the world below, carefully, carefully, lest their passage be detected. She found very little beside disappointment.

Skiljansrode—that Gradwohl had created, and she had shaped into an engine of silth-managed technology, and that Edzeka had developed into her personal technical Community—was no more. A gutted ruin, the surrounding snows littered with the corpses and machines and airships of those who had brought it low. Edzeka had been overconfident of her fortress, it seemed. But as she had promised, the warlock had paid a high price for his vengeance.

He had survived the quirky engine she had created in hopes of controlling him. Had outlived it and had prospered. As Bagnel had reported.

Bagnel's pessimistic reports were not pessimistic enough. Exploring the rogue areas, she found them stronger and more numerous than he had suspected. They had installations everywhere. But, she was pleased to note, not all were protected by suppressor systems.

She found no trace of Grauel, Bagnel, or the missing bath. That did not surprise or dismay her. She had not expected to find them easily.

She pinpointed the rogue installations upon a mental map, then went on to explore everything the meth had in orbit. She was quite surprised to discover that no weapons had been orbited since the defeat of the Serke. Perhaps silth disunity was of some value after all. Maybe they had not been able to agree on the best ways to shut her out.

She sent stealthy ghosts out to cripple what few systems did exist in tiny sabotages that would not become apparent till the weapons were actually used. She sent more down to the world to do the same to the rogues' suppressor systems. She pursued her quiet, undetected guerrilla campaign till she neared collapse from exhaustion. Then she rested. And when she could do so, she went on.

She was not discovered during her preparations. It was

what she wanted, and yet she was not entirely pleased. What she could do so could the pawful of Serke exiles hidden with *Starstalker*.

It was time to begin the scourging, the scouring, the cleansing. Time to let the fire fall, though it was no wind she sent down upon the world of her birth and hatred.

She did what no other silth had ever imagined or tried. She summoned the system's great black and sent it down against her enemies.

The death screams of rogue minds reached her there in the void, so numerous were they and so terrible were their deaths. So great was the horror that it reached that deeply hidden place where her compassion lay. She called out her hatred, hardened the shell around it, and continued the killing till she had cleansed every installation she had been able to locate.

At the desert base of the brethren, after their destruction of Maksche, her rage had led her to a slaughter of thousands. A slaughter so great it had shaken the world almost as much as the bombing of TelleRai. Against this kill that was but a fleck in the eye of a murdered beast.

The rogue world went mad. The airwaves went insane with confused messages, frequently cut short. And because Skiljansrode was dead and there was no one else to intercept their messages, the silth remained ignorant of the terror that had been loosed.

Black and terrible as the killing was, rogues survived. Marika released the great black, rested, allowed the remaining rogues to absorb her message. Recovered, she searched again, and found many more installations, every one defended by active suppressors.

Panic fogged the New Continent. It was so powerful she could not see how the silth could not sense it.

She summoned the great black, sent it down again, and delivered a new message. Only the most powerful batteries of suppressors could withstand its grand, dark fury.

Again she released it. And still there were rogues. She

nurtured her hatred, lest it bleed away before the task she had set herself was done. No half measures this time. No getting distracted and going away before the job was finished. No matter the cost to herself or the homeworld.

She reached with the far touch, probed those installations that had withstood the great black. *Kublin. Littermate. I have come home. You have roused me this time. This time there is only one way you can survive. Return me my meth.* She gave nothing away by admitting her presence. By now they would know their enemy down there. Who else had the dark-sider strength to do such slaughter?

The rogues responded just as she had expected. They tried to destroy her. But it took them hours to locate her, hours she used to recover her spent strength. Then they discovered that most of their weapons had been incapacitated. Their beamers did nothing. Their missiles exploded in their silos. And when they had failed in their counterattack the far touch came down again.

I am here, Kublin. Littermate. Warlock. And you are dead unless I receive my meth. Think of sleeping with the worms, coward. Think of this whole world sleeping with the worms. It will, if that is what it takes.

By now the Communities were aware that something terrible was happening. Their best fartouchers found her there in orbit and recognized her. Panic spread with the speed of lightning. It exceeded that of the rogues, who remained armed with the illusion that they could fight back.

Voidships rose from the surface. Marika sent one harsh, intransigent warning.

Most of the voidships turned back. The few that did not perished in the grasp of the great black.

Marika searched for and found Bel-Keneke and prodded her with the far touch. *Gather the most seniors of the Communities. There will be a convention.* She closed herself to any response.

She reached elsewhere. *Kublin. Littermate. Deliver Grauel, Bagnel, and the bath named Silba to the Reugge cloister at Ruhaack. You have one day. Then you die. And all who stand by you die with you.*

She continued launching periodic attacks upon rogue centers where she had been unable to detect the presence of her comrades. With practice she found that the great black could be pushed through the shielding of even the most powerful battery of suppressors.

She rested yet again while her senior bath managed the wooden voidship, then sent, *Bel-Keneke. I will be coming down soon. The most seniors had better be gathered. I will have no mercy upon those who do not appear before me.*

Then back to another message for Kublin. *Kublin. Littermate. I am coming down. If my meth are not at the Reugge cloister I will have no mercy at all. There will be no place you can hide. I will hunt you down to the very last of you.*

She began a leisurely descent, allowing those below ample time to respond, either with attacks or surrender to her will.

There were no attacks.

Chapter Forty-Two

I

There were darkships everywhere around the Reugge cloister, and scattered about the fields outside the town. Fields, she noted, that showed signs of beginning to thaw. Maybe the mirrors *were* working. The air did not have its customary toothy bite.

She saw witch signs of orders of which she had never heard, of Communities great and small, gathered from the ends of the world. She sensed more darkships in the air, hastening to the gathering, coming from afar. Her command had been unrealistic. It was physically impossible for some to reach Ruhaack in so short a time.

She drifted into the landing court, noting that the cloister itself was free of snow. The court had been cleared for her arrival. Silth were arrayed in accordance with the demands of ceremony for the arrival of a great most senior. She was grimly amused because they accorded her that honor.

She sent ghosts scurrying through the cloister, detected no signs of treachery or foolishness. For all the talent amassed, not a whiff of a trap. "As strength goes," she murmured. When the wooden voidship grounded she told her bath, "All of you stay close to me. For your own protection." She glanced skyward. Both mirrors were visible. Each seemed as brilliant as the sun itself. A world with three suns. Nowhere in her far travels had she encountered anything as strange as that.

Purely for the drama of the moment she pulled down ghosts from the upper air and made them shimmer about her. She stepped down from the darkship.

Bel-Keneke came to meet her, a silth grown old in a very short time, fur ragged, gray, body quaking as she approached alone. Marika glared, unable to restrain her feelings completely. She stood with ghosts glimmering around her, crawling through her fur, motionless, speechless, waiting.

Bel-Keneke croaked, "The convention has begun assembling in the great hall, Marika. Not all have arrived yet, some being impossibly far to begin. But all have promised to come, and I am told that all who have not yet arrived are in fact hurrying here as fast . . ."

"I am aware of that. Hear this. Henceforth you will address me as mistress of mistresses. That which you feared has befallen you, and that which you fled has overtaken you. Lonely, lonely, the stars come down, and the fire washes away the sins upon the earth. . . . " What in the name of the All was she saying? Marika controlled herself. "You stirred the darkness and wakened its wrath. You have brought it upon yourselves. You would not let be. You have forced me. From this moment I am most senior of most seniors. And I intend to proclaim a new order. Those who find they have no desire to embrace it will soon be reunited with the All. I am out of patience, out of tolerance, out of understanding. Lead on to the great hall, Bel-Keneke. My old friend, upon whom I bestowed all blessings."

Bel-Keneke turned. She walked, bowed as though by the weight of time, her shoulders drawn as though she expected to be struck. Fear trailed her like an evil perfume.

The most seniors were gathered in the great hall, indeed.

As Marika stepped in she recalled it as it had been after the kalerhag of the Serke and the fire set by those who had taken themselves into exile. Half ruined, choked with burned corpses. Alive with the stench of death.

Death lurked there now, slithering around behind the smell of meth fear.

She examined the silent silth in their shivering scores. So many. And so many of them so very old. And all of them so very frightened.

She stalked to the high seat that Bel-Keneke occupied in ordinary meetings of the Reugge council and seated herself. Her bath and Barlog moved in behind her, their weapons held ready. Barlog, she sensed, moved back behind everyone, not really trusting the bath to stick. She waited silently, her touch roaming the cloister. She could find no Grauel. No Bagnel. No Silba.

So.

Some shaking, deputized silth moved toward her. She raised a paw, freezing them where they stood. They dropped their gazes and waited.

She grasped a powerful ghost from high above, drew it down, tamed it, and sent it wandering rogue territory, into the installations she had not yet destroyed, amid the enduring terror and confusion. And she found an old gray male who could be none other than Kublin.

So old ... But she, too, was aging, for all silth had their ways of staying the teeth of time. How many years did she have to tame this mad civilization and prepare it for what would come upon it from the stars? Maybe not enough.

That was the task left her, after she had fulfilled her duty to her own. To sculpt this world a single face. For the alien was coming. Sooner or later. The meth were known, now, through her own doing. Seekers would find, as she had found the Serke, given determination and time.

Kublin. Littermate. I see you there. You are running out of time. Where are my meth?

He started, amazed that she had found him. He shouted panicky orders. Rogues ran hither and yon.

*There is no mercy in me this time, Kublin. Littermate.
This time, if I must, I will make you die a death that will
balance my past foolish mercies. Unless you surrender
Grauel, Bagnel, and Silba, you are doomed and damned.
Do not persist in your stupidity. You are strong, but I am
stronger. I cannot be stopped. I am the successor to Bestrei,
and I am ten times stronger than ever she was. I am not
constrained by her ancient codes of honor. I have a hunger
in me, littermate. It is a hunger for your soul, like the
hunger of the grauken, and I am barely able to restrain it.
Bring them to me, Kublin. Bring me my meth. Or I surrender to the grauken within me.*

Immensely powerful suppressor fields rose around the
installation, forcing her out. But she was strong, and went
more slowly than they hoped. Before she lost touch she saw
females, silth, moving near Kublin. They were all very old,
very ragged. Their apparel was Serke.

So. As she had suspected, that struggle was not at an end
either. Only a pawful remained, but they went on, trapped
in the destiny they had woven for themselves.

What better place to hide than upon the world that had
spawned them, far from the deadly hunter of stars? Was
Starstalker concealed right here in the system? In the
shadow of a distant asteroid, somewhere where no voidfaring silth bothered to go?

That answer would come soon enough.

Marika stationed her tame ghost near the installation and
held it there with a thread of touch while she returned
herself to flesh and the grand convention she had
summoned.

They were conversing, some in soft tones or whispers,
most with the touch. Snatches quickly patched together in
one grand consensus. *Doomfarer. Jiana. That look is upon
her, stronger than ever before. Something dire is about to
happen.*

The reek of fear in that great hall was ten times what it
had been upon her entry.

From her place Bel-Keneke made a sign, sped a feeble,

frightened touch that told her that the last of the most seniors had arrived. Marika rose. She chose to speak instead of touch, and to speak in the tongue of common meth instead of any silth language. "Pups in gray mange, with your fur falling out, why are you so afraid? What is one savage from the wilds of the upper Ponath? Look. See how amusing, in her country clothing, her savage bloodfeud paints, carrying her weapons like some common fur trapper. Is this an object of fright?"

Her voice hardened. "I am reality, who has been baying along your backtrail so long. I am that which you fear, and I have overtaken you. I am not pleased with you. You have been in command. You are responsible. Your Communities have done foolish, stupid things, over and over and over, and then you have insisted on compounding them with more follies and stupidities. The story is always the same. Always the story of silth greed. Always the story of silth manipulation and maneuvering and treachery, never the story of meth thinking of tomorrow, never of meth facing reality and the future and *seeing* what lies there. I have preserved you and preserved you, and for what? Why? You will not learn. Perhaps you cannot learn.

"This is a new age, sisters. Can you not understand that? We are alone in this universe no more. We must sculpt a single outward face."

"I sent you a messenger, to apprise you of that, and you saw in him only one more opportunity to vent the greed and treachery that lies coiled about your hearts. You saw nothing else, and you heard nothing at all."

She glared down at the packed, silent, frightened silth. She sensed that some were considering attacking her. If they dared, as a group, they might end their terror forever. But not one among them had the courage to be the first to move.

"I read your hearts. As you are afraid of me now, so you stand convicted of the crime of cowardice in the face of the rogues who would have wrested your world from you. *Had* wrested it from you, save for small regions where they allowed you to abide till they chose to eliminate you. Again and again I gave you the chance to destroy those who would devour you, and always you squandered it. Again and again you allowed them to regain their strength, and each time become stronger, while you snapped at one another's backs and tried to steal starships or lands or whatever it was that for the moment seemed more important than the survival of your Communities. You will not save yourselves."

She stared, dared. No one responded.

"You do not protest the indictment. Not one of you, though some are less guilty than the rest." She reached into the void, pulled. "You would not learn, would not live together, would not defend yourselves. If you have no other value, then you might at least serve as examples of the cost of stupidity to those who will come after you." She yanked viciously. The great black struggled, but it came. "We cannot rebuild the world with you, that is obvious. We will see if it can be done without you."

They did not understand for a while. Then they understood only too well. The otherworld filled with outraged, terrified touch. And they remained true to what they were. They panicked rather than do what they needed to save themselves. They would not join even then.

Marika hammered another layer of armor around her heart. She told herself they were poor silth, that they truly deserved what was to come. But she hurt. She could no longer love herself.

She drew Barlog and her bath close to her, to envelop them in her own protection, then unleashed the fury of the great black.

You experience true darkwar, she flung into the horror of screaming mouths and twisting bodies and flying blood. *I bring it down upon you, for the race.*

It lasted far longer than she expected. When it was over she felt hollow, wasted, as though the massacre had been a futile and pointless gesture, little more than a pup's destructive tantrum.

Her companions did not speak to her. The bath eased

away, overcome with horror. Barlong seemed more disgusted than horrified. Marika did not think much of herself at that moment, but she refused to turn inward, to scrutinize her feelings and motives.

"They wanted a doomstalker. A Jiana. They insisted. I have given them one. Come, you. We have business with the rogue."

As she walked to the courtyard and darkship, stepping over and around still forms, Barlog finally said, "Marika, they will not suffer this. You have sealed your doom. You have cried bloodfeud upon all silthdom."

"I know, Barlog. I know. But they'll have to work together if they're going to finish it, won't they? They'll have to eliminate the rogue at their backs before they dare turn upon me, won't they? In order to destroy me they will have to become what I want them to be, won't they?"

A wild awe filled Barlog's eyes as she realized that Marika had walked into this knowing exactly what she did.

"I have them by their cropped tails, Barlog. And I am not going to let go till they have remade themselves in the image I want. I have more surprises waiting for them. . . . But you need not be any part of this. You can retire to the packsteads on our world out there. It's not the Ponath, but it's . . ."

"No. We have lived together—so many trouble-filled years. So much blood. We will die together. I insist. I have nothing else."

"If that is what you wish. Come. Let's go find our friends. And lay my family to rest."

Barlog shuddered.

II

Kublin had not exhausted his arsenal, nor would he surrender. He was as stubborn, was as much Jiana, as Marika was. He had his own dream of the shape of the future and was as determined to give it form.

But he did yield. A little.

Marika hammered at him a week, reducing his final strongholds one by one, slaughtering his followers. Then she laid siege to his final redoubt, a place far beneath the earth shielded by suppressors so powerful even the great black could not penetrate them. Marika brought in laborers and voctors by the thousand, began digging.

A deputation of terrified rogues came out. They brought Grauel, Bagnel, and the bath Silba.

Only Silba was alive.

She then understood why the coward had been so stubbornly determined. He had had little with which to trade.

Grauel and Bagnel had died before her return to the homeworld. Kublin had had no counters with which to play a trading game.

He had feared her fury would be inflamed all the more.

It was. But it became a directionless fury, a rage against circumstance, which burned bright swiftly and soon guttered into despair.

Marika took up Silba and the bodies of her loved ones and withdrew into the void. Bagnel she set sailing among the stars.

"Go, old friend," she whispered, and fought a sorrow greater than she dared admit. They might have been wonders. One death, among all the thousands she had engineered and witnessed, had stolen away all purpose, all caring. "Sail among your dreams. Among our dreams. And may the All reward you with more than all you lost for my sake."

A small part of her urged her to go back and ravage the world as she had ravaged the rogues and most seniors and her own Community, to take a vengeance that would not be forgotten while eternity lasted. But Bagnel's ghost visited her and whispered to her in sorrow, in the gentle way he had learned in his later years. He was never tilted to the dark side, for all he had shared her life. He would not have himself avenged. He could forgive even stupidity.

She battled her hatred for her world, her past, and all that had been denied her because she was what she was. She thought often of pups never born, and wondered what they might have become.

She watched Bagnel's body drift till she could no longer find it with the touch, then climbed into the Up-and-Over and fled toward her far stronghold, her alien starship fortress that orbited a foreign world and star.

"Let *them* deal with Kublin," she said. "I have no home and no race. I will go back there only one more time."

She would keep Grauel there, preserved in the void. And when the time came for Barlog to become one with the All she would go back, and the two old huntresses would go down to the Ponath, to the Degnan packstead. They would receive a proper Mourning, with all the Degnan unMourned, and their ashes would be scattered as was fitting for the most respected of the Wise. That she would do, though it cost her everything. They had kept their faith. She would keep hers.

On the resting worlds Marika questioned the bath Silba, and learned that the rogue had subjected her, and Grauel, and Bagnel, to every torment and indignity in an effort to learn about the aliens and about her. Bagnel and Grauel had died by Kublin's paw, as he had used his wehrlen's talent to force a crude truthsaying. Silba had been immune, being silth-trained. She believed that Kublin had learned everything known by the other two, and much from her as well, for he had been a crafty interrogator.

Marika worried, for she did not know how much Grauel and Bagnel had known, nor could she predict what Kublin might make of it. She should have gone ahead and destroyed him.

Already her most ferocious oaths were sliding from her mind. She was thinking that, one day, she would venture back with some of those weapons the rogues had dropped upon TelleRai. A few of those would dig Kublin out of his last fastness. If the silth themselves did not complete what she had started, to free themselves of one half the family so they could devote their attention to the other.

III

A nasty surprise awaited Marika.

She might have made a heat of the moment vow to retreat from the universe. The universe had made no such promise to her.

The starship was not alone in orbit.

It took her a minute to comprehend what she was seeing. *Starstalker.* The long-missing Serke voidship. Here! But that could not be. It had to be hidden in-system back . . . Maybe. And maybe it had been waiting for her to show, and had pulled out while she was preoccupied.

She sent ghosts skipping across the void, felt them rebound. *Starstalker* was bound by suppressor fields as powerful as those shielding Kublin's headquarters. The voidship bristled with technological armaments.

She did not waste a second. She summoned the system's great black and hurled it. *Starstalker*'s suppressor fields bowed, but held. A trickle of silth distress leaked into the otherworld.

Marika overcame the great black's reluctance and slammed it in again, harder. *Starstalker*'s fields creaked. Panic radiated from the voidship, from the orbiting alien derelict. Marika pressed harder still, and kept the entire Serke compliment preoccupied with resisting the great black while she pushed her darkship to one of the alien's locks. She touched Barlog. *Go inside and kill Serke. They will be too preoccupied to defend themselves.*

Barlog went. She stalked passages, firing short bursts at Serke sisters, and exchanged shots with a pawful of unskilled rogues not directly involved in resisting Marika's assault.

Each silth slain weakened Serke resistance to the great

black. It was now clear that the suppressors would hold only while the Serke supported them by pushing at the black themselves.

The Mistress aboard *Starstalker* panicked. She broke away, abandoning her sisters aboard the alien. Marika touched Barlog. *Take care. Starstalker is running. I must pursue.* But once *Starstalker* pulled away it no longer lent suppressor protection to those aboard the alien. Marika flung a pawful of lesser ghosts into the starship's passageways.

But then *Starstalker,* under lessened pressure from the great black, opened fire with its brethren-type weapons and forced Marika to dodge while it ducked into the Up-and-Over on a line she could not calculate. In parting, the voidship dispatched a covey of rockets toward the alien.

Marika could not stop them all.

She threw her darkship toward the alien, flinging a touch ahead. *Barlog! Are you there?*

Barlog could not respond. She was not silth.

Marika snatched a ghost and sent it inside. She found Barlog trapped in a damaged sector, still alive, but unlikely to remain so for long if not helped. She sped an enraged promise of damnation after *Starstalker,* a promise to end its tale.

She took the voidship in hard, quickly, and sought a lock through which she could enter. The first few she examined were damaged beyond use.

Inside. She raced along metal corridors, climbed ladders that rang beneath her boots, skipped past dead meth, flung ghosts this way and that, searching out safe pathways. . . .

She arrived too late.

Barlog lay sandwiched between buckled plates of steel. She screamed when Marika tried to shift the weight. Marika screamed with her, cursing the All. There was nothing she could do. She did not have a healer sister's skills. She had not taken time to learn them. None of her bath had the talent.

She settled down and gripped Barlog's paw. Over and

over she apologized. "I'm sorry, Barlog, that I brought you to this end."

Barlog replied, "Do not blame yourself, Marika. I chose. Grauel and I both chose. You gave us a chance to return home. We chose not to go. It has been a long life filled with wonders no Degnan ever dreamed of. By rights none of us should have survived the invasion of the Ponath. So we cannot complain. We had many borrowed years. Our deaths have been honorable, and we will be recalled as long as Marika is recalled, for were we not her right and left paws, her shadows in the lights of Biter and Chaser?"

Barlog gathered her strength. Marika gripped her paw more tightly. She said, "I do not want you to die, Barlog. I do not want you to leave me here alone."

Finally Barlog replied, "You were always alone, Marika. We but followed you down the pathway of your destiny. We leave one request. Take us back to the Ponath. Not now, but someday."

"That will be. You know it will be. If it is the only thing I accomplish in what life is left me."

"Thank you, Marika."

Neither said anything more. Marika did not want to speak for fear grief would betray her, and she lose the concentration she lent to watching for a return of *Starstalker*.

In time Barlog shuddered, whimpered, clutched her paw tightly, and went to join the All.

Marika could maintain control no longer.

Chapter Forty-Three

I

Marika presided over an abbreviated Mourning down upon the colony world. She had the ashes of Grauel and Barlog stored in flasks that she placed aboard her darkship. Then she took the darkship up and out, to the stars, and till her bath rebelled she hunted Serke. She became more cold, more deadly than ever before, and saw little purpose to life other than the final destruction of the last six or seven of the old enemy.

When the bath refused to be driven farther she returned to the battered starship and lurked there sullenly, solitarily, becoming social only when preparing to launch another search foray. She often talked to herself when alone, debating taking her huntresses home. The part of her that insisted on waiting till they were avenged always won.

If she would not go of her own choosing, the homeworld would summon her.

There was a flight into the dust cloud, sniffing cold spoor, and another team of bath who tired of fruitless, driven pursuit. She turned back to the starship, and as she approached it she received a touch.

A darkship with a crew symbolically selected from four dark-faring orders awaited her. It bore a desperate petition from the new most seniors of the various Communities, the silth she had expected to come hunting, but who never had.

What was this? Some cunningly laid trap?

She approached the meeting with extreme caution.

The Mistress of the courier ship was a Redoriad survivor of the battles with the Serke, one Marika knew and had little cause to suspect—though she had participated in Balbrach's attempt to steal the derelict. Her skills in the void were second only to Marika's own. She said, "You see before you the only Mistress of five sent who survived the effort to escape the homeworld. We all carried the same plea. Your talent is needed at home, Marika."

"For what? What has happened now?"

"The brethren. Of course. You were right about them. Somewhere, somehow, while silthdom diverted itself with other matters, they built a starship modeled on the alien. It appeared a month ago. It carried many brethren whom we could not harm and weapons of the alien sort. Many silth have perished. They seized the mirrors and orbital stations. Now they are down on the planet, attacking us everywhere. They have powerful suppressors that take our talents away and force us to battle them in their own fashion. Though you hurt them badly before, they have gained strength because they have won the sympathy of the bonded population."

Marika recalled the attitudes of her elders when she was a pup. The Communities had not ever had the hearts of common meth. "You would not listen, you silth. You would not learn. I do not want to come. The homeworld has done nothing but cause me grief. Yet I have made promises to my dead. I will come. And I will die, I think, for if none of you can destroy them, what hope for me alone? For if this is a lure into a web to avenge those I punished for their stupidity and cupidity, what chance that I will prevail? The bait would not be set out till the trappers felt certain of their ground."

The Redoriad ignored her suggestion of potential treachery. "You have the wooden darkship. The rogue cannot see you in the void."

"Little good may that do."

"You will come? For certain?"

"I said I would. Let me rest. Let me grieve for myself and all my stupid sisters who would not hear my warnings, so beg me now to kalerhag for their salvation. I should allow them to be eradicated. I should hope a smarter generation would arise after them. But I will come. I have nothing for which to live. Nothing but the destruction of my enemies."

"This is not true, mistress. It has taken a disaster of grand magnitude to convince the sisterhoods that the solitary voice crying warning held more wisdom than all their ruling generation. They believe, Marika. They beg you to take the mantle and show the way, to forge the new unity. . . . "

"I do not want to lead. I never wanted that. Had I wished, I could have taken command long ago. All I ever wanted was to walk the starpaths with my friends, finding new things. I have been allowed little opportunity to chase that dream. The wickednesses of silth have compelled me always to turn elsewhere. And now they have robbed me of all who were dearest to me. Then when they must pay the price of their folly they beg me to save them."

"You are bitter."

"Of course I am. But enough of that. Tell me what you know of the orbits occupied by the rogues." She did not believe treacherous silth would have craft enough to weave a luring tale with sufficient verisimilitude to include properly shaped imaginary rogue orbits. She would go, but the Redoriad's report would tell her what she faced.

II

Marika paused on a world a short jump from home. She rested her bath well. She carried a doubled and heavily armed crew. The Redoriad she sent ahead to scout. Shortly before she expected the Redoriad to return she took her darkship up and gathered ghosts for the Up-and-Over.

The Redoriad appeared. *They are in polar orbit,* she reported. *Inside the orbits of the smallest moons. They are arming the mirrors and stations, though there are not really enough of them to operate all the systems. Touch I had with the surface was grim. Several small sisterhoods have been entirely destroyed. All the larger are in trouble. The only damage done the rogue ship was by a homecoming Mistress who committed kalerhag when she saw she could not reach the surface. After her rites she plunged her darkship into the rogue's drives. It cannot maneuver. Unfortunately, it remained in a stable orbit.*

Marika thanked the Mistress, then questioned her closely about the rogue ship's orbit. She wanted to arrive near it, to allow it no time to respond to her appearance.

She skipped to the edge of the system, took control of a great black, then made the long jump, mind tight upon the innermost of the homeworld's minor moons, which orbited inside geocentric altitude and well askew from the equator.

She came out within a mile of the moon and hid behind it. It was fewer than a thousand miles from the rogue, and would move closer. She hurled the great black the moment she regained her equilibrium. She drove it with all the strength her hatred could inspire. She ignored the rest of the system. If she did not beat that ship nothing else would matter.

The Redoriad Mistress was right. The ship was brethren from its conception and mimicked the alien in line and armament, though it was smaller. It began firing soon after she started her approach. It had not had much trouble detecting her.

She moved in fast, though, directly toward the ship's stern, where there was a cone of space in which it was difficult for the ship's weapons to track her. She evaded or destroyed what little did threaten her, then entered a smaller cone where no weapon could reach her at all.

She probed the ship's suppressor fields and found a crack where the sister had smashed her darkship. She flung the great black at it, set it to ripping metal and the flesh beyond.

She brought her darkship into physical contact with the rogue's stern. Rogue weaponry on the moons and stations dared not fire upon her there.

Marika touched her reserve bath, who would have to play the roles so long filled by Grauel and Barlog. *Plant a charge.* They hurried out the arm touching the starship. Once they returned Marika drifted a short distance away.

This would surprise the brethren. They still expected silth to think like silth. That made them vulnerable to more mundane techniques.

The explosion left a satisfactory hole in the starship's skin. Marika drifted to that gap, tethered her darkship, and threw herself in amid the twisted metal. Her bath followed her.

The great black made the ship's interior a place of madness. So condensed was it there that the place seemed thick with a noisome, hate-filled fog. The bath teetered on the edge of insanity. Marika had difficulty maintaining her sense of direction.

She found a pressure door through which she could enter that part of the starship that retained hull integrity and opened it.

Rogues waited on the other side. Their determination collapsed, though, in the fog of the great black. They did not wear suppressor suits. Perhaps they had grown lax within their orbiting fortress.

Marika allowed the great black to spread through the vessel, overcoming without killing. Many of the crew went mad. They fired at one another or shot themselves. They screamed and screamed and screamed. The bath captured and restrained those they could.

The control center was a greater problem. It was shielded by independent fields. Marika could find no weak points. She did not want to damage the ship any more, but had no

choice if she wanted her way. She sent two bath to fetch
more explosives.

Rogues in suppressor suits counterattacked from the command center while they were away. Marika and the remaining bath exchanged fire with them till they lost their nerve.
One bath and three rogues were killed.

The explosives arrived. The moment the charges blew
Marika shoved the great black into the control center. She
followed. She had to slay only one more of the brethren to
force their surrender. Five minutes later she had them out of
their suits and the great black off seeking other rogues'
nests.

She found those everywhere. Most she did not attack
because they held too many hostages. She would not force
grand sacrifices unless she could break the rogues no other
way.

She set the shadow loose upon the world, in places where
the rogues were strong, till all was confusion down below.
Then she sent the great black off to its home system.

She examined the ship's control center. It duplicated that
in which she had lived so long, reduced in size. "Wake them
up," she told the bath, indicating prisoners who were unconscious. Those who retained consciousness she told, "Take
your stations."

They moved reluctantly. A few refused. She drew a small
ghost inside, chose a male at random, and made him die
slowly.

She demanded, "Anyone else want to be a martyr to an
idiot cause?" She extended a paw toward one who seemed
senior.

He moved to a position.

"Good. Now activate all secured systems. This ship is
going to do what it was designed to do."

Males eyed her blankly.

"You'll buy your lives by destroying those who summoned
you." She wrinkled a lip in amusement.

No one argued, though many sets of shoulders tightened
in anger and resentment.

"Good. You know me well enough not to waste time arguing. You may begin by recalling those who have taken control of the stations and mirrors."

The senior male replied, "They will not come. They have orders."

"They will not come, *mistress*. Recall your upbringing. Annoy me again and you will enjoy a long life as my personal bond. I am not pleased with you meth. I am tempted to see that your lives are very long and extremely unpleasant."

"They will not come, mistress. They have orders to remain where they are, no matter what they hear."

"Very inventive. We shall have to convince them, then. Prepare a rocket. We will destroy the Hammer. Send the order. Give them one minute to respond. Then launch."

The senior rogue started shaking.

Typical male fear fit. They had no choice but to entrust tasks to cowards. They were all cowards.

"I am watching you. While you work recall that I have spent years studying the ship on which this one was patterned. I will know what you are doing." She stopped, flipped a ghost at a male doing something surreptitious. He screamed. "You see?" She ordered the bath to hang him from the overhead. "Your friend will sing songs of agony while you work. His screams will serve to remind you who rules and who obeys."

She patted the senior's shoulder. He shuddered. "This time you pushed too hard. You made the Communities beg me to deal with you. You sealed the doom of all brethren. Even those we silth think good, I suppose. You were given countless chances to learn and refused all of them. In the Ponath, where I was whelped, we destroyed an animal that threatened us. Immediately. Sentiment did not stand in the way. Life was too fragile, too difficult." She patted his shoulder again. "Be of good cheer. You will participate in great events. You will see the end of an era. You may become the only brethren left alive. I might set you loose later, to wander the world and bear witness to the fury of silth aroused, to the fury of the All, when meth dare defy the natural order."

Some of the males looked at her as though she were mad. Most tried to evade her attention. The senior started to rise, lips back in anger. Marika gestured. The hanging male shrieked. "Such is the fate of those who will not obey. Those who will will survive. Destroy the Hammer. The dome on Little Fang will be next." She whispered to her senior bath, "I am leaving for a moment. Watch them."

She stepped out of the control section, closed her eyes, opened to the weak touch she had felt a moment before.

The Redoriad Mistress had entered the home system.

III

What is it? Marika sent.

You may have sprung a trap.

I knew that when I came. But the males were here. How otherwise?

I came back too soon, too tired, hoping to be of aid. I dropped out of the Up-and-Over too soon, and askew from the ecliptic. Chance showed me three starships very like that which attacked the world. They are lying quietly out there.

Marika grunted, reflected a moment. *So. Did they detect you?*

I think not. I remained only a moment. Barely long enough to note them, probe them, and get out. They are not alert.

Interesting. Were they shielded?

No.

Stay where you are. It is dangerous here still.

Marika paced. A trap. With the deadly part awaiting a signal from in here. A signal already going out at the velocity of light. How far? She queried the Redoriad Mistress. Many, many hours. Too far for them. They had been too careful in hiding themselves.

The fools. She closed her eyes and summoned the system's great black. It did not take long.

She returned to the control center afterward. "Have they been stalling?" The rocket had not launched.

"I think so, mistress."

"So." She waved a paw. "Like that. That easily. Your ships in hiding have been destroyed. They were not alert. They did not have their shields up. You gain nothing by trying to stall till they get here." She faced the bath. "I want all the brethren aboard gathered here. I will give them the chance to die for their beliefs, or to make their peace."

The senior male looked grim. Marika said, "I told you to destroy the Hammer. You have not done so." She waved. The dangling male howled till the senior closed a circuit that launched a rocket.

"Now the dome on Little Fang. Orders to return here, then one minute, then launch. I want the orders sent on a frequency open to everyone."

The senior growled, "You are enjoying this."

"Very much." And she was. She was free of restraint. There was no one whose opinion concerned her. This would be done her way entirely. She would shatter their power, and humiliate them in the process. And she would enjoy doing it.

There would be no mercy this time. This time she would redesign the world.

It took only four rockets to convince the brethren that their position was hopeless. Marika made it seem obvious that she was willing to sacrifice everyone in the stations.

A few hundred meth died. And the void around the homeworld was hers.

Once the brethren from the mirrors were safely away, inward bound, she loosed the great black and finished everyone who had held the stations.

The senior male protested.

"I promised them nothing. Only you who are here." She

stared down at the homeworld, at the place where Kublin cowered. He would not respond to the touch. But he never did.

She had a rocket carry a greeting down.

The explosion, half an hour later, was most gratifying. But it did not neutralize Kublin's installation. She sent another.

A tendril of touch reached her. A fartoucher sister down below sent her the gratitude of the Communities. The message sounded terribly contrived. Marika responded, *You are not yet saved. That from which you fled has overtaken you. That which you feared has befallen you. I have the rogue ship now. And there will be real changes before I abandon it. You had a choice. The brethren way or Marika's. You chose mine as the lesser evil. Now you must live or die with it.*

The second missile detonated over Kublin's headquarters, highlighting her position of strength.

That weapon did not break through either. She ordered a third launched.

She reached with the touch. *Kublin, this is only the beginning. The bombs will fall forever unless you surrender. There is no other way to save the brethren. Your trap has been broken. Your ships are destroyed. You are powerless. It is you, or all tradermales.*

His response would reveal the extent of his commitment to his dream. If cowardice ruled him completely, he would stay down there till the bombs reached him. If he screwed up his courage and came forth, and surrendered, she might allow his followers life.

He would receive her message, of that she was certain.

She watched the senior tradermale closely as he released each of the missiles. The ship boasted a great many. The rogues must have found themselves a world rich in uranium, and must have developed the skills to manufacture them. She recalled those they had used to try destroying the mirror project. How primitive they had been!

After the twelfth bomb struck down into the molten fury

left by its predecessors Marika received a touch. *Enough,
Marika. Stop. I am coming up. Full surrender. Just stop
destroying the world.*

A darkship will pick you up. She touched the Redoriad
Mistress, instructed her to descend and collect Kublin.

It would be hours. She took the opportunity to rest.

IV

A touch from the Redoriad. *I have him, Marika. In chains.
He is cooperating. He seems shocked.*

Bring him up. Touch me when you clear atmosphere.

When that touch came she resumed bombing the more
stubborn brethren facilities. She expended all the remaining
rockets, without much concern for whom they might harm.
Installations across the world perished. The surviving
tradermales would find themselves hammered back into the
past century.

That ought to convince all meth that she ruled the future,
that she would accept no arguments.

The rogue senior reached his limit. He could not believe
she had done what she had done. She asked, "You would not
have employed the weapons against different targets? Is
your thinking so parochial? If meth are to be changed, they
must be convinced that they have suffered from the fury of
the All itself." She ordered him to prepare beam weapons
for use against surface targets. "I wield that fury. Let the
world placate me."

He refused. Even in the face of unending shrieks from the
hanging male, she refused. "String him up," Marika
ordered. Once he was up she made him scream too. She told
his crew, "I need meth able to operate the beam weapons."

They would not aid her. Killing some did not move them.
They believed they would be slain anyway. Why help her?

A touch reached her. She told her bath, "Our guest is
about to arrive. Meet him. Be careful. He is wehrlen."

Kublin entered ten minutes later. Marika did not recognize the creature he had become. For an instant she feared she had been tricked. But on closer examination she found the feel of the pup well hidden behind the surface of this ragged, graying male.

"Marika, you broke your word. I surrendered. You sent bombs down anyway."

"What would you have done differently? I gave you countless chances. You abused them all. Each time you made the reestablishment of order more costly."

"You are destroying everything, Marika."

"Perhaps."

"Do not obliterate the memory of the good you have done, Marika."

"The good has been forgotten. No one cares. I turned back the ice, and they fight for the power to control it. Meth care about me only because I represent power. They either want to take it from me or want to profit from my possessing it."

"Then why do you fight those who would free the world from the old silth wickedness?"

"Some things are worse, Kublin. Some things go against nature."

"It is too late for you, Marika. You are one meth trying to slow a flooding stream by bailing with a bucket. You cannot halt what has been set in motion. Silthdom is dying. And you are more to blame than I."

Marika leveled her rifle.

"You initiated the mirror project, which required so many changes in society. You made it possible for those who share my beliefs to move freely, telling males and bonds that there is hope for a world not always crushed beneath silth paws."

"It was you tradermales who made an unholy alliance with Serke and . . ."

"Perhaps. But we would not have won the hearts of millions without your contributions, Marika. Without you we would have been nothing but what those old ones planned to become: replacements for silth. New oppressors. You made us over into liberators."

Marika slipped her weapon off safety. Her paws shook. Old memories from her early days at Akard howled in the back of her mind. Madness peeped out of its deeps. Ghosts of silth long gone muttered *Jiana!*

"Killing me will solve nothing, littermate."

"I will not be betrayed by my softness toward you again, Kublin. If you counted on that when you surrendered . . ."

"I did not. I never have. You can kill every tradermale there is, Marika, but you will not stop it. Because you yourself have been the principal agent of the change. I have done nothing but channel it. You are the Jiana and you have reshaped the world already."

"Do not call me Jiana!"

"Why not? Can't you face the truth?"

"Do not!"

"You know the truth in your heart, Marika. Who but a doomstalker leaves all who cross her path dead upon her backtrail?"

Marika's bullets ripped into him. Her aim climbed. Bullets hammered the control center, racketed around, cut brethren and silth down. Even she was grazed by a ricochet.

The pain restored her sanity. She flung her weapon away, leaped to a silth she had injured, tried to help her. Her fury was spent. She became businesslike, shouting orders. The other bath eyed her warily. "Do not stand around! Help these meth."

She was disgusted with herself. In a moment anger returned, but it was a cold, reasoning anger that had little to do with hatred, that was turned inward.

Jiana, yes. At least on this small scale. Many meth had been injured needlessly.

To escape her shame she ducked through her loophole, into the peace of the otherworld. After a time she grabbed a ghost and raced through the dark, flitting from station to station, mirror to mirror. The crews there had begun to recover. Electronic chatter filled the ether.

Electronic communications. How things had changed during her lifetime. In her young years, at Akard, telecommunications had been a rarity, a carefully kept secret. There had been little of anything technical or mechanical in silth life. The whole world had been, in a way, a restricted technological zone. Roaming the world now, she found new technology everywhere, affecting every life, brought on by the demands of the long winter and the mirror project.

Electrical, petroleum, or gas heating had replaced coal and wood in the homes of many meth. Agriculture and mining had become mechanized. Once even the vast cloister farms had been worked by methods little different than those the Degnan had used in the Ponath. Only wealthy orders had possessed draft animals. Industry did not at all resemble what she recalled. She had to look long and hard to find a true dirigible airship. The great sausages had been retired from all but the most remote enterprises.

She should have paid more heed during her rare visits home. A drop to Ruhaack, on the borders of civilization, and a monomaniacal hunt for rogues beyond those borders had not been enough to show her the broader picture.

All that. All her fault, in a way.

The past was gone. And the past was silth.

Kublin might be right. Unless in her madness she had destabilized the new civilization so far that it would collapse.

She returned to her self, surveyed the control center briefly, stared at Kublin's still, mutilated form. That, at least, she had accomplished. The future would not be his. Down on the homeworld the rogues were on the run. This time the silth would show little mercy. They had learned. They would finish the job before returning to their feuds and their fear of her.

She no longer cared. Let them go on. Let them hunt her. It did not matter now, and once she was gone it would not matter ever.

She reached down to the world with the touch and announced that she was returning to the starship.

She sabotaged the brethren ship so it could not use its weapons and left the males alive as promised. She took to her darkship and the stars. But her heart kept swinging back to Kublin and she knew that dead he would haunt her more virulently than ever he had alive.

Chapter Forty-Four

I

Years came and went and were lonely. Marika grew older, and was all too conscious of aging. Contrary to her expectations, darkships continued visiting the alien. Few had permission from home.

In the quiet following the horror on the homeworld all voidfaring silth turned outward, away from yesterday. A new era of exploration began. Silth soon probed far beyond limits reached in older times. Marika herself occasionally ventured out, guiding favored Mistresses through the cloud to see the shoals of stars beyond.

She undertook no new explorations. She did not stray far. *Starstalker* remained unconquered. But she listened to others avidly, and insisted explorers maintain meticulous records.

Many who visited came to learn. She taught, if less than eagerly. These were young silth, of a new generation, less shaped by ancient thinking, more flexible and less afraid. They wanted to pick her brain for what she had discovered about those-who-dwell, about the dark side, about undertaking extended journies through the void. Many wanted to serve her as bath, for she continued growing stronger as she aged. Those who served with her could expect to grow stronger themselves. Somehow she opened new paths in their minds.

She was alone seldom, yet always lonely, like some legendary hermit of old tales, seated on her mountain, tutoring all who came seeking knowledge. She had no joy of it, but taught all comers, hoping to shape the new generation. They paid for their education by helping to recover, rebuild, and unravel the mysteries of the alien starship.

"We must cease to be narrow," she preached. "Narrowness nearly brought us to destruction. We must know the tradermale mentality as we know our own. We must eschew contempt, for others have skills of their own that are as wonderful and mysterious as our own." Her use of old-fashioned backcountry words like tradermale amused the new silth. Such language was an anachronism. The ice had devoured those who had used it.

Marika had become a bridge to a vanished culture, last of her kind. The far frontiers of civilization, the low-tech zones, were gone forever.

She had peace, but there was no Bagnel, no Grauel, no Barlog with whom to share it. There was no friend to help cushion the future.

She retreated increasingly into ritualistic patterns set by her foresisters. The young silth were baffled by the paradox: Marika proselytized new ways while devoting herself privately to rituals and mysteries already old at the beginning of history. There were whole days she spent open to the All, alone in celebrating traditional mysteries.

Old ways banished the troubles of the spirit haunting her. She now understood the old sisters who had tried to force her into certain shapes when she was young.

There were times, too, when she took the wooden darkship out alone and drifted through the system contemplating the void. She could not believe that, had it not been for the endless winter and the fury of the nomad, she would now be among the oldest of the Degnan Wise. The Marika within did not *feel* old. Only the flesh did.

She was waiting too. Marking time. She knew the All had not finished with her yet.

II

A Mistress named Henahpla, a footloose explorer such as Marika once had hoped to become, brought the word. Aliens in the cloud. Far down the heartstream of the dust and gas, where it was densest, giving birth to new stars.

The cloud was Henahpla's stalking ground. She knew it better than did Marika. Marika closeted herself with the Mistress. "Where?"

Henahpla sorted charts for which she was primarily responsible, indicated a particular star. "Here. One ship, like this one."

Marika knew the star. Hers had been the first voidship to visit it. It had one planet in its life zone. "A resting place. I will post it off limits till we see what they are doing."

"They are looking for something, mistress. They are searching, not exploring."

"How do you know?"

"I am an explorer, mistress. There are ways things are done. If you do not fall into one pattern you fall into another. I know searching. I search before I explore, lest I stumble upon *Starstalker.*"

"Uhm." Marika had a theory about *Starstalker*'s disappearance. Would this encounter confirm it? "I want you to do a reconstruction of that ship. Some of the sisters who were with me when I visited the rogue aliens are still here. We will see. . . . But I should go see for myself, should I not?"

"Mistress?"

"There are aliens we do not wish to meet again. And there

are those who built this ship. The enemies of the others. Did you get any feel for their plans?"

"None. I stayed only long enough to see what was happening. I think I departed undetected."

"I had better eliminate any information pointing toward the homeworld. Just in case. Then we will go see these aliens."

Marika passed the word. Silth began examining mountains of records. No questions were asked—in Marika's realm orders were carried out without them.

When she rejoined Henahpla she found half a dozen darkship crews assembled, eager to share the adventure. Marika could not in good conscience deny them.

They would venture out anyway, under pretext of going somewhere else.

She followed Henahpla into the Up-and-Over, nervous, yet feeling refreshingly alive. Was this the mission for which the All had saved her?

The voidships plunged into a system naked of an alien. There was no evidence that any had visited.

Searchers for sure. How long before they located her derelict? *Home,* she sent. *Let them come to us.*

The alien was there waiting when she returned. His ship was almost identical to her derelict. It was approaching the wreck, but had to do so constrained by physical laws that did not inhibit silth. Marika skipped through the Up-and-Over, hastened home.

The alien matched orbit, but did nothing else immediately. The creatures were cautious.

Marika hastened to the communications section of the derelict's control center. That had been in use for years. "Have they tried to communicate?"

"Frequently," an old male replied. "We acknowledged receipt, but put them off pending your return."

"Open channel and proceed. Test your knowledge of their speech."

The ensuing dialogue went more easily than had Bagnel's

on the alien world. These creatures used the language of the derelict's crew. They were more polite. Marika suggested several direct questions. The aliens responded directly. "They have my permission to come aboard if they like."

The aliens accepted immediately.

Marika met them as they entered the ship. She felt young again, fired by the old excitement. *This* was what had lured her to stalk the stars.

The aliens wore suits recalling those the rogue brethren had worn in battle. They removed their helmets and stood looking at the meth looking at them. Marika lifted both paws. An alien female responded by raising her right, stretching thin pink lips over very white teeth. Marika nodded, indicated that they should follow her. She led them to the control center.

Sometimes the aliens seemed amused, sometimes they seemed baffled, by the repairs and modifications the males had made. Marika watched closely, but did not trust her judgment of their reactions. They were too similar to meth in appearance. It was too easy to assume they should think like meth.

In the control center she told the old male, "Ask them if they are of the Community that built this ship."

The senior alien seemed to understand the question. She responded affirmatively. Marika said, "Tell them they may examine the machinery. Watch them closely." She herself activated the alien's final report.

The six outsiders divided, began doing this and that. Marika suggested, "Tell them about the encounter with the Serke so they may see our perspective."

The outsiders paid little attention. They chattered excitedly as they brought up data no meth had been able to access. They seemed pleased by what they found, and not at all distressed by the vessel's fatal encounter with a startled Serke Mistress.

"They call it a piece of living history," the translator told Marika. "A ship lost for several of their generations. I suspect they are not inclined to long-term feuds. After all, the event antedates your own birth."

Marika grunted, not entirely satisfied. The roots of her feud with the Serke antedated her birth. Today six or seven of them survived. And she was the last of the Reugge, more or less.

She had made several efforts to learn what was known of the alien language. She had had little success. Now she determined to try again.

Silth intuition told her good things were about to happen, that she had come at last to the time for which the All had saved her.

A species from another star! A species created by an entirely different evolution, yet star-faring like the meth!

Puplike wonder overcame her.

III

They called themselves humans. Their forebears sprang from a far sun they called Sol, more distant than Marika could imagine. None of these humans had seen their dam sun. Their race occupied a hundred colony worlds, in numbers that left Marika agog. She could not imagine creatures by the trillion. At their peak, before the coming of the ice, the meth had numbered only a few hundred million.

Marika was much more comfortable with these aliens than those she had met before. She learned their language well enough to converse with their senior, who called himself Commander Gayola Jackson.

The outsiders could not believe silth did what they did. "It smacks of witchcraft," Jackson insisted. Though the word translated, the two races invested it with widely different emotional value. What was fearful fact to one was almost contemptible fantasy to the other.

Marika envied the aliens their independence. Their starship could stay in space indefinitely. Commander Jackson had no intention of departing before exhausting the potential of the contact. She sent a messenger drone to her seniors.

Marika felt comfortable enough with the "woman" to permit the drone's departure.

Four years fled. The living legend began to shun mirrors.

Marika rolled her voidship, sideslipped, surged forward. Her students slid behind and beneath, nearly collided. She was amused. They were learning, but the hard way.

She glanced at the axis platform. Commander Jackson was shaking. The only human ever to dare it, she could not acclimate herself to silth dark-faring. Marika began rolling as she aimed the tip of her flying dagger at the heart of the system. *Go home,* she sent.

The touch was another thing the humans had difficulty accepting.

So much for enjoying herself. She could stall no longer. It was time to hear the latest bad news.

Marika gathered ghosts and hit the Up-and-Over. Stars twisted. The derelict materialized. Jackson's dread formed a miasma around the darkship. But she would not yield to it. She ventured out as often as Marika would permit. There was a bit of silth in her, Marika thought. The stubborness of silth.

Marika left the alien female in the paws of her bath, entered the derelict. Now, more than ever, the old starship was the heart of dark-faring silthdom. An incredible sixty voidships called the relic home. . . .

It was a completely unforeseen result of Marika's struggles with the landbound silth of the homeworld. The terrors she had loosed back when had birthed an isolationism with which star-faring silth could not and would not deal. One by one, one darkship after another had broken with its dam Community rather than give up faring the void. Only a very few Mistresses fared homeward anymore.

A dying breed, Marika feared. No more were in training.

Marika entered the situation room, which had been refurbished by Jackson's people. A half dozen of her folk's starships orbited with the derelict now. Each of the room's ends boasted a vast three-dimensional star chart. Each time Marika viewed one she felt a pang of loss. That Bagnel should have missed this!

The meth end of the room was crowded with agitated silth.

"Ruthgar gone," Marika observed. "And Arlghor?"

An elder sister replied, "It is as you suspected, mistress. Someone is sealing the voidpaths." Golden trails emanated from Marika's star and zigzagged toward the meth homeworld. Though Marika's folk had little intercourse with the dam planet, anomalies in that direction had caught their attention and had led them to investigate. Eight of the marked routes boasted stars hidden inside magenta haze. Those stars were the primaries of the worlds where dark-faring silth rested. Darkships sent to investigate those worlds had not returned.

The elder sister asked, "Will you do something now?"

"No." She did not know what to do. Sending more investigators would be like throwing stones down a well.

Everyone assumed *Starstalker* was responsible. Marika had grimmer suspicions. The old enemy, with no more than seven very ancient silth to operate it, could not have the power to make deathtraps of so many worlds.

"And Arlghor?" she repeated.

"Nothing yet."

She grunted. It was not yet Arlghor's time. Soon, though. Soon. She strode to the far end of the room. Commander Jackson was considering her own portrait of peril.

Hers was a more vast star chart, filled with clouds of light. Individual pinpricks were hard to discern. The magenta there floated in puffs and streamers. "No change?"

"No. No incoming information."

"That disturbs you?"

"We are a minor mission, far from home space, but there should be courier drones. All we hear is what your people bring us. They don't understand us so their reports make little sense."

For three years Marika's protégés had been visiting and trading with the human starworlds. Marika did not understand the news they brought either, but it was evident that the human rogues had come out of hiding and there was a great struggle on.

"Ruthgar is gone," Marika said. "Arlghor is next. If it goes I may leave this ship to you."

"Would that be wise? If what you suspect is true..." Jackson paused. "To hell with regulations. Marika, you've never seen a warship. These ships here are scientific and exploratory craft. Small ships, armed only lightly. I'm not supposed to admit that anything nastier exists, but I don't want you jumping into something blind."

Marika eyed Jackson. Small ships? Lightly armed? That world she had visited had not shown her anything more sinister.

"They'll be ready for you if they're working with your enemies."

True, Marika reflected. The sealing of the homeward starlanes might be meant to draw her into a trap. But just *Starstalker*? Would the alien rogues think her worth the bother?

Where did she stand? Damn! She had sworn to ignore the homeworld, to let it go to the All. If the Communities allowed yet another rogue resurgence, so be it. She owed the fools nothing more. But if *Starstalker* had acquired outside allies... Had she an obligation to defend the race?

This would become more than a power struggle. Humans were enough like meth that they could not ignore a power vacuum. Jackson's people, nominally friendly, were trouble enough.

She and the woman had become friends, but there was little love lost elsewhere. Silth would be silth, especially in the far reaches of the dark, too often upon the human worlds they visited. Admonitions had little effect. They inundated the humans with arrogance and contempt, for the creatures had no silth class. They were little more than brethren technicians, working with their hands.

Marika sometimes wanted to shriek in frustration.

Perhaps it was in their genes. Perhaps she was more a sport than she suspected.

Chapter Forty-Five

I

Marika sensed a darkship approaching. She ignored it. She continued guiding three young Mistresses through maneuvers. They were doing well in their ghost-fencing.

She was old and feeling it, and thinking of recording all she had learned, all that had made her first among silth. All that had made her the most terrible silth of all time. She was considering revealing all her secrets. She thought such a document might illuminate a pathway, might betray the pitfalls and long ways around that she had encountered.

What might she have become had she lived in another time, free of constant strife? What might she not have done?

Mistress?

Yes, Henahpla?

The last route has been closed.

I suspected as much. Excellent move, Flagis! The youngest Mistress had used the Up-and-Over to seize a position of advantage. *You have the makings of a strategist.* She fended Flagis's ghosts deftly. From the summit of age each probe seemed entirely predictable. *Practice among your-selves now. Exercise restraint. I will tolerate no accidents.* The young occasionally let pride carry them away and began trading blows seriously.

Marika brought her darkship beside Henahpla's. Rude wood beside finely machined titanium. But the witch signs attached to Henahpla's darkship were as old as time, crafted and blessed in the ancient ways.

My voidship has more character, Marika thought. More style.

The human senior is concerned.

Then we must ease her mind. Marika slipped into the Up-and-Over. She was inside the derelict before Henahpla reached orbit.

Jackson did seem rattled. "What is it?" Marika asked.

"A darkship returned from the human side of the cloud."

"Bad news?"

"There was a big battle. My people were not victorious."

"But still no message direct?"

"No. They've forgotten us."

"What might this defeat mean?"

"That depends on the magnitude of the disaster. The rebels are outnumbered. They were never likely to succeed. The aftershocks will be more political than military."

Marika nodded an understanding she did not quite pos-sess. She guided Commander Jackson to the situation room and pointed out the fact that the last route to the meth homeworld had been closed. "The last route they know," she added softly. "I can get there if I have to."

Jackson sucked spittle between her teeth. The habit irri-tated Marika. The creatures possessed no self-discipline. "Will you flank them, then?"

"No. I'll wait."

"I wonder."

"What?"

"I can see that you want them to come to you. But that might not be wise. You are not familiar with our warships."

"We shall see who distresses whom." She foresaw no

difficulty dealing with human ships if it came to that. She was silth, darkwalker, strongest Mistress of the ages. The void was hers to command.

Those who had put the stopper into the bottle lost patience when she did not try to break out. Ten days after they closed the last route they invaded Marika's star system.

Alarms howled in ship-night. Mistresses and bath scrambled from their quarters, raced to their darkships. Calmly, Marika strode to the situation room. Commander Jackson arrived before her. Already the human end, bustling, had adjusted to local scale.

It was real! Not the false alarm Marika had expected. But . . .

"One ship," Jackson told her. "Destroyer size. Already deploying riders. We'll have singleships in our hair in an hour. I hope it's just a recon pass." She indicated dots radiating from a common origin. "I have to get my ships out of orbit."

Marika was irked. Why hadn't her patrols warned her? They should have done so long before the humans detected the arrivals. She hurled anger outsystem, though her pickets were too distant to receive a general touch. "They're going to run?" she asked.

"I have to protect my people." The human scientists were evacuating the derelict hurriedly. "We can't do much more than get killed if they attack."

Baffled, Marika shook her head. She examined the situation, wheeled, stamped away to her wooden darkship. She cut the bath's ceremonies short, drove into the void toward the incoming raiders.

A picket's touch found her then, reporting the arrival with overtones of bewilderment. The Mistress had detected nothing until a small human ship almost overran her.

Marika shivered with a chill that penetrated her golden shield. The aliens did not touch. The touch's absence rendered them invisible to Mistresses less talented than she. She should have realized.

She deployed her companion Mistresses.

Ghosts flung outward discovered an inward-bound formation of six small ships. Behind them, more sedately, came a second formation of one large ship, two a third its size, and four more small ships. Marika did not understand. Commander Jackson had spoken of one ship, a "destroyer," arriving.

Go!

Darkships vanished into the Up-and-Over.

Marika emerged into fiery confusion. Webs of light clawed the void. Missiles were everywhere. The smaller human ships were almost as nimble as darkships. She drove toward the biggest ship. A moment later she felt the touch-screams of dying silth.

The size of the main enemy ship awed her. It was long and lean and cruel, like some monster ocean predator. Its mass had to be several times that of Jackson's biggest ship.

A small ship exploded.

Another darkship died.

She had underestimated them. Terribly.

She flung a wild touch across the void, grabbed the system's great black, yanked. This was no time for finesse.

A medium ship turned her way, accelerated incredibly. How had it detected her so easily? She grabbed the Up-and-Over, skipped, regained control of the great black. The ship found her again and closed swiftly, but the great black came too. Marika skipped again, flung the great black.

A strange screaming filled the void.

These humans touched when they died!

Their screams went on and on and on as their ship began breaking up.

Why so long?

Their dying tore at her nerves, distracted her from the broader struggle. . . . Crewed by the dying, the disintegrating human ship ripped past, drives accelerating still, carrying the remains outsystem.

A bolt of light stabbed so close Marika imagined crisping heat. She tore her attention from her victim.

A small ship was almost atop her. She ducked reflexively, fired her rifle as it screamed past, and only then thought to fling the great black.

Tortured screams flooded the touch.

That was the last small ship of the main force. Marika probed for the leading group. It too had been hard hit. Three survivors were streaking back toward their dam ship.

Victory. But at a terrible price. She could not find half a dozen Mistresses.

The main force turned. Marika ordered pursuit abandoned. She wanted no more losses.

She trailed the enemy's withdrawal, watched him recover his surviving rider, then his singleships. The smaller vessels all nestled into recesses in the larger's flanks.

She tried for the main ship's drives, but it kept her too busy evading fire to concentrate.

Riders recovered, the destroyer pulled away. Marika found its acceleration astounding. Such power!

The starship vanished. Like a darkship leaping into the Up-and-Over, yet with a twist that seemed to rend the fabric of the void itself. Marika shuddered to a shock that recalled nearby thunder. But there was no sound out there in the dark.

II

"They got whipped, but they'll be back," Commander Jackson prophesied. "They learned what they wanted to know."

"Uhm." Marika conversed in monosyllables, gruffly concealing her uncertainty. Seldom had she been so uncertain of her capacity to cope., The incredible, powerful technology behind that killing machine!

"They'll come ready to fight, Marika. I wish I had orders."

"Why did the smaller ships cling to the large one?"

"Economy. Military grade hyperdrives are costly and

bulky. So each hypership carries riders equipped only with cheaper, less massive system drives. *Military* grade system drives. A Main Battle carries riders on its riders."

Marika sighed. Despair began worming its way deep into her soul.

The destroyer had been gone four days. A ragtag fleet of voidships dropped from the Up-and-Over, badly mauled. Marika hustled her Mistresses out to meet them.

"They're from my homeworld," she told Jackson. "All who were able to fight their way through." They were, in fact, the last star-faring silth save a few crews exploring and not yet aware that the beast was afoot.

"The voidship *Starstalker* has returned to home space. Accompanied by your enemies." The news the touch carried was almost too grim to bear. "Silth talents have been of little value against alien technology in fighting on the surface." The Communities were struggling bravely and desperately, but with scant hope. The general populace was giving no help. Even the long loyal brethren faction was making only token efforts at resisting.

Marika cursed the All within the shadows of her heart. She, the rebel within silthdom, had been by time and circumstance hammered into a symbol of everything silth. She had become the adhesive bonding harried silthdom together. How had she come to this?

She knew the message borne by the homeworld Mistresses. The Communities were struggling on in hopes she could, once again, stay the jaws of doom.

What was the point? The All seemed determined to see an end to the silth ideal.

She took the wooden darkship into the void alone, beyond the touch of those waiting aboard the derelict. The ashes of Grauel and Barlog rested at the axis. She faced the urns.

Grauel. Barlog. We are returned to where we began. Savages surround us. And this time there is no Akard to send help.

There is a difference, Marika. They war upon silth alone.

True. But without us what would meth be? And how long will it be silth alone?

Silence.

She cruised the dark till exhaustion turned her homeward, not once finding an answer she wanted. There were options, possibilities, and some things that had to be attempted whatever befell, but all outcomes depended upon Jackson's people.

She strode down the arm of the voidship, poised over the last of her pack.

There was no choice. She had promised. She had to take them home.

Jackson told her, "It's insane," after Marika dismissed the assembled Mistresses. "Your silth sorcery won't mean a thing against a rebel fleet. Please wait."

"Your people have shown no interest in what is happening here. There is no point in waiting."

"They must be hard-pressed. It's hard to defend everything when marauders . . ."

"Take the struggle to the marauder. That is what I have done all my life. To the sorrow of thousands. No. No, my human friend. This I must do, though it means my end. I have my obligations. To my huntresses who have fallen, to my Community that is no more, to all meth and silth still living. I was created by the All to *act*. If I achieve no greater victory, I must break through and scatter these ashes before I rejoin the All." None of the Mistresses had questioned that. They understood.

"What you call kalerhag is an obligation?"

Marika eyed Jackson warily. Even the humans? "What makes you mention kalerhag? It is a forgotten rite."

"I doubt that. I cannot speak your language, but I can follow conversations. Kalerhag is a growing theme. The bath especially are talking mass suicide if your mission fails."

Was it engraved on the genes? Kalerhag had been out of

vogue for ages, and most recently discredited by Serke behavior in the face of absolute defeat. Yet it became attractive in the face of the terrors borne by these aliens. "It could be," she murmured in her own language. "Should honor and the need of the race demand."

Forget that. That was not a good way to think when there was a strike to mount. She dared think of nothing but conflict. The voidships were poised. The best of the best Mistresses, Henahpla, Cherish, and Satter, were ready to launch the first phase, down interdicted voidpaths, behind a trio of great blacks. Soon horror would stalk the stars.

Marika's own approach would pursue a starway only she knew, only she had the strength to fly.

"Where there is life there is hope. An old saying among my people."

"We meth are fatalists and mystics. Symbol is always more important than substance."

"But suicide . . ."

"Not suicide. Kalerhag. Sometimes to defy, deny, even defeat fate, one must rob it of its prey."

Jackson shrugged. "Perhaps. Some of our ancestors venerated such gestures."

Marika grunted, withdrew. She assembled her crew, including redundant bath and a back-up Mistress, in the sanctity of a small compartment set aside for ritual. Soon most of the silth aboard had crowded in or were watching from beyond the hatchway. The humans respected that time and stayed away.

Henahpla, Cherish, and Satter were long gone. The principal follow-up forces had departed. The passageways aboard the derelict were naked of silth. Only a few old brethren researchers maintained a meth presence. Marika was about to leave.

She did not expect to return.

Jackson's messenger caught her at the lock, about to share golden liquid. "Mistress, the Commander must see you before you leave."

"Must I?" She did not need her despair reinforced by Jackson's negativity.

"It's critical."

Marika found the Commander in Communications. She sensed bad news immediately.

"My superiors have spoken at last, Marika."

"Sending bad news, of course." She had ignored the arrival of the courier drone.

"It's not good. There has been a change of government." Government was a concept Marika still did not understand. "General orders to the Fleet Arm are to undertake no hostile action till the State stabilizes and determines policy. I am able to defend myself. Nothing more."

"It could have been worse."

Jackson lifted an eyebrow.

"You could have been ordered to turn on us." She strode out, using old drills to calm herself as she hastened to rejoin her bath.

Alone.

In the void there would be little time to worry about betrayal.

III

Marika drove the darkship as hard as ever she had, hastily scouting the strike points assigned Henahpla, Cherish, and Satter. Each had employed her great black properly. A dead ridership drifted off each rest world, still tainted by last touch-screams. She snarled, an ice-hearted Ponath huntress with the blood of foes upon her fangs. The last weapon.

She grabbed the Up-and-Over, racing along the secret pathway to the homeworld, satisfied that her strategy was sound.

She should arrive first, armed with a great black dragged in from another system. Henahpla and Cherish should appear shortly afterward, armed with great blacks of their own. Satter would grab control of the home system's own black. Four of those monsters ought to be able to overwhelm everything in their way.

She drove hard. Her bath protested. She rested when she must, and resented every minute. Later, she rested one jump from home, after neutralizing a ridership.

All was timing now. The others had to be in position. If they were delayed, her next move would prove disastrous.

The time came.

Nervousness fled during the passage. She maintained an iron grip on her great black. Elation grew. The wait was at an end.

She paused on the brink of the home system briefly, wishing she dared make certain of the others. But the Serke aboard *Starstalker* were certain to sense the new great black.

Into the Up-and-Over, her mind fixed on Biter. She would use the moon for cover. Out of the Up-and-Over.

She almost lost the black in her astonishment.

The void was aswarm with aliens. Several of their ships were as dreadful as Commander Jackson had promised.

An electromagnetic storm exploded. Her appearance had been detected.

She hurled the great black.

She eased nearer Biter till she hovered in shadow just yards above its barren surface. Spears of light stabbed the night, coming nowhere near her. Beyond the moon, *Starstalker* flung panicky signals at its allies. The voidship began to move.

Terror and agony flooded the otherworld as a huge alien ship died. Thousands aboard, Marika reflected. The agony of their dying seemed to touch other humans elsewhere on a subconscious level. Their reactions were slow, tentative. She yanked the great black and hurled it at *Starstalker*.

Panic filled the otherworld.

The Serke voidship vanished. Marika was astonished. She had not thought those old witches possessed the nerve to take the Up-and-Over so close in.

She threw the great black at the largest alien she sensed.

Fire erupted upon Biter's face. Light lances dragged drunken scarlet feet across the monochromatic moonscape. Glowing balls welled by the dozen, yielded by missiles unable to target the wooden darkship.

Marika shifted her attack to a third warship.

A beam struck close by, followed by another. They might be guessing, but they were guessing well.

Out on the margin of touch she sensed another great black. One of her point Mistresses had arrived.

Where was *Starstalker*?

A beam seared the void only yards away. A missile boiled Biter's face close enough for the fringe gases to buffet her. All through nearby space small attack vessels were closing in.

She flung the great black once more, then gathered smaller ghosts and darted into the Up-and-Over. A missile erupted close by as she went, disturbing her concentration. She lost the great black. It fled before she stabilized her darkship and reached for it again. She cursed, moving nearer the surface of Chaser.

She sensed two great blacks under control out on the lip of the system. Soon, now.

Still no evidence of *Starstalker*.

She captured a large ghost and flung it into the drive of a medium-size alien hustling toward Biter. It went drifting toward the homeworld, unable to alter course.

She turned to another, again ruined a drive.

The crowd around Biter began turning her way. She ruined a third drive, aboard a ship headed toward her, then grabbed for the Up-and-Over, darting well inside the orbits of the smallest moons. That far in she would be unable to take the Up-and-Over again.

She started down. Best deliver the ashes while the alien remained distracted and confused.

Her latest victim bored into Chaser, igniting a geyser of fire.

Alien ships darted around, trying to locate her. Angry

radio blasts filled the ether. Marika continued to marvel at their numbers and sizes. The damage she had done amounted to nothing. Everything they had must be here.

She felt *Starstalker* return, felt Serke minds questing. And in the same second two great blacks arrived among the foe. A third appeared only two minutes later. One set upon *Starstalker*. Terrified, the Serke fled again.

The rest of the starfarers should arrive soon.

Marika had no time to follow the struggle. She was going down as fast as she dared, yet not fast enough. The touch of a weary surface silth reached her, warned her that ground-based aircraft were being prepared to intercept her.

She raced toward the sea east of the New Continent, holding that touch with the surface.

The news from below was not good. Only a pawful of silth survived. Most were in hiding, scattered among the populace, pretending to be displaced workers. The alien was in complete control and looked likely to break faith with his Serke allies.

Perfidious males.

Marika felt the approach of the enemy aircraft while she was yet two hundred thousand feet up. She hurled ghosts. Aircraft dropped. How arrogant of them! Not one of their starships or aircraft was equipped with suppressors.

Maybe they did not know. Maybe the Serke were exercising duplicity of their own, counting upon her to batter the alien, and the alien to destroy her, leaving them to pick up the pieces.

She reached the surface unscathed and raced over gray waves edged with fire. One of the ships she had injured was coming down, trailing thunder.

The action beyond the sky was brisk. Three great blacks had ruined the alien's confidence. And now the main forces of darkships were arriving.

But their ships, all their ships, were titanium.

IV

The shore cliffline reared ahead, giants wearing boots of foam. Beyond, the land betrayed patches of green. Marika was pleased. Here the ice had lain fifty feet thick the last time she had come by. For all that had happened, the mirrors remained active.

She was a long way from the Ponath. Fast as she rushed along, the night was faster. It overtook her before she reached her ancestral territory. There in moonlight the land yet lay skeletal, not all the ice gone, but enough so the heads of hills and bones of dead forests had begun to show through. She slowed, searched for the packstead.

Again and again aircraft came to challenge. None of those that detected her ever came within eyeshot.

The ice had changed the land. Little seemed familiar, though the hills above the Ponath reared naked above the remaining ice. Bald heads where once had stood impenetrable forests. She slowed, uncertain she had reached the right country.

She had flown too far west, for she came upon the promontory where Akard had stood. The ice had left no trace of the fortress. She turned eastward, thinking how puny were the works of meth in the face of the slow fury of nature.

She found the packstead easily, then, for something turned within her, connecting with the land of her birth. Her life there rushed through her mind, a torrent. How did that pup become the hard, cruel bitch riding the night above?

She summoned her back up and ordered her to take over as Mistress, to drift slowly above the site, fifty feet up. Marika went to the axis and collected the urns containing Grauel and Barlog.

Holding those urns, she gazed at the sky. The continuing struggle scarred the outer darkness. She opened, allowed the touch to overwhelm her.

Half her Mistresses had been destroyed. Satter was among those lost. No other Mistress had been able to take control of the system's great black. But the survivors battled on.

The alien had suffered as heavily. A score of crewless starships drifted aimlessly, complicating the battle situation. The struggle remained close despite the technology and numbers ranged against the silth. Henahpla and Cherish, recalling what Commander Jackson had told them about warships, were trying to intimidate the enemy by concentrating on vessels capable of carrying riders away.

Perhaps that was not the wisest tactic, Marika reflected. But she let them continue, with just a light touch to let them know she would be back among them soon.

She opened the urns and sang an ill-remembered memorial chant. The breeze around the darkship wafted bits of meth dust. She continued on into rites of Mourning for the entire Degnan pack, which she had owed for so long.

"I kept my promise, as you kept yours," Marika whispered to the spirits of the huntresses. "We kept faith. Fare you well wherever, and I pray we meet in another life, to hunt the same trails."

Fighter aircraft were coming up from the south and in from the west. Another flight circled over the distant sea, hoping she would flee that way. Up in orbit others were thinking of her too. *Starstalker* was keeping close track.

She scattered the last ashes, sped one final farewell, then resumed her place at the tip of the dagger, well satisfied that she had fulfilled her principal obligation. Now she could join the rest of silthdom in death.

She had the golden bowl passed, for she felt a need of renewed strength. She had begun to feel her years. And she could not convince herself that self-sacrifice was the only remaining answer.

Ready?

Her crew responded affirmatively. Some even seemed eager to fling themselves into the jaws of the All. There were no doubts in their minds. They would die here, heroically, o

ater, if vanquished but unslain, in some grand and foolish
ceremony.

Marika hurled ghosts wherever aircraft were approaching, scattering wreckage over land and sea. Then she
climbed rapidly, calling on her back up to assume the
Mistress's duties again.

She stretched herself to the system's bounds, searching
or her old dark ally. The great black fought her angrily.
She refused to acknowledge its desire to be left alone. She
dragged it toward her.

Then she opened to the battle.

It was even no longer. Henahpla had been slain. Cherish
had but two bath remaining and could not manage her black
while struggling to control her voidship. Several faint hearts
had fled for the derelict.

The outcome was no longer in doubt if one were silth
enough to read it.

Starstalker began guiding alien warships to intercept
Marika.

She whipped the great black in on the Serke voidship.
They shrieked and jumped away, but not without having
smelled the rotton breath of death. Not distracted by having
to manage the darkship, Marika kept watch. She hurled the
black the instant she sensed *Starstalker* returning from the
Up-and-Over. Again she got her blow in. Then again, and
again, and the fifth time *Starstalker* did not gather ghosts
fast enough to escape.

Marika brushed the Serke voidship once more to make
sure it would not recover, then let be. Let them think, and
worry, and wonder if their allies would save them or let
them die, adrift a few thousand miles from the homeworld
they had come so close to recapturing.

The warships above were sniping at the wooden darkship,
though Cherish valiantly strove to distract them. Rather
than assume control of the darkship, Marika began flinging
the great black among those who awaited her. Her hammer
blows caught them off guard. In minutes they began to
scatter.

Despite the evidence that the struggle would end in their favor, alien ships began leaving the inner orbits. A quick scan told Marika they were removing their jump ships from danger. The riderships would have to carry the brunt.

She might die here. She might be defeated. But already she had won a great victory for Commander Jackson's people. If they took advantage.

She reached orbital altitude despite all that could be thrown her way, though she lost two bath and had to resume control of the voidship before she wanted. She clawed her way into the shadow of one of the smaller moons, dodged from it to another farther out, part of her mind wielding the great black, part seeking ghosts with which to take the Up-and-Over. She wanted to get into open space now, to steal maneuvering room.

Ghosts were scarce. Most of the surviving Mistresses had fled, stripping the surrounding void. She would have to wait till more drifted in.

She pranced around the little moons, among the wrecks of alien ships, at times pretending to be debris. She sent a dozen ridership crews to whatever those creatures recognized as their maker. Always she inched away from the homeworld. Always the All stalked with her, though she was so weary she thought she would collapse any moment.

Cherish died, her soul parting from her flesh with a last scream of touch encouraging Marika to fly away, to regain the derelict and thence mount another offensive. There were a few Mistresses among the stars, wandering. She could bring them in, train them to the great blacks, and finish the massacre begun here.

Marika returned a gentle, thankful touch as Cherish melded into the All. There was one silth who, like herself, never yielded.

She gathered ghosts.

She was alone in the home system, the only darkship still in action. The aliens were closing in. Even those vessels that had withdrawn were returning to taste the kill.

She threw the great black one last time, then jumped

CEREMONY 273

ragging the monster with her a hundred million miles
utward.

She waited.

They did not come. They had lost touch.

She had the senior bath pass the golden liquid again. And
en she jumped inward again, dropping not four miles from
tarstalker and a bevy of small alien attendants.

Good-bye, old witches. Old enemies. You lose again. She
osed the great black and took pleasure in the screams of
e dying till enemy fire came so near one of her bath
omplained of scorched fur.

She skipped into the Up-and-Over, reversing the route
e had used to approach the homeworld.

Chapter Forty-Six

I

For all good news there must be bad, for all good fortune balancing evil. That which Marika garnered a week after fighting her way free of the homeworld was the worst.

Alien warships had beaten her to the derelict. A Main Battle was there, with riderships deployed, and it was evident that several Mistresses had stumbled in to their deaths already.

Tired of fighting, of killing, of struggling on when there seemed no end to the struggle, Marika nevertheless jumped in, leaving the Up-and-Over so near the derelict the aliens remained ignorant of her advent.

The starship had been pounded into scrap, as had the starships belonging to Jackson's expedition. Nothing lived except on the planet below. Marika reached with the touch and found a few silth, but no starfarers. All those had been driven away.

She drew the system's great black, disposed of the crew of the Main Battle, then took the Up-and-Over while the riderships bustled about in panic. She jumped to another world and found another alien waiting there, fully alert. She departed rather than fight. She needed rest.

A second and third world proved equally perilous. The supply of golden liquid was getting low. And her bath had been exposed to space too long. She had to get down.

There was but one place left to flee, a world Henahpla had discovered, hidden on the far side of the cloud. She had designated it as a last hiding place if ever she were ousted from the derelict.

Could she survive so long a passage?

She made it, barely, but had to be aided down to the surface by the few silth who had reached the world already. She collapsed once she was down, was only vaguely aware of the chatter of silth afraid she would be lost to them.

She wakened occasionally, took a bit of broth. She suffered spates of delirium in which she believed she was arguing with Grauel, Barlog, Bagnel, Gradwohl, Kiljar, or even Kublin. She believed she was delirious when she overheard the ongoing argument polarizing the makeshift encampment.

Once she staggered from her shelter and tongue-lashed the Mistresses and bath, damning them for yielding to despair, but they did not understand her tangled Ponath dialect. She collapsed before she could make them understand. They restored her to her pallet and resumed their defeatist chatter.

Later, a Mistress came to inform her that another two darkships had come in. She observed, "I think you are suffering from more than exhaustion, mistress. A pity we have no healer sister."

Marika tried to rise. "I cannot be sick. I do not have time."

The Mistress pushed her back down. "A tired body is fertile for disease, mistress. Rest."

"I have never been sick. Not a day."

"Good. You have a strong soul. You will recover more quickly."

Perhaps. And perhaps her malaise was all of the soul, she

thought. Lying there, she had too much time to reflect. Jiana. How she had bristled at that label in younger years. But how right they had been. They had smelled the stench of death in her fur. She could deny it no longer. Doom had come irrespective of her conviction.

Even now she fought confession. But how could she deny truth? She had been the heart of it all along, and her backtrail was strewn with bones and ruined cities. Yea, with ruined planets.

She should have perished in the Ponath with the rest of the Degnan pack. Grauel and Barlog should have abandoned her when first she had offended them with her wickedness. She should not have been born. She or Kublin.

The debate among the sisters continued without respite, swinging sometimes this way, sometimes that, toward resumption of the struggle against the alien invaders, or away. Marika charged into the lists in a rare lucid moment, after days of introspection.

"It is too late for our kind. We are obsolete. The doom of silthdom was sealed when first the Serke encountered the alien. We can struggle on but gain nothing, like the Serke themselves after they were found out. We are what? Eight darkships? Nine? Can so few turn the tide? Of course not. Why even try? We are not wanted at home. Time has passed us by. The race have turned their backs upon us. We are orphaned and exiled."

They heard her without interrupting, as befitted a most senior. Their deference irked her. She was not deserving. "Do you understand? We are silth. Silth have no tomorrows. If we live, we leave no legacy. The homeworld and colonies are lost to us. We cannot breed. We cannot recruit. We are the last of our kind. Understand that. The last. Representatives of the end of an age. If we continue the struggle we will serve no one well, silth or the race. In the broader view of the race, we can do nothing but harm. We must let the race go. Let them learn the new ways of rogue and alien. We must not torture them further, for they will need every hope to survive."

Marika settled to the barren, rocky earth of the campsite, her energy expended.

Not one sister spoke in opposition, though in a strictly silth context her remarks amounted to heresy. She took a series of deep, relaxing breaths.

"Good, then. Let us examine our position. I doubt we will find we have supplies enough to last long. Decisions will have to be made around that fact. I have a task for a volunteer. A darkship will have to sneak back to the homeworld, to the edge of touch, to carry the news that Jiana will lead till the end."

Still no sister spoke.

"We have all been doomstalkers," Marika suggested. "Making tomorrow by fighting it. Come, sisters. Let us see what supplies we have and can recover."

They began to murmur as they worked, questioning her sanity. Those who had argued against going on had, perhaps, counted on her to overrule them. Now they wondered what had become of Marika the tireless, the unyielding, the savage, feral silth who had grown up to become the very symbol of conservative silthdom.

II

The date Marika chose was an anniversary of that on which the nomads had stormed the palisade of the Degnan packstead for the final time. So many years ago. Her silth life had been hard, but life would have been much harder even in a peaceful Ponath. She would not have lived this long had she not been driven forth.

The place Marika chose lay on the far side of the dust cloud, facing the banks of stars she had hoped one day to explore. She viewed those silvery reefs and shivered with lonely sorrow. So much missed because she was Marika. Talent was more curse than gift. Only lesser Mistresses had won free and had gone thither in stalk of wonder.

That vast starscape recalled Bagnel and shared dreams, and things that never were, and thoughts of Bagnel stirred other sorrows. She did not want to face those now. Not at a time like this. She would face Bagnel soon enough.

Come together.

One by one, nineteen voidships drifted together, till each dagger tip floated just feet from Marika. A thistle head of darkships. Their refurbished and polished witch signs glittered in the light of massed stars. And not a one present but by choice.

Nineteen voidships. Certainly all that still existed. Marika had gathered them for months. Not one voidship remained unaccounted for. But for a scatter of ground-bound silth in hiding among the turbulent underclasses, these constituted all surviving silthdom.

Jiana. Jiana indeed.

A short distance away a silvery speck glistened as it shifted slightly. It was a captured messenger drone, reprogrammed. It was observing. Recording, for the posterity of a race about to enter upon an entirely new age. Marika wanted this hour remembered.

The drone would carry its tale to the homeworld. Marika supposed the few surviving rogues would cheer when they deciphered its message.

Thistledown adrift among the stars. She was afraid. All the sisters were. But it was too late to turn back. It had been designed that way. There could be no changes of heart. The golden fluid was gone.

Let she who knows the song begin to sing. Let the All harken. The final ritual is begun.

For all the talk, for so long, not one of the sisters had known the Ceremony entire. It had been that long since its formal usage. But snippets gathered from the memories of nineteen crews had been enough to restore it.

Marika made her responses abstractedly, contributing to a growing envelope of touch that softened the fear. In a way it reminded her of her Toghar, the ceremony by which she had achieved her official entry into adult silthhood.

Kalerhag. *The* Ceremony. The most ancient rite, dating back to prehistory. It could be and could mean so many things. This time, stepping aside to make way for the new and the young, the oldest of its functions.

Not the end she had foreseen. But now, surely, the best thing for the race, sending the old ways out in honor rather than hanging on and hanging on the way the Serke had done, working only evil. Let the new way have the full use of its energies. It would need them to deal with these rogue aliens, and with Commander Jackson's people, who were sure to come hunting their enemies.

As peace enveloped her, Marika found she could wish her successors the best of luck. Anger and hatred went with the fear, and she found she could forgive them most of their wickedness.

Momentarily, she wondered if Kublin had settled into the same frame of mind in his final minutes.

The golden glow surrounding the sisters began to fray. Their fur stirred in the breath of the All. The darkness closed in. Marika, whelped of Skiljan, a savage huntress of the upper Ponath, possibly the strongest and greatest silth ever to have lived, faded quietly into the All, her battles finally done. Her last thought was a curiosity as to whether or not she would find Bagnel waiting on the other side.

III

Courier departs.

Nineteen darkships drift on the edge of the cloud, very, very slowly separating. They are lost, but they will not be forgotten. They will become legend. And the legend says that Marika did not die at all, that she is only sleeping, and that when the race of meth have fallen into their darkest hour she will come out of the great void with her witch signs shining, her bloodfeud dyes fresh, and her old rifle newly oiled. And the enemies of the meth will be swept away before her.

So ends an ancient age.